MUSIC FROM THE
FIFTH PLANET

Anne Nicholls began writing as Anne Gay, changing her name after marrying author Stan Nicholls. Her first published science fiction was the story "Wishbone", which appeared in the *Gollanz/Sunday Times Anthology of SF Competition Stories*, followed by more stories and the novel *Mindsail*. Other novels include *The Brooch of Azure Midnight*, *Dancing on the Volcano* and *To Bathe in Lightning*.

Anne was then hired by LineOne to edit *The SciFi Zone* website, which she did for four years; she has also written self-help books, including *Make Love Work For You*.

In recent years Anne has been active in the David Gemmell Awards for Fantasy organisation, and has exhibited her paintings on the subject of Chronic Fatigue.

MUSIC FROM THE FIFTH PLANET

ANNE NICHOLLS

Introduction by Justina Robson

Cover painting by David A Hardy

The Alchemy Press

The Alchemy Press, Staffordshire, UK

www.alchemypress.co.uk

Acknowledgements

I'd like to thank all the people who've been so supportive during my writing career from editors to publishers. These include all the folks mentioned in the *Origins* section at the back of the book, but with a special thank you to Jan Edwards and Peter Coleborn of The Alchemy Press.

On the speculative fiction writing front, I'd also like to thank Justina Robson for her introduction and for being such a supportive member of the SF Writers' Group, along with Freda Warrington, Jenny Gordon, and Chris and Pauline Morgan. Their feedback over the 24 years I was a member proved invaluable.

I'd also like to thank Paul Simon, singer/songwriter extraordinaire, for giving me the courage to stop shoving my manuscripts in a drawer and start sending them off. And, of course, for all the inspirational music that's accompanied each stage of my life.

Dedication:

To our dear future: Jacob and Mia Fifer,
to Marianne and Nick Fifer
and to my ever-supportive husband Stan Nicholls
with love always

Contents

Publication History

'By Right of the Stars' (as by Anne Gay) © Anne Nicholls 2010. First appeared on The Alchemy Press website Wildstacks

'Howie Dreams' (as by Anne Gay) © Anne Nicholls 1989. First appeared in *Arrows of Eros* edited by Alex Stewart

'Pixellated' © Anne Nicholls 2015. Previously unpublished

'The Cunning Plan' (as by Anne Gay) © Anne Nicholls 1998. First appeared in *The Mammoth Book of Comic Fantasy* edited by Mike Ashley

'The World of the Silver Writer' (as by Anne Gay) © Anne Nicholls 1989. First appeared in *Digital Dreams* edited by David V. Barrett

'The Seeds of a Pomegranate' © Anne Nicholls 2013. First appeared in *The Alchemy Press Book of Urban Mythic* edited by Jan Edwards and Jenny Barber

'Bride of the Sea' © Anne Nicholls 2001. First appeared in *Phantoms of Venice* edited by David A. Sutton

'Dragon's Breath' © Anne Nicholls 2013. First appeared in *The Alchemy Press Book of Pulp heroes* #2 edited by Mike Chinn

'Wishbone' (as by Anne Gay) © Anne Nicholls 1987. First appeared in the *Gollancz/Sunday Times' SF Competition Stories*

'Fair Phantom, Come I' © Anne Nicholls 2015. Previously unpublished

'Eyes of Day, Eyes of Night' © Anne Nicholls 2012. First appeared in *The Alchemy Press Book of Pulp Heroes* edited by Mike Chinn

'Dragonsbridge' © Anne Nicholls 2012. First appeared in *The Alchemy Press Book of Ancient Wonders* edited by Jan Edwards and Jenny Barber

'Buried Flame' © Anne Nicholls 2015. Previously unpublished

'Roman Games' (as by Anne Gay) © Anne Nicholls 1988. Previously published in *Other Edens* edited by Robert Holdstock and Christopher Evans

Introduction

I first met Anne Nicholls in the mid 1990s. She was in the process of writing her third novel, *To Bathe in Lightning,* and had achieved success and a steady readership with her first two planetary romances, *Mindsail* and *The Brooch of Azure Midnight*. We were attending a writers' workshop at the home of Freda Warrington. I was thoroughly overawed to be in the presence of published authors – at the time I was still well away from achieving such a feat myself – and so alert that I can remember a lot of that meeting now, in particular the combination of kindness, insight and resolve that Anne brought to the group. What I lacked in experience I tried to make up for with home baking, and I'm delighted now to be able to write this short introduction for a collection of Anne's stories. It would be okay to read them accompanied by baked goods, too, as most of them are enormous fun and just the thing for a short tea break from life's troubles. The ones that I can't classify as fun deal with material that's too serious for LOLs, they're beneficial in different ways.

Reading the collection put a lot of smiles on my face. Not only because Anne writes with wit and insight but because I was able to recall how many occasions we'd sat and laughed in crit meetings and that everything she brought was interesting to listen to. She has a whimsical imagination and loves to fuse the magical and the mundane into wry comedy. This can tend to the black and the gothic in patches, but never at someone's expense unless that someone really deserves it. Often they do. In 'Pixillated' a group of fey creatures are bribed and cajoled into correcting the injustice of human corruption by their canny 'gardener', Gran. Gran pays with compost for the reinstatement of her daughter and the righting of a scam, but not without a great deal of slapstick and good-natured moaning. A similar vein of down-to-earth magic appears in 'The Seeds of a Pomegranate' where again human crimes pull djinn and other beings into their midst. There's a strong sense that the magical and the divine really struggle in today's world, overlooked, ignored, dismissed and belittled – they've become strangely common folk.

Humour is not her only strength – and the stories which are less entertaining and more provoking display Anne's keen insight into the darker aspects of human nature, particularly within romantic relationships. Her narrative of an abuser's inner world replete with their self-regarding justifications and excuses is horrifyingly exact in both 'Dragonsbridge' and 'Silver Writer'. In 'Dragonsbridge' a victimiser becomes a victim of his own making, so mired in his illusions that even after he is offered redemption he can't recognise it. The collusive self-doubting and explaining-away of the abused is equally well-noted in 'Silver Writer' where Anne examines the role of fantasy in creating relationships and romance and the way in which this can work as powerfully against someone as for them. These stories have a powerful hunger for a reckoning at their heart, but instead of giving an easy moral platitude they offer glimpses of the wantonly incurable – incurable monsters, incurable romantics. Anne is at her finest when displaying and dissecting these viciously intertwined brambles of human making, showing how the dream of reality and its truth can be so far apart between one mind and another, something which also makes her novels well worth tracking down. She allows hopes for escape, for some of the people, some of the time. There is justice some of the time and some of the time there is only the horror of a twisted vision. Her writing on the vulnerability, the fragility, of human nature is extremely moving.

There are stories where the bad guys get their comeuppance, however, presented here in several adventure tales of fantasy, science fiction and derring-do, including an outing with Sherlock Holmes. Although all of these stories have a period feel to them – a kind of boisterous Indiana Jones quality with their exotic settings and pulp speed – they also have a timeless appeal; we rescue child slaves from pirates in China in 'Dragon's Breath'; witness the rites of passage of a desert nomad as he seeks magic to save his people in 'By Right of the Stars'; and ponder the possibilities of alternate lives with Dr Watson in 'Fair Phantom, Come I'. All of these are beautifully written; Anne evokes setting and directs action with great skill so that the tales flow along at an effortless pace from daring beginning to satisfying end. I wish she would write more adventure stories! Plus, I don't think I've read anywhere else a scene of such innovative graphic pleasure as that in which a man enters a hall of heroes *wearing* his dragon companion as a cloak ... that was worth the admission fee just on its own. And I defy anyone not to love a story about a faithless, chain-smoking nun duelling a dragon in secret whilst crossing Italy by train ('Roman Games'). These stories are a box of delights. Do try them.

Anne has also done lots of other great things, as you can see from her CV below. I don't think I can improve on the facts, nor need to, so here are some Anne-facts quoted directly from the author herself:

Anne Nicholls began writing as Anne Gay. She changed the name after marrying author Stan Nicholls. Her first published work of speculative fiction was the story 'Wishbone', which appeared in the *Gollanz/Sunday Times Anthology of SF Competition Stories*. A slew of other stories was followed by her novel *Mindsail*. This ran to four editions and reached the *Sunday Times* best-sellers list just above Dick Francis. He was at #65 on the way down from #1, though. Other novels, *The Brooch of Azure Midnight*, *Dancing on the Volcano* and *To Bathe in Lightning* followed, receiving wonderful reviews including in the *Daily Telegraph*.

At the dawning of the age of connectivity Anne was lured

into the web. Internet Service Provider LineOne hired her to edit *The SciFi Zone*, which she did for four years, relishing the privilege of interviewing luminaries such as Terry Pratchett. She was delighted to present the Karl Edward Wagner Lifetime Achievement Award to Anne McCaffrey, who revealed that she always ordered signed copies of Anne Gay's books.

LineOne became Tiscali. Now Anne, with her degree-level training in counselling, became their agony aunt. As TalkTalk they're still using her problem pages fifteen years later. The Department for Education, Schools and Families head-hunted her to be their online agony aunt too.

Between well over 150 radio and TV appearances and dozens of features in the British and American press, Anne has also found time to write two self-help books. The print editions of *Make Love Work for You* have sold in English, Spanish, Swedish and Chinese. The e-book editions of this and *Is Your Family Driving You Mad?* are just out.

For the last seven years Anne has been active in the *David Gemmell Awards for Fantasy* (www.gemmellawards.com), where the prize-winners are chosen by international vote. She has had two exhibitions of her paintings on the subject of Chronic Fatigue Syndrome and continues to enjoy writing.

Justina Robson
June 2015

By Right of the Stars

I'd never seen anything like it. I was just sitting there at a long table like everybody else. Something massive and strange passed outside the ice-encrusted windows. I slid my old dagger out of my boot and slipped it up my sleeve. Inside our cavern heads turned until everyone was staring apprehensively, reaching for knives and swords. Even so they flinched, and so did I, as the monster slammed open the door. Tall, it was, with a strange peaked head and leathery skin scabbed with snow.

Behind it, the northern lights crackled green. The sudden gust made the lanterns flicker and the fire flared. For a moment no one moved.

Then the monster ducked inside and back-heeled the door. Into the silence a deep voice said, 'Sorry about that. Wind ripped the door right out of my hands.'

And hands there suddenly were, rising to fumble at the claws on its breast. Hands all brown and strong but human-like. All at once the skin unfolded and we saw it was great blue-black wings that spread wide. One mighty beat and the creature speared upwards, beak gaping and eyes scanning the assembly.

Then we could see a man who'd been under the bony-headed creature, a slim fellow but broad-shouldered, with a lean tanned face and eyes as dark as pitch, as the giant bird-lizard flew up and away from him. Men gasped and ducked as it circled over the long tables, shedding snow and dancing round the stalactites with clacks of its long jaws, lazily ducking a knife Ostal threw. Then it slipped nimbly past the leather curtains and was gone into the bigger cave beyond.

'Don't mind Teri,' the stranger said. 'He likes fish better

than flesh.'

Only now did another man find his voice, Wotansmund, a powerful man in a spangled green robe, standing at the far side of the room in front of a board lined with arcane symbols. 'This place is private!' he burst out angrily. 'What right do you have to come bursting in here where you're not wanted?'

The stranger raised his eyebrows. Without the bird's wings cloaking him he shivered, but he answered readily enough. 'By right of the stars,' he said, and his dark eyes were steady in his wary face.

Laughter roared through the cavern. Each and every one of us at the tables laughed, the initiate-master loudest of all.

But the stranger didn't laugh. He raised his hands and drew a square on the air. It shimmered and opened...

*

Beneath a burning sunset, wave upon wave of red sand stretched to the far horizon. A strange shape filled the foreground. It took a moment for the men in the cave to realise it was an animal with a long, curved neck, seen from a saddle of crimson silk. The stranger, slim inside his robes, slung bags and rolls over his broad shoulders, then reached forward to caress the shaggy head.

'Further I cannot take you,' the camel said in a voice as dry as the whisper of sand. 'My enemy the sea would swallow me if it could, as it did once before, so very long ago. Aren, it will swallow you too if it can. And down there my other enemies will kill to stop you because they fear their end. But it is the only way for us to find freedom.'

From the crest of the last dune Aren followed the camel's gaze. Here the land rolled downwards, growing green and lumpy with date-palms and orange-trees as it neared the coast. The last shadows lengthened and the first stars peeped over the dunes in the east. From up here Aren could see the shame of his people: white walls girdling the town. All the way from one headland to the other the walls rose strong and proud, fencing off the port and the bay. But a smile flashed across his face as he realised that in their arrogance they hadn't posted a guard. It wouldn't take him long to scale the walls. Within, ten thousand stars burned yellow to challenge the god's jewelled heavens. Lamps, he suddenly realised. The lamps of those who hated the desert. Hated him.

'How can I leave you?' Aren whispered.

'You must or I'll die, and so will you.'

'I *will* die down there,' said Aren, gesturing with his chin at the scarlet sea.

'Then I'll die with you. Not the same day, not the same hour, but I will die, and all my dwellers with me. Go, my hope. Go, so you can come back to me.' And Aren felt the sand trickling down under his touch until the camel and the saddle were only veils of dust sifting away on the hot air.

*

By the time he'd walked down past the groves and the trading-ground, it was dark. The salt, moist breeze was rapidly cooling and the stars twinkled dimly, put to shame by the lanterns and cook-fires of the town by the sea. South-west and north-east, cliffs reared jagged for a hundred leagues or more. Only here could the traders land. Only from this one, noisy, smelly, smoky port could Aren sail to find what he needed. And until he'd found it, he could never come back.

But the gates were shut. From below and above thick white bars closed the entranceway. In the light of the quarter -moon the walls glittered restlessly. It was hard to focus on them. None of his people had ever been allowed so close to them. They seemed to writhe beneath Aren's gaze.

Then two lamps opened above the gates. Startled, he stepped back. He felt exposed, as though those lamps were looking at him.

They were. Flat, reptilian eyes, moon-shot and cold. Tempting, taunting, the top bars raised and the lower ones fell and he knew it was a trap. The mouth of the giant snake dripped with venom as the jaws widened further to lure him in. All around, the little snakes that made up the wall squirmed and thrashed to reach him with their needle-sharp teeth. Small wonder there were no guards. Who needed soldiers to keep the desert out?

Aren leaped back as the forked tongue slashed towards him.

Panting a little from sheer terror, he sank down cross-legged on the road. He too was taunting: he sat just out of reach, watching the thick black tongue sweeping out, but however hard it tried to catch him, always stopping short. Acrid venom flashed like opals, trying to blind him, bind him to the snake's will, but Aren had the serpent's measure. Where he sat, it couldn't drag him numbly to its maw. But it tried and kept on trying as the ghostly moon swung up the sky, wreathed ever more thinly by the coils of cooking smoke.

Slowly the sounds of the town faded. One final argument between shrill and gruff voices, a last, lilting song, one tired ringing of cymbals, the little ones girls played between their fingers before they sought sleep on their pallets on the flat roofs. Only now the port was sleeping could he hear the lullaby: the soft susurration of the waves. Too soon, too soon the tide would turn. If he missed it...

In time Aren smiled a little smile to himself. He wasn't sure it would work here, the sand-magic, in earth that was compacted with dried dung and crumbling leaves. A mere handspan beyond that scything tongue, he dug his fingers below the hard surface, calling the desert that lay sleeping beneath.

Watching as the snake's jaws grew tired and the tongue could barely raise the energy to slash out at him, Aren called a little of the desert's power and by touch wrought a tube. His slender fingers tapped here and there and tiny holes appeared down the length of it. With a gentle twirl he widened the tube's end and suddenly he put the thing to his lips.

Eldritch sweetness filled the air, soft and slow. It was

almost a flute-song yet not the sharp sounds of music made by man. Gently swaying, Aren played the endless hush of the sands, the poignant sighing of the breezes that ululated around forgotten spires of rock. The melody rose and fell, rose and fell, gentle as a sleeping baby's breath.

The little snakes' heads drifted back and forth, back and forth, remembering the days in the wilderness, before they'd been prisoned by men. Hated men, who trapped them always beneath the burning sun, never let them find shade in the noontime or warm crannies when darkness brought the chill. When the sandstorms hadn't stung, because they could burrow down to safety. When they could feast on desert rats or sometimes tunnel into a fallen gazelle, no one to tell them when they could and couldn't eat.

They yearned for the desert. They strained towards it, towards the song that called them. Even the mighty snake, Queen of the Wall, swam back into a sand-sea of memories that went back before her egg, before the egg of her dam, and her egg … Queen of the Desert, then, with all the wide spaces trembling beneath her mighty sway.

Aren played on, now louder, now softer, until the moon had sailed down behind the western cliffs and the sun sent his first faint messengers through the dim charcoal sky. And in the last darkness before the dawn his song grew softer yet, so soft the snake-wall couldn't hear what they craved, that threnody of freedom that came out of the wilderness in the east.

Then one, then two, then hundreds of white asps wriggled and stretched and snaked towards it. All thrashing at once, they freed themselves from enchanted knots and surged to Aren's flute. But before they reached him, long paces before they could engulf him, he spread his fingers and caught the dawn breeze. He held the flute high and turned it to channel the song of the air, then lofted it behind him. Grains of sand shimmered in the last starlight and sought their home, and the comber of snakes broke around Aren and was gone.

Last of all Queen of the Wall oozed towards him. She

hissed, and words whispered into his mind: 'You have freed me, Power of the Desert. Take this against your need.'

Then she too was gone. Only a sliver of white was left, a dagger made of a tooth, with a hilt of opal that held stars in its milky depths.

Aren walked into the town.

*

Already the first lights of coming day shone out through the windows. Families stretched and yawned and quarrelled, and babies cried for the warmth of their mother's milky breast. People like his people, but not like. Here was no sharing. Here the people took. When the people of the desert came with their treasures, the arrogant people of the port kept them waiting in the trading grounds outside the White Wall of Shame. After all, they were only barbarians.

A carving of ivory, elegantly shaped by days and weeks and months of craft? The port's traders sneered and offered coppers. The people of the desert were hungry? The traders sold them rancid coconut and mouldy dates. 'Nothing good comes out of the desert,' they said, but they took the goods anyway and gave starvation in return. Great slabs of salt, the two huge panniers that were the 600 pounds a camel could carry, went for half a bolt of shoddy cotton. Ice from the Mountains at the heart of the world, packed in oiled silk and skins and straw and mud and cloth that must be constantly cooled by water? A silver for a piece the weight of a tall man. For every item, bronze bowls and shapely pottery, strong nets for fishers, cakes of dye and perfumed essences, the traders lied, 'Can't give you more than I can get for it.'

But now the Wall of Shame was gone, and the people of the desert would deal directly with the shippers. The merchants' stranglehold was loosening, but it wasn't broken yet.

And Aren, all alone, would be fair game for any of the port's leeches who saw him. Light as wind he trod, ducking past flame-lit windows and hiding in shadows, heading for the caravels and the galleys down at the wharfs. The streets were so narrow that hanks of dyed wool strung across drying-poles made a shifting roof between walls he could touch with either hand. Slipping down an alley under the pearly grey skies, he saw a pot-bellied child drawing in the dust. Its eyes widened but he winked and put his finger to his lips. And swiftly he sketched a smiling camel that got up and plodded away. Rapt with wonder, the toddler followed it into the pre-dawn dimness and Aren eeled down a gunnel that was narrower yet. But it was rich with the scent of straw and dung that meant a stable.

And a stable meant donkeys. Donkeys that worked at the docks. He was close!

And he was seen.

A stocky merchant in rich clothes came out of a lamp-lit doorway and stopped abruptly. For a heart-beat the two stared at each other. Then the broad man yelled, 'Raider!'

Aren whirled and doubled back but now two others burst into the alley. Eyes glittering with hate, they jabbed towards him with their scimitars as if they couldn't wait to get close enough to run him through. The merchant stepped backwards and servants pushed past him, almost tripping each other in their haste. Aren was trapped.

He leaped upwards. Hands and feet splayed against opposite walls, he pushed himself up and up until he reached the overhanging roofs. Beneath him the mob bayed. One of them even copied him but didn't climb far before slithering back down.

Aren grabbed the coping-stone on one side and hauled himself onto the flat roof. Maids were folding blankets and rolling up mattresses, and one was cooking over a brazier. He ran past them just as the two servants burst up from the staircase.

'He's here!' yelled one, smiling broadly and tossing his knife from hand to hand.

The other didn't bother speaking. He moved aggressively sideways, blocking Aren.

Who jumped from mattress to mattress, right over their

heads and onto the stair-housing.

'You can't get away from Brahim!' yelled the talkative one, jerking his chin up to point at the other men pouring from the stairwell. In the first rays of the sun their sword-points glittered like stars. The merchant himself was smugly in their midst, urging his servants on.

Aren leaped down on them, his weight knocking three to the ground and sending the others off-balance. He ripped a hilt from one's grasp and whirled it in an arc. His own knife was in his other fist. Leaping forward, he cannoned into his closest foe, then lashed a foot into another's knee.

But he was penned by the mass of them into the corner where the girl was cooking. She huddled away from him and he flashed a grin at her. She was desert-born, a slave. Her fine features and the bruises on her arms said so. He flicked his sword under the rim of the broad pan and boiling meal scalded the front rank. The sole of his boot kicked embers that spun into the air.

And he sprang to the rim of the wall, jumping down onto the roof of the donkey-stable. It was thatched, and he went straight through, landing on a heap of straw and palm-fronds. Embers rained down with him. Tongues of flame licked shyly upwards, then gained confidence and roared into pillars of fire. The donkeys were braying and kicking in terror. Aren hurled burning fronds at the base of the locked doors, then bashed them with a pitch-fork, levering them apart.

In a charging river of hooves and teeth and flesh he burst out of the blazing stables and through the throng outside. Some were fetching pails of water. Some were striving to stab the son of the desert. But all of them were yelling hate.

He leaped aback a bolting mule and urged it downhill. He'd left the sword behind when he'd grabbed the pitchfork but the knife, long and deadly, was still in his grip. Leaning his weight sideways, he turned the mule round a corner, its hooves scrabbling on the stones of the quayside. Lines of loaders leaped aside as he galloped through, their burdens spilling to slow the pursuers.

On board the ships, sailors in strange clothes were already about their work. At one, not quite the farthest, they'd already cast off the bow-line and were struggling with the thick aft cable round one bollard.

'A fortune if you'll take me with you, lads!' yelled Aren.

Quick as a mosquito he sprang from the mule and ran up the cable to land panting on the deck a moment before the rope was cast up beside him.

'Show me the fortune,' the first mate said. 'Better be worthwhile if you want us to outrun that lot.'

Chest heaving, Aren fished inside his robes. Nobody saw what he was doing. They all thought he was just scrabbling around to find what he wanted. When he withdrew his hand and opened his fingers, red gems sparkled on his palm.

'Right then,' said the mate in his gravelly voice. 'Guess the captain won't mind. But I can't hurry the wind.'

Aren took one look back at the yelling mob, hundreds strong now, dashing towards them through the melee on the quayside. And raised his arms, back and then forwards, pushing the wind from the desert. The sails cracked and filled and out swept the caravel ahead into the bay, faster than any galley could follow, though they tried. 'Remember my name, you desert mongrel!' howled the rich merchant, leaning out from the closest galley in their wake. 'Brahim! The man who's going to kill you!'

Racing past the headlands, the caravel heeled on the waves as the men on the steering-oar tried to turn it. Aren saw what they were doing, and swivelled to funnel the winds north and eastwards, parallel to the shore. Only when the last galley had dropped behind did he sink to the deck, exhausted.

He had no idea how he looked. The clothes he wore were charred. Blisters rose on his arms and tears from the fierce winds carved white streaks through the soot on his face. His long hair was grey with ash, and the palms of his hands left bloody prints on the planks.

Curious and unhappy, the captain came aft to where he slumped. 'What's all this about a fortune?' he asked harshly, in a tongue that clearly wasn't his own. 'It had better be worth it because that port's closed to me now.'

Wearily Aren moved one hand, and a trail of rubies fell from his grasp. 'Those do you?' he asked.

With a tilt of his head the captain signalled the mate, but thought better of it and picked up the gems himself. Seven of them, each the size of a desert quail's eggs. He rubbed the blood off them and squinted through their incandescent hearts.

'So what did they want of you?' the captain asked, signing now for the mate to bring food and water for their captive. Or was he their passenger?

'I've removed their Wall so you can deal directly with my people now. They won't rob us – or you – any longer. They wanted revenge.'

'That true?' the captain said, as his officer strode the shifting deck with a loaded tray. 'Is the Wall gone?'

'Didn't see it,' the burly mate said, kneeling to touch wet cloths to the stranger's wounds. 'Should'a been on the cliffs but it weren't there. Thought it mighta been misty, though.'

'Where you headed, lad?' the captain asked absently, spinning round to check that the Wall no longer glimmered on the cliff top but the cove was well behind them now. The fabric covering his legs was light-drinking black and his shirt was white silk. Aren swigged water and examined him. His beard was the colour of wheat and he dressed like no one Aren had ever seen.

'North, where the snow comes from, and the sky is green and yellow and the sun doesn't set at night.'

'We wasn't headed there.'

'But you could be?'

Now the captain was polishing the rubies with a fine lace-edged kerchief while the burly first mate tried not to seem like he was staring. 'Or I could tip you over the side and take the rest of them jewels.'

'But you won't.'

From the crow's nest the watch called, 'Sail ahoy!'

They looked where the boy was pointing, at the triangular sails behind. The caravel was carving the rollers well enough, but at a speed the faster ships were easily overhauling.

'Make me more of that wind!' snapped the captain.

'I can't. I'm worn out.'

'I'll hand you over to them.'

'You've helped their enemy, captain. Think they'll stop with taking me?'

Grimly eying their twin pursuers, the tall blond man stowed the fare into his cummerbund. 'More sail!' he yelled. 'Clear the decks for action!' and to Aren, 'Can you fight?'

Closer and closer came the two ships, lean, raking biremes with flashing banks of oars. Sailors were in the rat-lines, cutlasses bared and grappling-hooks darkly fanged against the bright horizon. Within minutes they'd be upon them.

Calmly Aren ate and drank and in the bustle of arming the crew, the captain forgot him. Aren prowled down into the holds, smelling out what was there. Piles of gazelle-horns spiralled in the light of a swaying lantern, and bales of cured hides sent their ripe musk into the gloom. Sacks of salt. Ivory and brass. Vast bowls of copper from the heart of the desert. Aren smiled, and opened the hatches.

The captain – Aren hadn't even had time to find out his name – yelled, 'Batten 'em down!' but Aren strode to him and whispered in his ear. The captain called, 'Belay that! Get to your stations!'

At their master's command the steersmen heaved on their boards and the ship reeled aslant, furling all sail. The galleys swept past, the larboard one so close that the caravel's stern raked the oars to splinters. Over heeled the ship, sending Brahim and his men tumbling. On the slave-decks rowers screamed as their chests crumpled, and so fast was it travelling that the oars on the far side had already dipped so it swerved away, crippled. Blood streaming from a gash in his head, Brahim the merchant raged his vicious spite.

But the other galley slowed and backed water and then it was alongside. The grapples swung and bit the caravel's rails. A wave of sailors leaped aboard. Steel met steel amid the ringing battle-cries. On the poop-deck the captain hacked, his steersmen at his side. Blood stained the decks. A hand flew and flopped to tangle empty in the ratlines. And nowhere could the captain see Aren, the cause of all his troubles.

Now the one-winged galley had limped to their other side. Once more the grapples hit the rails. Brahim the merchant was busy at the forefront, urging his soldiers on. The defenders' forces were split. Slowly they were being pushed into the middle. In a moment they'd be back to back, surrounded.

Then they heard a sound, felt it rather, a resonance that sounded like a wet finger on the rim of a glass, only deeper, far deeper, deep enough to shudder bones. For a heartbeat nameless dread stopped the fighting but Brahim cursed and thrust forward, impaling a defender and kicking him off the point of his scimitar. Then the slash and thrust renewed with clanging savagery.

Suddenly Aren stood on the deck at the head of the open hold. Round his throat was a necklace of lion's teeth. In his left hand he brandished the Queen of the Desert's tooth, and balanced on his right was a bowl of shining bronze. Round and round the rim he sent the serpent's tooth, making that unearthly sound – or part of it.

Because the rest was quivering through the planks. A torrent of hoof beats, a deafening waterfall of snarls. Ghostly gazelles plunged and bucked. And the skins of desert lions filled with their ghosts and smashed outwards at the attackers.

Yelping with fear, some tried to flee. Some hurled themselves from one deck to the other, and some fell to be crushed between the hulls. Others battled on, too fearful of their lives to look aside.

But not Brahim. Berserk, he jinked past a lion and carved

his way towards Aren. Cords stood out on his bull-neck and his scimitar darted gracefully through one target to the next.

Then he was before Aren. He saw the desert-man armed only with the things which brought forth such hideous, deathly music. With a sudden smile on his sweating face, Brahim lunged.

Aren swayed a fraction and plunged the serpent's tooth through Brahim's shoulder. The merchant fell back, the tooth still in his flesh, and the music stopped. Skins fell to the deck, but the human dead were still dead. Aren saw Brahim struggling to stand. He yanked free his serpent's tooth. Grinning, he gonged the bowl on the merchant's temple, and Brahim toppled.

*

The captain – Aren discovered his name was Jan – was all for taking the galleys as prize-ships, but Aren tilted his head to where other sails now poked above the horizon. 'No time. But free the rowers. It will slow them down.' Briefly all was chaos as the last of the enemy were locked below their own decks, Brahim hurled ungently on top of them, while the rowers cheered and Jan's crew snatched what they could. Not much, but still a worthy haul.

Hoisting sail, the caravel headed north and east once more. Jan had his men clear the slain from his decks. He only shrugged when the mate wailed, 'All them skins is full of holes!'

'Ours aren't. Cram on the canvas.'

*

The caravel sailed north. Once a storm all but swamped them, and once when they stopped in a cove for supplies, bad water sickened the crew. Still they seemed to have outrun pursuit. Jan kept a wary eye on the desert man and didn't try to rob him.

They dropped anchor in Amsterdam to offload, and there Aren found a berth on a whaler heading for Stavanger. Three days he waited for the whaler to set sail, and all the time he turned his eyes from the hostel on the Ijssel Meer to watch for incoming shipping, but he didn't see the galleys. Nor did he see Brahim, shivering, lurch down the gangplank with one arm in a sling off a brigantine that had made port at Le Havre.

But Brahim saw him.

*

At Stavanger Aren came off in a bum-boat, and felt clumsy when his feet touched the frozen earth. Ice slicked the quayside and the mountains back of the fish-stinking town reared white spikes to the ever-dark sky.

The food was wrong. It lay cold and heavy in his belly. The furs he bought with the rubies of his blood weighed so much he felt swaddled and ungainly so he wore only the thinnest. The one piece of iron he'd brought – a needle suspended in a small bamboo cage – pointed the way.

People told him a blizzard was coming. Don't leave, they said. Watch out for the elk. They'll trample you. The wolves will hunt you down. Stay away from the dragons because they're always hungry for travellers. And the trolls – but they wouldn't talk about them.

But Aren remembered Brahim, and climbed out from the town to set his ambush.

Up into the dark-firred mountains where the winds smelt of snow and even the food tasted of pine-resin. Far off a wolf -pack belled, and in the next valley a male howled back his loneliness. Aren was camping by the thread of a waterfall spilling out of a half-frozen lake when he heard wings above the crackle of his fire.

He sat very still, one hand pushing down into the soft earth below the ash, where his fire had melted the permafrost. Wise enough not to stare into the flames but outwards, beyond the golden circle of firelight, he scanned the skies. Wind stirred the tops of the fir-trees so they seemed to try and catch diamond-bright stars. The aurora borealis sang in shifting curtains of rose and emerald.

And there in front of it was a moving patch of blackness. The blackness grew until it had head and wings and a long, spear-like tail. Aren sat very, very still, humming.

The blackness had shining eyes that gleamed brightly in the light of the fire. It perched on the rock which helped shelter Aren from the cold, and said, 'You're not trying to kill me! That's very polite of you. Perhaps I won't have you for supper.'

Aren's hum rose in his throat until it was words. 'I bring greetings from your cousins in the sunny lands to the south.'

'Cousins?' The dragon cocked its head and its eyes shone like stars. 'I have cousins?'

'Indeed you do. They have hides of amber and red and copper, but they don't have the plain elegance of your ebony skin.'

'Is that manners or is it flattery?'

'That's for you to decide,' said Aren with a crooked smile. 'But you're letting my supper burn. Would you mind if I took it off the spit? You're welcome to share it, of course. It's fish.'

The dragon, its body not much longer than Aren's but lighter with its bird-bones, hopped down the other side of the fire, ungainly until it had coiled its tail neatly round its haunches. Its toothy jaws made some difficulty in speaking but it managed. 'I love fish. Too cold to catch it this time of year, though. The water makes my teeth ache.'

'Not if you have some twine and a hook. There should be more come morning, but for now, let's eat.'

*

Above the eastern mountains the sky grew pale and yellow but west over the wild seas, stars still sparkled around the crescent moon. After a long night swapping tales, the dragon was asleep, curled almost round the fire to hog the heat, but Aren had kept to his own spot and slept with his fingers still in the fire-warmed earth.

The earth trembled softly to footfalls coming closer. Aren woke at its message. Soon he heard harsh breathing as seven men toiled uphill. He peered cautiously over the dragon's bulk at them several bow-shots below. Sure enough, Brahim was there, fat in his frosty furs. His arm was out of its sling and the gash on his forehead had healed to a thin white scar. Two pale men were in front of him, others with darker skins straggling back behind.

'You're tickling me,' grumbled the dragon.

'We've got visitors. The fat one wants to stop me.'

'Stop you what?' said the dragon, shifting his head round on his long neck to peer sleepily at the newcomers below.

'Stop me learning how to trap words on parchment so no-one can cheat my people any more.'

'Don't they do this word-trapping closer to your home?'

'They do, Teri, they do. But it seems there are different ways of trapping words. Way up here their magic looks different and it's so far from home that our goods are worth many times what folk nearer would give. And it would take many magicians to change one language to the next for all the lands that lie between. Each might lie or cheat and if we don't understand all their word-magics, how would we know? So the desert sent me to find out the word-magic of these ice-mountain people. Brahim and his people have robbed your people and mine too many times for us to let them get away with it any longer.'

'They're not my people. And there are seven of them and one of you,' said Teri, the point of his tail beginning to twitch. 'How do I know you're telling me the truth?'

'I've told you my story. Here's the Queen of the Desert's tooth. What does it say to you?'

Teri took it in a forepaw, sniffing the long spike with its tip of venom ever ready. Cold-blood to cold-blood, creature of myth to creature of myth, truth ran from the fang to the dragon's mind. 'Let's eat them!' Teri exclaimed.

'Let's not,' said Aren. 'There's more fish on the lines. Will you frighten away the men of the north? I'll take Brahim.'

What they had believed was a rock suddenly became a man beside a dragon. The men of the north were terrified. Both made religious signs, then one ran while the other threw a spear in panic. It fell far short. He drew a sword. So did Brahim and some of the others.

Teri leaped aloft. His wings cracked the air as they opened wide. So nimble was he that he made a game of dodging their missiles or catching them to rain them back down. He enjoyed frightening them off and swooped cheerfully down the valley.

Only Brahim kept coming. Sweat dripping from his crimson face, the fat merchant waddled up the hill, scimitar in hand. 'Got you, you son of a diseased camel! I know your game and you're not getting away with it!' he puffed.

He must have felt secure in all those layers of fur, in all his years of running his town and cheating his victims. But the desert man brandished Queen of the Desert's fang like a dagger. From its tip flew a spot of venom that landed unerringly in Brahim's eye. It sparked like an opal, shone like a star. He screeched and fell to his knees, pawing at his face.

No more than Brahim had Aren expected quite that. Brahim knelt weeping. At first he keened with pain, or that's what it seemed like. Then his cries turned to sobs.

'What have I done! What have I done!' he wailed. 'No wonder the desert hates me. It'll swallow me up, swallow all of us, and there'll be nothing but sand forever.'

'We of the desert have your place, and we of the sand our own. Treat us fairly, Brahim, and we'll trade with you and with the ships. Rob us and you doom your kind.'

Swiftly Aren pulled in his fish-lines and started breakfast. Neither he nor Teri noticed when the hidden man crept out and led Brahim away.

*

I saw the stranger clap his hands and the window closed. Now there was just tables and chairs and a man in light furs. Silence hung in the cavern but for the wind rattling the door. Wotansmund began to say, 'You're not welcome —'

Then a swoop and a splash and a caw of triumph rang out from the lake in the back cavern to remind us that the stranger was not alone.

The initiate cleared his throat and grasped the fronts of his spangled robe in a considered pose that was supposed to show his importance. 'You're not properly welcomed, I should say. Come in and warm yourself by the fire. A stoup of mulled ale and a platter of pork-belly?'

'That's very kind,' said Aren, and slipped neatly between the rows of benches.

'What – ah, what did you think to find here?'

'I've come to learn your mysteries, the mysteries of words trapped on parchment so lies cannot stand.'

'And what would you give for this?' asked Wotansmund, clearly thinking of rubies and magic.

'Your mystery of trapping words should be free for everyone, don't you think?' asked Aren, quietly. 'That way you and we can both benefit.'

'What of your mysteries?' asked the initiate, fire catching in his greedy eyes.

'Come to the desert. You can learn our ways in half your lifetime.'

'That's too high a price!'

'I've paid it already, paid it in a thousand stars.'

From the inner cavern the dragon crunched bones.

Hastily Wotansmund said, 'So you have.'

We all sneaked our daggers away and picked up our pens, Aren among us, smiling softly as he brought a new magic to the desert.

Howie Dreams

Howie Dreamed and I smiled. It was a good Dream, cheerful and bright with colour. I had made the best Dream I could for him, sorry that I couldn't be with my friend at his first big performance on stage.

For ninety seconds his synapses caught movement before it could escape down his nerves to his muscles. The action was cerebral, the reaction a physical fact. He would wake self-confident and positive, at concert-pitch, and he wouldn't know why.

I would.

That's why I smiled.

Tiptoeing out of my spare room, I slung my travel case like a bandolier, and took my only prototype with me. Nothing nasty showed on the detectors so I braved the bitches on watch in my garden. I used to be afraid of them, of all dogs, but now I knelt to cuddle them, Minerva with her soft black coat and Athene all white-furred over her metal skin. Still I petted them goodbye. Howie might need them here. Besides, I couldn't take them into battle. Timenda sum, et dona ferente, and it was no two-bit wooden contraption like the Trojan Horse either. My dear bitches went back to burying some bones under the chestnut tree and I wondered who they'd been.

At the outer wall I peered at my security bracelet. It showed me the view through the eyes of the metal lions. Everything checked out. But the moment I stepped beyond the garden gates I burst into sudden flames. I bit down on a gasp but my shield held. It kept out the worst of the heat and light from the laser attack. My heart threatened to choke me. Who...?

The lions defended me with ultrasonics aimed at the laser's source. I heard the man vomit. I think it's eleven cycles a second that does that. My lions can't kill on the street. Penalty for death on the footpath, £2,000. The puke would cost him a modest fifty. And when my shield had gone out and I was back in normal cloudy daylight, my lungs sucked in cooling air.

Hefting my cases, I stepped into Rosalind's old banger, looking everywhere to check the baddie had no friends along. What I was carrying would change the world – I *hoped* for the better. Had the assassin known? Worse, *how* had he known? And the million-dollar question: who had sent him?

I changed cars seven times on the way to the unsuspected airport and threw my heli-tickets in a rubbish bin.

I was off to the first World Dream Fair.

*

Vienna, city of dreams – with a small 'd', until tonight. To the west, the dark hills distant under the violet sky, and the Danube, reflecting in amethyst the linden-scented air. Nearer, on the opposite bank, the Danube Tower and its warm-lit revolving restaurant. Viennese whirls with a vengeance. The Prater Park, where screams and laughter are the same thing, and the stately Riesenrad wheeling tourists high above the amusements.

The last time I'd been here, this side of the river was woods between the canalised arms of the Danube. Now it was the Wälderschloss Hotel. Imagine a Disney palace disguised as a faerie tree-house, right down to a jolly statue of a Valkyrie with a spear – better than Tinkerbell for keeping you safe – and you've got it. If you can afford it.

Like me. This was *my* Dream Fair, real rags-to-riches stuff. Well, more terraced house to penthouse. Or like it says on the quiz shows, my starter for men. Assuming everything went to plan. I could hardly believe I'd made it happen at last. I wondered who had sent the man to kill me – and if he was here.

I even let the doorman carry my bags for a tip. Harry

Lime would have been proud of me.

*

The opening ceremony was perfunctory. Hardly anyone ever turns up to things like that, least of all to listen to a sales pitch.

Why do so many men think women are untrustworthy? And so many women feel threatened by their sisters?

Cunning: I had a couple of guys on the platform with me: be-suited with distinguished silver highlights and rising exec in tight trousers. That should please everyone. They were nice guys too. And there was Regina and me to lead the chat. She's beautiful, Regina, with her slim young Germanity smart in short hair. Regina doesn't believe in make-up but then, she doesn't need it. I'm tall and in my thirties and striving for glamour. But then, I'm not as pretty.

Of course, there were the drinkers by the bar at the back, with sporadic types dotting the empty rows. A doctor or two, perhaps, a sprinkling of shrinks, and the mostly-empty seats reserved for an indifferent press. Was it one of them who was out to get me? No, they didn't look like killers. Just freeloaders, I hoped.

And up front where the lights were bright, there were five men and a token woman, all looking unnaturally keen ... to entrap us.

Which is why we'd bothered to hold the ceremony in the first place. It's nice to know who your enemies are.

*

Howie rang my mobile right when I didn't want him to.

He was tall and funny, his body sliding warmly on mine as we danced. Crystal archways glittered against the velvet night. The music soared, rich on the coloured air. The chandeliers were dimmer than the lights of the Altstadt a Danube away.

France smells of Gauloises; Spain is hot dust, black tobacco and sweet soap. Vienna smells of lime-trees by the river and cream coffee perfumed with traffic. We'd recreated them all. With Walla – his name was Walla – I danced through all of them, but the businessmen stayed in clumps for safety, in corners that reminded them of home. They didn't know the psychology of smell. They seemed to feel threatened by emotional technology, especially in the hands of women, as if any of us not a secretary or a cleaner was out to get them. I only wanted to rid them – and some of the sisters – of reciprocal fear.

They were the self-interested ones. The communicators explored each other's cliques. Regina matched steps with Jo-Beth, still noting, as I did, who was which.

Most of us were in party mood, even the ones caressing their fantasies on leaf-screened balconies. Weren't the dampers humming merrily in the raftered branches, just to reassure us that our laser-guns wouldn't work? All my people, and all my guests, were as safe as I could make them. I thought. I'd hoped Howie was OK back in London. I shook my worry off. He had my defences, didn't he? And the meetings at this Dream Fair should sort out the wheat from the chaff.

Our arms like stoles, Walla walked beside me through a skein of leaves. Walla sounds like Valour. We felt as if we'd known each other forever, each life impossible to imagine without this sudden friend. Yet still we were a little shy, like kids in Sunday clothes, as we melted towards a kiss. We touched like butterflies, testing. His lips were warm on the side of my neck, getting closer…

That's when Howie rang.

For a second there I sank my head on Walla's shoulder. Resigned, I sighed an excuse. Walla smiling – how? – shrugged and said, 'Zee you later.' He sounded mostly American but looked mostly Slav.

Did he mean it? I couldn't tell any more once the leaves dappled closed behind his retreat. I have to fight off mistrust too.

I answered my bracelet. Howie's face lightened the LED screen if not my frustration. Of course my shield wouldn't work here with the dampers but I knew he wouldn't have belled me if it wasn't important.

'Danan. Got me. Ey've got me, Dian!' His eyelids drooped. His head lolled suddenly onto his chest.

My bracelet said it was in Germany. The place Howie was in, not the bracelet. Hell, I was disorientated. I'd better get myself together. Howie wasn't worth much in cash terms, only a million or so. Nothing compared to his intrinsic human value. And if I hadn't got what They wanted – Oh God, let Them want money! – no doubt the sisters would get it for me; Kyoko and Regina, Hélène and Indira, half a dozen others. I'd done the same thing for Gianna before now. Let it be money…

But it would wreck my bargaining position – all our positions.

Besides, Howie was my friend.

'Sup?' he groaned. They pushed him – a dark, dirty hand. Howie jerked suddenly from side to side: they were trying to shake him awake. A startled blink opened his face to a reality he didn't like.

'They want it, Diana. Machine. You. Don't let them –'

Howie was switched off. My bracelet went dark. Through the crystal-floored terrace I looked down past the net of Wälderschloss branches. They were concrete, steel, I don't know. Stronger than oak, or mountains – but I felt I was falling, straight onto the Valkyrie's spear. It was aimed between my legs.

*

It was first light before They called again, that hideous time when the nightmare still lurks; the monster, fear, dripping in the mind and the sun too far away to drive it beneath the breakers of the subconscious. Gianna and I were still arguing; Regina back in Bonn; Hélène's lover in Dijon, in a flat above the city wall, all of us tuned in for the message. There had to be a message …

I couldn't trace Howie from my home. We had to triangulate the message at its source. So much depended on it.

Kyoko phoned from the lobby. The sound of it wrang our hearts. White-masked geisha, antennae quivering in her pearl-strung hair, she said, 'A package. Come by taxi, No. 74.' She actually said 'no'. 'The driver, she was phoned to pick it at the airport from left luggagings. Money was there, and package, key was left in lock.'

Very efficient. You'd never know she was blind.

Reception sent it up. A heart-attack for Gianna and me though we were both expecting the knock.

'Special delivery,' said the bellboy sleepily, dithering artistically until we gave him a tip. Then he thanked us with polite surprise.

We weren't expecting what was in it.

Howie's little finger. I gagged. The box in the padded envelope was sticky with his blood.

I wouldn't go any further, not even watch the message, till I had Howie's tape faxed to me. And the finger – Howie's finger – analysed and put on ice. Fingerprint and tissue-type, it was Howie's all right. It matched. It would be able to box arpeggios again – if ever we got the rest of him back in time.

No analgesic in the blood.

My stomach echoed to Howie's pain. I was afraid for us, too, all of us: the mothers, the shop girls and factory hands, the fishwives at the docks and the bankers, the teachers, the politicians – all of us threatened by the men who had Howie and what They could do with my machine. And by the women who'd handed him over.

No one knew what had happened to him. He'd never made his concert. The scanners, the bitches, the lions – none of them showed anything at all. So it had to be one of the girls who worked with me at Somequa Dreams. A friend. Great.

Why? This counter-counter espionage could wreck all of our Dreams.

Literally. The tape in the box showed Howie naked on a dusty floor. He was curled up foetally. Someone hooked his hand out with a wire coat-hanger. Left hand for rhythm, thumb and three fingers now, a massive scabbing clot where his fifth finger had been, counting as a pianist which Howie usually was.

The hanger disappeared from sight. Still unconscious, Howie withdrew his hand and cradled it on his opposite arm. Dried blood crusted his chest and thigh.

In his pain I mirrored the gesture.

Gianna's tough. Her aunt was in the women's radio station in Rome that was blown up by the Right. She said, 'No cry. Listen.'

I stopped, and we did.

One of those voice machines that make you sound like a robot used to. Impossible to tell for sure but I thought it was a man.

It said in German English, 'You, Dinah Schlate. We have your traitor-friend. You have only one finger of him. How you want him back – by instalments? Another finger at nine o'clock. Listen him. He have screamed.'

He had. I heard him. My friend. The close-up was sickening: Howie, white and sweating, mother-naked, his hand foreshortened, held down by a crate-staple. A huge axe drifted down to touch his finger for aim: the little finger, pinned too, fresh-bruised by the wire.

Up – down. The finger flopped drumming onto the hollow crate. Howie screamed against his will.

'In slices,' said the mechanised voice. 'He is playing no more the piano.

'Or, bring us now the machine, the new, not the one with which you must have wires to the head, but the sending one for Dreaming when you are awake or not. I have many plans for it…

'Alone go to the airport with the machine. Fly to Düsseldorf with the 6.30 machine.' He meant plane this time. 'You get a message there if you are alone coming. No lasers, no shield, or bye-bye Howie. No tracers with you, or bye-bye Howie. You get not his body back.'

The scream replayed, echoing on a plain concrete wall.

Not quite plain. It had Howie's blood on it.

I was shaking. I can't convey the horror of that voice like Sparky's piano. I really didn't need Gianna shouting over the hiss of the blank tape, 'So let him die. *Ecco,* is revolution, no? Lose Howie. Is not important. Machine is and you. Not a man.'

'He is! He's my friend!' I yelled in spiralling rage and fear. 'Oh, shut up!' as she started again in machine-gun Italian.

When I rang Regina, she hadn't been able to track anything. Nor Hélène's lover at Dijon University. I mean, how could you with an anonymous package?

I cancelled the lover, and Regina jetted back to Vienna. That little time had passed, less than half a night: she would have to be me at my Dream Fair. Hell, I was livid. And guilty, too. If it wasn't for my Dreams, They wouldn't have wanted Howie. Or what my Dreams could do…

I wondered hollowly what They would do to me. Sulking, Gianna drove me to the airport, even crosser when, on Their orders, I handed her my bracelet. No shields now, and now phone. They'd said. So this was what isolation felt like.

*

Düsseldorf. Glass and steel buildings, Volkswagens hooting on the bridges. Industrialisation in Early Smog. The taxi-woman wore a skirt and peasant blouse, very fetching. She took me, like a message at the airport said, to a kiosk on the Kö, where the machine-voice ordered me about on the old-style sound-only phone. I had to follow His commands, she followed mine, rushing me to a café – where I waited hours for the next call. The taxi-driver had endless coffees with Kirschtorte and cream. She could afford it as the minutes clicked her meter. I swear it turned into a kilometre.

I thought about Howie, and sweated. Machine-voice and axes, and what might have happened as nine a.m. came and went.

The machine to cheer up the world sat idly in its boxes.

My fear must have showed. She tried to cheer me up. Lovely Gitta, meter maid, told me all about her Dream. 'Oh, it was wonderful. My husband, he snores, you must know.' Actually I didn't but I can't say I cared. She went on to my apathy, 'He collects the mats on which you stand the beer-glasses in the bars. He goes often with his friends to many bars, to collect them, he says. When he home comes —' she was proud of her tourist English '—he does not ask me how went the day for me or Karin. That is my daughter, she is at the high school. He lays the mats on the new table I have bought and tells me about them. I am not interested longer – at first, yes, but now he has thousands. He laughs and smells of beers, you understand? He is pleased with himself and wants not to listen, only to talk. He earns not much money and gives it all out on the beer.'

Uncertain of my attention, here in the potted music and palms as the air slides from morning coffee to lunchtime wine and Howie could be armless, she says, 'You are sure is here the café where your friends phone?'

And I say, 'Yes. But I don't know when.' Because if I reveal the kidnap she will call the police and bye-bye Howie.

She smiles innocently. 'We have time for a coffee then. Would you like another?'

And when it comes and the phone call doesn't, she drags my attention back with fluttering gestures and feminine laugh. It has a certain sleazy fascination, this girls together talk of her Dreams. Will she regret her confidences later?

All the time I keep thinking of Howie and that awful joke: 'Doctor, will I ever be able to play the piano again?'

*

I was contemplating dying when she finally drove me to the pick-up point.

The Howienappers had sent me from phone-booth to old-fashioned phone-booth, outside banks, the Trade Fair, Wimpy bars and jewellers. I was jittery, afraid, oppressed by women's guilts. I could have screamed from the tension but at each new contact I squeezed calmness into my voice. They would be tense too. If I wound their springs any tighter Howie could...

Howie. His defenceless eyes at Their boot-toes. The flat, friendly stomach where I leant my head, stripped of its flesh. If I didn't make Their Dreams come true, I'd have balled up my friend's skin in my hand and torn it away to discard it. My friend, almost the most wonderful person I'd ever met. Irritating and aggravating, not of one flesh like my sisters but learning from me and teaching me. We liked each other, not sexually, but as people sharing the same race and planet. And he was one hell of a laugh on a good day.

Was?

I could have made the Dream-way without his backing, but not spread it as wide as we have. He believed – believes? – in respect for the individual, as I do. Don't you like people who think the same as you?

Dear Howie, what are They doing to you now?

That axe … in the taxi my stomach shrank too.

*

At nightfall, by the sunset-flamed Thyssen Tower, They told me this address. They'd proved I wasn't bugged and I wasn't followed, and in the red-reflecting kiosk They sent a shudder of more fear to pump up my heart. He said, 'I can see you. I watch you. I know exactly what you do.

'Now. Do this right. You come now here, to this address. Because I still you watch.'

And when I whirled round, His unseen eyes could have been anywhere.

I make Dreams. They made me a nightmare. I can still feel it everywhere, following me from inside. They say rapists watch. We are afraid.

Gitta slid the taxi down a wide street on an industrial estate. There were trees and regimented flowers between the factories. Mind, they're all like that – until the next time some kindly government knocks them flat. Some holy war, a mushroom cloud, and thou, my love, goodbye. And there were eyes in the gathering darkness.

I sneezed from soot and soap powder drifting down as thunderheads squashed the air. Gitta looked at me in the mirror as we were sucked towards Their lair, and said, 'You are all right?'

Whose side was she on?

I nodded. She accepted it, knowing it was far from the truth. She chatted to comfort. 'That Dream I was telling you. I cannot afford a personal Dream, but my friends get some sometimes from a man she knows. I borrow her machine. My husband would be very much angry if he knew. But he doesn't. He sleeps like a – tree?'

Her intonation rose to ask me if I understood. I nodded again, appalled.

'It is another lover every night. It is not always clear; it hurts my head a little, but it is worth it. It is so good, you know? It gives much pleasure to my friends and me.

'Last night it was a man; my husband only not my husband, kind and handsome, you know?'

I could imagine. I'd seen pirate-Dreams before, fuzzed and darkly sexual. Gitta grinned, embarrassed but conspiratorial, and said, 'Tomorrow, if you would like, ring the taxi company and I will lend you one. It will relax. I felt him very powerful,' she went on. 'He made me feel safe. You like men like that?' In the twilight she thought I knew what I said. 'It was very good, he liked to make love. My husband, he likes to have sex, when he wants, like he wants. I am not in it, you know? Only an opening for him. Maybe he was different before, or maybe I only remember him how I expected him to be when I did not know what questions to ask.

'But that Dream! He knew just what I wanted. The man made me feel safe. I mattered to him. It was very good to have someone strong to look after me. We had many children. I look after him, too.'

In the mirror as the hoardings slid by, hiding His eyes, her eyes crinkled while she smiled. She was in love with a cheap fantasy, and tonight would darn the socks of the man she mistook for her lover. A deadly romance to stop her changing her life.

I knew who'd made the Dream. Who else?

The kidnappers. People who cut off fingers and people's minds.

What would They do to me?

*

Empty factory, boarded up. Inside – strip search, done by Gitta, and after all that money from me too. They paid her well – also my money – and final indignity of her pudgy, cake-wielding fingers, she even searched inside me. I almost threw up. Then They sent her away. After all, They didn't want any women cluttering up Their far-Right plans. A needle…

When I woke up, I was somewhere else, and it hurt. Even if Regina traced my greedy taxi-driver, she'd never find me now. Even the air smelt different – essence of rural mould. It was very quiet. I wondered why They needed me so far from humankind. Maybe from here nobody would hear me scream.

They left me a tee-shirt and knickers. The red tiles were cold under my feet when They let me see Howie – by phone. I didn't know where he was either, only that there was no time-lag on the phone. Precision – somewhere in the Western hemisphere. Ace.

I tried to make a joke for him but I couldn't get the words out. He looked awful. He still had nine fingers though. He said one word: 'Don't.'

I did.

I got out the Super Acme Dreama Deluxe – that wasn't its real name. That was just me, trying to raise a smile. Would you call a bringer of hope and joy by an acronym like SADD?

Oh, I grieved for it as I took it out of its white cases. It was meant to be such a good thing, to take the sting out of relationships and float them along on a river of understanding. With everything, even the opposite sex.

They made me force unreality into its circuits. Believe me – my Dreams had never been untrue, until that night. I was terrified.

I demanded the head, preferably separate, but They weren't as literal as me. Firmly attached to His sergeant-major's body, His head wore a gorilla mask. It looked very odd with His suit and tie and shiny dead-crocodile shoes. Frightening. His friend with the axe came too.

'If I'm to make your Dream right,' I said to his deception, 'I need your eyes and your temples uncovered.' Smart, don't you think? Then I'd be able to recognise Him for my retribution.

They made me align my machine in the light but focus it in total darkness so I never saw His face. My horror grew – out of his invisible, tangible presence, His desires, His domination – and His axeman stalking unseen.

I pressed the buttons that blocked out His conscious self – rather more thoroughly than I had led them to believe. I had to leave enough of Him on top to speak if the guard asked Him to. Before the lights went out, this one was a leering Bavarian spirit in macho studded black. I wondered what his coarse breathing was now.

Gorilla didn't like even the minimal contact of the beams as I tuned them in. He was hostile, more than suspicious. I was frightened for Howie and myself.

But I said, 'Words are not something that people have in common. Words reflect experience. I'm a woman, smaller than you, younger than you, from a different culture. I have less acquisition of wisdom; I'll never be as powerful as you obviously are. Your meanings won't be the same as mine. The best you could hope for is that they'd overlap. And you want better than that, don't you?'

Treacle and truth mixed up like a half-chewed sandwich. Soothed to merely terrifying, He still objected in the heavy breathing dark, 'But I am told your good machine needs no personal matching.'

'Not for giving the Dream, no, though it's better.' I wondered if he could smell the fear on me. 'But for making a Dream perfect to your order…'

They like order. His body might be an NCO's but His

thoughts were definitely officer class.

But he'd never played at semantics.

*

It was easier to breathe when They left me alone with the light-switch. Their sweat and aftershave and body-smell still tickled the hairs in my nose with the scent of rubber mask even after the soundproof door closed off Their footsteps. The neon light was as welcome as sunshine. I felt its release in the slackening of my rib-muscles but freedom was a distant country.

I played back his dream. Still small 'd'. He wanted me to capitalise it.

What it was scared me more than Howie in his grasp.

First, pump up His executives' self-esteem: Hitler Jugend in saddle-stitched suits. Send them out invincible, conquering sales, subverting their competitors.

And the Dreams were: look at the evidence of your eyes. How many women architects? How famous? Where were the Schillerins? The Goethe-esses? Can you name a lady Turner?

But the horrifying thing was: the Dreams were for women too. To teach them they couldn't do it, whatever it was. To teach them to love looking good for men only and not for themselves. Look: the make-up houses would buy it. And the sellers of domestic gear. Just think of their increase in sales if all women can do is look good for playing house.

To show women couldn't be plumbers, because they weren't. How cosy, how easy – don't fix it yourself. Leave the cold floods round your ankles to a man. He'd mend that pipe, and you'd be glad of his company while you made him coffee. There's moral support if you like.

And on and on. Back to feather dusters and antimacassars; sex as a cage – if we were good. Farewell to research, or finance. Each of us isolated and shrunken to cowering in our homes – because we were afraid of the big bad world outside.

I love Howie. There's a lot of men I love.

I love my home. But not when it's my prison.

44 / Anne Nicholls

I didn't think much of His colour-scheme either.

The table was bolted to the floor. Chair ditto. There were no windows and the food came on plastic plates. I was very alone.

I started building the plan of His Dream, the furniture if you like, the characters you can't see because they're you. I even trained His bully-boys in how to use the machine to blare out a Dream to whoever walks by, which is what He wanted. Never mind if they fall under a truck in this sudden Dream, or spend their last pfennigs on fashion, not food. His thugs were fine technicians, though. With all the sensitivity of a tractor.

I ate, I slept, and nightmared of less Howie and more axe. I tried to give Regina and Gianna the time to find us by delaying and procrastinating but the thought of Gianna's laserettes and the backlash of male fury wouldn't let me stop entirely.

Every now and then They let me phone Howie.

He had septicaemia. He looked like a stick-insect on a diet. I downed tools – well, brain – until They let him have a doctor. They were always worse when Gorilla wasn't there.

They countered, 'We'll chop his hands off, swish, with the axe. You go on now.'

I said, 'Howie'll die. I'll wreck the machine. *He* won't like that.'

They said, 'Then you'll die. Or you'll make another machine.'

'How can I?' I wailed. 'I'm only a woman.'

They believed that.

*

After that first time it was always light in there, even when I peed. My mind tramped in circles of no escape, and when Tampax appeared it was terrifying to know they watched even my most intimate acts. And by telephone Howie's body grew visibly frailer. In agony and guilt I worked in cold eternal light, faster, longer, to get us out of here. With penicillin and all, I was still waiting for him to die. What would I do then?

There were four hundred and seventy-five red tiles one way, three hundred and thirty-three and a half across the other axis of the floor. Every third tile was a dust-sucker. They knew that much about my Dream machine anyway.

I tried, to stop myself thinking too much about the wicked imbalance He wanted me to perpetrate on a world struggling towards fairness, I tried with pen and paper to work out exactly how many tiles that made.

It was only when I was too tired to think constructively. Never twice did I come up with the same answer. I'm an artist, a jeweller of thoughts, not a scientist, you see.

And always I knew They were watching me.

*

Howie began to make jokes. You could still play 'Chopsticks' on his dirty yellow ribs but his eyes no longer looked like London fog. Just a little, I started to hope. Maybe we'd make it – if Gorilla didn't come back.

The gorilla came to see me. An off-white safari-suit this time – very chic, but it still gave me the creeps to talk to a trousered primate. It was … inhuman. In separate corners, a devil and a skull held Their axes watchfully, as if I might karate Them from fifteen feet. His soldiers were as wary of women as He was. Why else would He be doing this?

He said, 'I am hearing reports. Your friend is better now. You waste no more time. Or my friend will make him worse. Our axe has two heads. Do you need your breasts, to work? I give you twenty-four hours, *ja?*'

Threat changed to gloat. 'We have mechanalysed the machine. It is copied now manifold. In three days' time we will have copies of my Dream that you make in every department-store in the German speaking world. Soon we will have a better, an English language one also. Then we will let you go.'

Why not? He could afford to do that. We would be negligible. Wouldn't we?

He tossed something on the table. Pinky and Perky

followed Him to the door, almost colliding as He stopped to stare at me some more.

He said, 'Expect no help from your lab. Somebody wants neither you nor your boyfriend back. They are saying you betray your cause because of him, and he is a traitor anyway to men.' He chuckled, the winner.

Again the door sealed seamlessly over my yells and I broke my nails on it in vain.

It was an old-fashioned giveaway Superman watch. After all that silent disorientation its tick was very loud.

*

I made Him his rotten Dream, just like He wanted it. I worked straight through, inspired by fear and long planning. Also appalled at the image presented of women – and of men. Neither gender could seriously hope to live down to it.

When I had finished I was so tired I couldn't stop shaking, let alone sleep.

What had I done?

Pirated Dream-machines and gutter-merchants already sold cheap and nasty Dream of power-sex, and like most inventors I tried not to feel responsible for other people's abuse of progress. Probably Oppenheimer felt the same.

Women like Gitta having dirty Dreams, quick coloured lustings by her beery snorer. Escapism, not action. Dash back to the cave, girls. Let's get clubbed real soon.

My weary thoughts wouldn't leave me in peace. More Dreams with the key I'd given Him? Bankers and traders plotting bad ideas into honest men's minds? Sneaky execs being double-double agents? Slip the guy a mickey, or take him to the feelies, then plug failure into his brain. No one would know with my new wire-less machine. True, it wouldn't work quite so well on women. We've always had to watch who's plying us with gin. Anyway, we're pre-programmed for failure. It just makes us work harder because we have to.

But I could imagine, as the old analogue watch ticked in torment away, the damage I was about to inflict on the world. And would the gorilla really let us go?

For escape I remembered:

Back in that terraced house, after processing other people's words all day, I'd made the first Dream in my bedsit. It was for Howie's sister, who lived in the room next door, while Howie was teaching music in Erith. Of course, I hardly knew him then.

Oh, nostalgia – Wedgwood walls and a cheeseplant. The good old days of poverty when nobody tried to laser me.

She was crying. Sweet twenty-three and on the shelf. Dressed in sludge brown for camouflage. Overeating as a defence: she could blame being fat for being lonely. The fact that she never went anywhere was nothing to do with it. I had to borrow sugar by the tonne before she'd even have coffee in my room.

I Dreamed her into liking herself. Not blushing if someone asked her the time. Not excusing her menial successes as luck. Not avoiding people's eyes as if they might leech out her soul.

By the time we went to Howie's first gig at a pub on Angel Hill she'd got as far as wearing red. And kind, grateful Howie made me Dream I liked dogs.

Superman ticked nearer to the Kryptonite. I was so scared I felt sick.

What had I done? Did Prometheus like the Blitz?

*

By the time the short hand was on Superman's kiss-curl, I was afraid millions of women were going to wish me dead. Gianna's *partigiane* would turn me into spaghetti. If I lived that long. If Howie did.

*

In pseudo-military uniform He came at last and clicked His heels not for my benefit but because it displayed His self-image. Swallowing, I played it for Him.

Gorilla liked his Dream. It was just like He wanted it, only more so. While He forced me into a sleep I might never wake up from, He chuckled over it.

Betrayal of (wo)mankind.

But I'd bought Howie's life and mine. I hoped.

Betrayal?

*

They left us on the banks of the Danube. I woke from drugs to linden seeds drifting like white cotton on my eyes. Hell, it felt like a hangover. My jeans were far too big – could you have eaten if you'd done what I had? And I vomited into the river up where it was still blue. Outside was very big. I was glad Howie held my hand. Nobody else would want to.

I told him between gasps, 'There were a hundred and fifty -eight thousand, four hundred and twenty whole tiles and half a one on the floor in that cellar.'

He smiled palely among the buttercups and said, 'My feet are killing me.'

Oh, the romance of it all.

We tottered into civilisation, or Linz as it was known locally. It looked good even on a dull evening. Howie and I looked like scarecrows. We got thrown out of everything but the station buffet and I phoned Regina from there to mobilise our detectives and a lawyeress. They let us reverse the charges but they wouldn't give us free coffee. Dear Austria. I wish my life was as tidy as you.

To kill the hour until she jetted in we walked round the town. Not the gabled museums or the onion-domed churches, but the shopping centre. By then it was raining torrents and the shops were Sunday-shut. Even the pigeons were sheltering from the rain, and mannequins smiled lonely from their spotlights in the dark.

I felt it first. Not the rain, but His Dream, splurging out into the sad, grey evening. Over-bright, over-amplified, but I recognised my own work as any artist does.

Any jeweller of thoughts.

Gorilla wanted plastic. Silicone breasts and Sindy clothes. Action Man in the office. No sweat, no periods, no brains. Moustachio'd lion-tamers, the Wehrmacht in the market, broadcast scatterwise to everyone not on his wavelength, with no fine tuning like headsets or personal technicians or all the research I hadn't done. Wifey in her nest and her man a hero every day. Psycho-masturbation.

I'd given it Him, Walt Disney-style, and studded it black with irony. But *He* hadn't seen that. He saw, like everybody does, what He already wanted to see.

In Linz, incredulous, snorting with giggles, Howie Dreamed.

And I laughed.

Pixellated

'I want—'

Nandi and Gina stared at Ellie. Neither of them had ever seen her like this: hair writhing like Medusa's, eyes hot as Tabasco with weeping and rage. This was definitely not a normal Thursday visitation and young Nandi hadn't wanted to be dragged here by a mother in a rage.

'I want—' Ellie's hands crushed the letter as though she were a champion pig-strangler. It was dated 3rd May 1997.

Gina put an arm protectively around her granddaughter, pulling her out of the line of fire. In the sunlit living-room silence stretched like ancient knicker-elastic.

'I want—'

'Day-Glo Delight!' sang a jingle from a ghetto-blaster passing the open window.

'Justice!' yelled Ellie, leaping up from the sofa like Sylvester making a bid for Tweetie-Pie. 'My bloody money, my bloody reputation and my bloody job back!'

Into the stunned pause that followed, Nandi whispered, 'Er, Gran! Mum swore!'

'I don't bloody blame her!' Granny Gina whispered back, and watched her daughter's fury with awe.

While Ellie is raging, let's set the scene, shall we? Number 73 is a long, low house that looks like a thatched cottage which just happens to be wearing tiles. While the house preens at its mullioned-window perfection in the duck-pond on the Green, let's dolly up the path between lavender and pinks. Hurry through the glazed front porch and turn left into the lounge. The decor is haphazardly Oriental but the untidiness is solid British craftsmanship. 70's soft rock plays gently on the stereo. Granny Gina is nothing if not a traditionalist. Through the back window is a garden with cherry trees and a herb-bed. Pan across the greenhouse and back into the lounge, where Ellie (33, brunette in chic scarlet suit) is failing to enjoy her well-deserved tantrum. Ellie's mother G – that's short for Gina as well as Gran – is around 50, in stretch jeans and a short purple kaftan. She stands agog, the first stirrings of anger play about her mouth and her eyes slit with steely determination. Nobody's going to screw her family and get away with it. Ellie's daughter Nandi (nine, willowy and blonde) breaks the tableau by backing away from her mother's windmilling arms, incidentally stumbling into G. They collapse onto the couch in a giggling sprawl and then fall guiltily silent.

Ellie shrieks, 'I don't know why I came here! Got sympathy on a meter, have you?'

G stands up and straightens her silk top over her opulent stomach. 'Sorry, dear. Tea and sympathy or gin and sympathy?'

Ellie glances at the four o'clock on her watch and says defiantly: 'Gin.'

*

'Run along and play now,' G says to her grand-daughter. 'And don't go near the greenhouse.'

As the child ran merrily away Ellie looked darkly at her mother. 'Haven't you got more sense than that? If you'd never said anything about the greenhouse, she wouldn't have dreamed of going anywhere near it! What, full of marijuana plants, is it?'

'Opium poppies, dear.'

Ellie took a breath to respond.

'And before you get your exercise by jumping to conclusions, Eleanor, remember when you used to have a sense of humour?'

Ellie sighed and took the glass G handed her. Gin and lemonade glinted like rainbows in the crystal. 'No, Mum, I don't remember. Had it amputated when they told me I was being sacked for embezzlement. I've been locked out of the office. They're saying by Monday they'll have enough to put me in jail. I've got three days to work out how to put it right.'

'You tell me all about it, love, and I'll fix it.'

Listening disdainfully to wailing sitars, Eleanor couldn't be bothered to reply.

*

Nandi didn't go anywhere *near* the greenhouse. She went *into* it, which was, of course, different. She wasn't being *naughty* or anything.

It was like a jungle in there. She couldn't see more than a square centimetre of blue sky. There was emerald-green, jade -green, sea-green, pea-green … and a smell unlike any other. It was a bit like bamboo and a bit like tea-leaves. It was hot, moist earth mixed with spicy flowers and – what's brown and sounds like a bell?

'Shut that door! It's freezing in 'ere!' said a voice, and before you know it, she had. That's what comes of having Ellie as a mother.

'Sorry,' said Nandi in her poshest talking-to-strangers manner. 'I didn't know there was anybody in here.'

'Well there is!' That was a different voice, but still quite high and squeaky.

Nandi groped for the doorknob behind her and said into the dimness, 'Who's there?'

'I am.'

'And me!'

'Yeah, don't forget 'im,' said a different voice entirely. It sounded suspiciously ironic, though.

'And I don't even have to mention me,' said the coolest male voice in the world. Small, but very cool.

'I– er–' Nandi peered into the depths of the greenhouse, which looked much bigger inside than out. 'I'd better leave you alone then. Sorry for barging in.'

'I never saw no barge. Did she 'ave one when she came in?'

'Yeah, kidder, where's your barge?'

The voices came from four different places, but try as she

might Nandi couldn't find the speakers because they kept being four *new* different places.

Nandi flounced back to the door. 'I don't like people making fun of me. I'm going now.'

'We're sorry. We won't do it no more.'

Nandi heaved a theatrical sigh. She was on the point of saying, 'Oh all right then,' when the third voice said, 'But we won't do it no less neither.'

Smothered chuckles surrounded her and the cool one cooed from among the tomatoes, 'Chill, kid. Take a load off. We're just having a little fun, but we'll be good now. Won't we, guys?'

'Sure, man. No problem. Ask the kid what she wants.'

'Ask her yourself.'

From somewhere near a petunia Nandi felt the surge of embarrassment. The third one mumbled, 'I can't do that! She's a – a girl!'

'Grow up! We're not going to ask her so you'll have to.'

No words, nothing but the sound of a suddenly dry mouth opening and silence coming out of it, the sort that sounds like one hand clapping in a deserted Buddhist grove.

Street-wise, Nandi pulled a face. 'Well if you don't want to talk to me I've got more exciting things to do.' She opened the door and said cuttingly, 'Like watching schools maths programmes.'

'S-s-s-s –'the shy one said.

Nandi didn't care whether 'S-s-s-s –' was shorthand for 'Stay' or 'Sorry.' She came back in. 'All right then, I will. But you've got to promise me you're not dangerous.'

'Wouldn't 'urt a fly.'

'Well, a fly we would.'

'True. But we don't like flies. We like girls.'

'Or a slug. I'd give a slug a run for its money. I 'ate them bloody slugs. But we wouldn't hurt no human girl.'

Nandi's face lit up and she sank cross-legged on the floor. Breathless, she said, 'Are you aliens?'

*

In the living-room Ellie let sheaves of paper cascade onto the crimson rug, a fall of humiliation that rustled gently in the breeze. 'So you see they can 'prove' I embezzled all the money they took for themselves now they've re-done the accounts. What is it people say? They've cooked the books.'

'Done to a turn on gas mark nine.' G laid a beringed hand comfortingly over her daughter's. 'Don't fret, dear. I'll sort it. Leave Nandi with me. You come back tomorrow. It'll be all right. You'll see.'

Ellie's thoughts stayed trapped behind her teary eyes. 'They've stopped my salary so the mortgage cheque bounced. I'm skint, Mum! I haven't got any food in the house because the bank's cancelled my credit-cards and I'll never get another job now. Come Monday I'll be doing porridge in Holloway. And my lawyer said to plead mitigating circumstances.'

'Don't worry, sweetheart.' G grinned. 'I told you I'll fix it.'

Ellie sniffed the lavender oil on her mother's incense-burner. Irony could have been her middle name. She picked up her patent-leather bag and said, 'Yeah. Right,' as she slammed out of the door.

*

After putting Nandi to bed ('There are pixies in your greenhouse, Gran!' 'Are there, dear? How nice.') G got herself a glass of burgundy and picked up her guitar. By candle-light she walked through the dusk and settled herself comfortably in the sagging chair in her greenhouse.

'Evening, guys.'

From the shadowy leaves four little figures rustled their way towards the cheery glow. In the pale, golden light eight little eyes gleamed within hooded blooms at the end of long, thin stalks. Whizz wriggled down with his back against a runner-bean stem. Prangle lounged on one elbow on top of a grow-bag, Nate sat cross-legged on a geranium and Tommo Tea-leaf leaned hipshot on a plant-pot, ready to retreat if things got tough. With their denims and embroidered leather waistcoats, their winkle-picker boots and Prangle's cool, slouched hat, they seemed eternally laid-back and young. Forty-year-old hippies. Not eight inches high, but hippies nevertheless.

'So, G, what gives?' said Prangle. 'The kid was real upset.'

'Got a bit of a problem, guys. Somebody's had it away with forty thousand pounds from my daughter's work and put her in the frame.'

Whizz took a long pull of his drink and raised his eyebrows. 'So?'

G shrugged. 'So I want you to fix it.'

She hardly saw Tommo sidle off out of sight, plugging his ears as he went. The others wouldn't meet her gaze. Eventually Nate twanged the stalk he grew from and said, 'We don't do *out there*, G. You know that.'

'Besides,' Whizz said, 'Ellie's a straight.'

G sat peaceably, waiting.

'Yeah,' said Whizz, 'them as lives with the straights, falls with the straights.'

G sipped her wine.

'So ... er ... g'night then,' Whizz added awkwardly.

'Not noticeably,' G said, and got out her guitar.

*

By the time the moon was waning they had an agreement. *If* she stopped playing *Kumbayah*, and *if* she brought them extra compost, they'd fix it.

'No compost 'til the job's done, boys,' G declared. She spread the print-out of Ellie's accounts on a board on the floor and popped the computer disk crisply on top. 'I don't want you getting high on working-time.'

'It's not *work*,' Nate said. 'It's *creativity*. We *need* a little inspiration.'

Prangle flittered forward and laid a pleading hand on G's foot. He twined his tether-tendril seductively around her toe. 'Oh come on, man! Enough with the heavy stuff, all right?'

Tommo said nothing because he still had moss stuffed in his ears, but from somewhere in the dark Whizz muttered, 'You tell 'er, Nate! No compost, no deal.'

Not everybody ends up dragging a sack of Southshire's Super-Gro down a long road before dawn on Friday. With the first rays of sunlight dazzling off the glass, G mumbled, 'I still think this is a mistake, but you don't get the good stuff 'til the job's done,' and shut the greenhouse door.

Why was she not surprised when Nandi woke her at ten o'clock, saying, 'Gran! The little men! They're all asleep!'?

G rolled out of bed with a face like thunder. 'I'll fix their wagon! But you, poppet, had better have some breakfast first.'

Before G had finished her coffee, Ellie burst into the kitchen. Today it was a navy trouser-suit, liberally spattered with leaves. 'Why the hell don't you trim those bloody plants in the front porch?' was her cheery greeting. 'It's like hacking through Sleeping Beauty's back yard!'

'Not if you're thinking happy thoughts, dear.'

In silent rage Ellie glared at her mother, helped herself from the coffee-pot, kissed Nandi rather like a bird might peck a spider, then snarled, 'It's worse than ever!' She brushed off foliage and paused only to pull a prickle out of her thumb. 'Kate rang me from the office to say they've found another ten thousand's gone walkies. I've already had the police round. Thank God they haven't got any real evidence or I'd have been sunk.' She eyed G's pyjamas hostilely. 'I might have known you wouldn't lift a bloody finger to help me!'

G raised a finger and drew a circle in the air. 'It's lifted, it's lifted. Give me time, for goodness' sake. We've got all week-end. Why don't you go and stay with that mate of yours in Bournemouth? Nandi's fine here, aren't you, little 'un?'

Ellie drowned Nandi's reply. 'But Mum! I can't do anything down there!'

'You can't do anything up here. At least down there you can get a tan.'

'Yeah, Mum, I'd like to go to jail with a tan.'

By eleven o'clock on Jail-Day minus three, G was showing Ellie carefully out through the side door. 'And you're sure it's that bloke Nick? The boss's new boyfriend?'

'Well everything was fine 'til he muscled in. Hadn't I just got them seventy thousand pounds of lottery money? Hadn't I got them another year's worth of statutory funding? It's supposed to be a flaming charity! It's not just me! He's robbing *orphans*, for crying out loud! Has the man got *no* morals?'

'Obviously not. Just forty thousand pounds. But you've left me the disks and he's bound to have left a paper-trail.' G handed her daughter a wedge of tenners out of a tea-pot. 'I'll be your contact address, all right? You keep well out of it so they can't suspect you of anything else and have a nice time in Bognor.'

'Bugger Bognor! It's Bournemouth.'

'Well if that's what they're doing to Bognor, you're right to steer clear of it. See you Sunday.'

*

It was still Jail-Day minus three. G left Nandi playing *Tomb Raider* in the living-room and stormed off to the greenhouse. Four hippie pixies lay in stoned postures. Prangle waved a nonchalant wing at her. 'Hey, babe! Come on in!'

'I'm coming in all right.' G's tone was as hard-edged as her spade. In her purple kaftan she looked like a harpy having a bad day. The four little beings tumbled horrified into the air. Whizz had to flap hastily out of her way as a wodge of compost flew out the door.

'We did it, man!' Nate yelled, fluttering right up close to her face.

She blew him into the grapevine. 'You did it all right! You made it worse, you morons! Instead of putting the money back, you lost even more!' Another shovelful of Super-Gro splattered onto the path outside.

Prangle drew himself up to his full eight inches and said, 'Woman! Give us back our compost or we down tools.'

'Down tools and you'll never see muck again. Until you get it right I'm withdrawing all compost privileges.'

*

Stalemate.

Friday lunchtime came and went. Friday teatime came and went. Every time G sent Nandi down to the greenhouse, the little girl came back saying, 'They're just lying around, chatting. They say it's your fault.'

'Well, never mind. Let's go for a ride in the country, shall we?'

As the hedgerows whipped past Nandi asked quietly, 'Is Mummy really going to jail on Monday?'

'Not if I can help it.'

The child's face screwed up in anguish. 'Why don't you *do* something, then?'

'I am doing something, dear. I'm buying garden gnomes.'

*

They were bright. They were plastic. And they were all over the place. Except in the front porch, of course. G wasn't about to ask for trouble.

As she put a particularly repulsive fisher-gnome beside the path with its rod hovering pointlessly above the crazy paving, she glimpsed four little faces watching her with expressions of horror. When they realised she'd seen them spying on her, all four of the pixies turned their backs. She had one moment's doubt as she eyed their rigid shoulders. Then she heard Prangle whisper, 'Act casual.'

So she put the four most garish manikins right in the greenhouse. Sitting on scarlet polystyrene toadstools, wearing yellow plastic hoods, grinning with polythene jollity.

She stood, hands on hips, surveying her handiwork. 'There you are, guys! Gnome from gnome.'

Nate flew up to hover furiously in front of her nose. 'That's *it*! That's the final bloody straw! Either those gnomes go or we do.'

'Suit yourselves.' G opened the door and bowed theatrically. 'After you, boys.'

They hovered straining at the end of their tethers.

G smiled with saccharine sweetness. 'Oh, I forgot. You can't actually go anywhere, can you? Still, there's no place like gnome. 'Bye!'

*

'What took you so long?' Prangle said when she finally showed up at midnight on Friday.

'Mopping up.'

'You? You've taken up nocturnal cleaning, G? Half the time you don't even clear up in the day.'

'Mopping up my granddaughter's tears. But don't worry. I'm not asking you for anything. In fact, come Monday, I probably won't be troubling you at all. Far too busy looking after Nandi while her mother Ellie languishes in jail. You remember her, don't you? Ellie, I mean? The one who used to make you clothes when she still believed in you? But don't trouble yourselves. She'll be quite happy sewing mailbags with a pack of murderers, I'm sure.'

G bent down to plant a kiss on the top of a yellow plastic hood. 'Good night, little gnomie,' she said, and turned to leave. She carefully didn't go near the accounting disk.

'What do you want?' Whizz said before she could shut the door.

'She wants the money back,' Tommo said.

'And the books straight.' That was Prangle.

'And the bloke what done it sorted,' growled Whizz.

'Yeah,' Nate said darkly. 'And no more *agnomalies*.'

G smiled and watered them. As she shut the greenhouse door, she heard a chorus of 'Hi-ho-o-o, hi ho-o-o-o, it's off to work we go.'

*

'Jail-day minus two,' G announced as she marched into the greenhouse – with some difficulty, most of the floor space being occupied by gnomes. Back in the house, Nandi was watching a *Star Wars* video and sucking her thumb. G folded her arms and stared downwards past the thicket of gaudy plastic. 'So what can you tell me, my little pixel manipulators?'

Whizz didn't answer. He was too busy executing breathless pirouettes on the round metal thing on the back of the computer disk. It wasn't plugged in but from his feet tiny sparks sprayed upwards into the Saturdayness of it all.

Prangle swept off his hat and bowed. 'Considering that for the past four years you've been so scared of Ellie that we have to lighten you on the bathroom scales every time she comes round, I think we've done a fine job for her.'

'So what's the snag?'

'Oh, no snag. Show her, Tommo.'

Whizz continued circling furiously on the disk. Tommo fluttered upwards, shaking pollen from a bougainvillea. The golden dust sparkled in a gleam of sunlight, highlighting a faerie trail from Whizz's winklepickers and out towards the distant City. Whizz stepped off the metal and tottered dizzily to a tiny stool in the corner, where Nate took out Whizz's gum-shield and fanned a cooling towel at him.

'See, G?' Prangle said proudly. 'That's the last of it. Sent all the data, checked it got there, every last pixel of it. Your daughter's version of accounts —' G glowered at him and Prangle hastily went on ' — er, the real accounts that is, well a copy's now lodged with the accountant who's supposed to be doing the audit.'

'And just in case he's a wrong 'un,' Nate interjected, still flapping his towel, 'there's a copy in the computer at the local nick. Who also happen to have a *Wanted* file on Naughty Nick. It's even a real one that we've downloaded from Scotland Yard. Happy now?'

G smacked her lips thoughtfully. 'Is all the money where it should be?'

All four of the pixies nodded vigorously.

'The real, physical money?'

Prangle thrust his thumbs into the belt-loops of his jeans. 'Er, the number-crunching money's in the right accounts. So can we get rid of these plastic gnomes now before somebody sees 'em?'

'The actual, printed, crinkly mazoola?' G insisted.

'Sort of.'

'Sort of as in it's still round this bloke's gaff?' G persisted.

Again the little men nodded. 'So what about these gnomes?' they babbled.

'I'll take 'em away.'

The little men cheered.

'But they're staying right outside until you've bamboozled the orphan-embezzler.'

Prangle pushed his cowboy hat back. 'Have a heart, G! We can't do physical stuff long-distance. We're going to need a telephone. And quickly. We need to get hold of some of the local talent up by where this Nick guy lives double-quick. Wherever that is. After tonight it'll be the dark of the moon and us pixies'll be knackered for long distance work.'

*

G took Nandi shopping. It was, after all, Saturday, and children think that's what Saturdays are for. Ice-cream, fashion-shops and extortionate CDs. It was tough work not thinking of Ellie's arrest in a mere forty-eight hours.

'Do you have to buy a telephone extension today, Gran?' the blonde girl said as they trailed out of the third shop that said it could order one for the end of next week.

'Indeed we do, pumpkin.'

'But if you want to make a call from the greenhouse, why don't you just walk back to the house?'

G opened her mouth but few rational explanations appeared on the tip of her tongue. Few as in none. 'Are you miserable, child?'

Nandi nodded.

'Then we might as well be doing this while you're not in the mood to have fun.'

But in the nearby market town, as fate would have it, telephone extension cables were not to be had. In the end, as Saturday afternoon blazed in a sticky too-hot-for-comfort way, G and Nandi were forced to set out on the motorway to

Computer Universe, some twenty miles distant, on the edge of the City.

G hoped they would make it before the shop shut.

Then as a traffic jam prisoned them on shimmering tarmac, she hoped they would make it before the radiator boiled dry.

Oops.

*

'G, I'm disappointed in you.' Prangle said on Saturday night. J-Day minus two, and dusk at that.

'Yeah,' Nate exclaimed indignantly. 'After all we've done you've gone and let us down.'

Tommo pursed his lips and shook his head reprovingly.

Computer Whizz was still reeling slightly from his earlier exertions. They hadn't managed to untwist his tether-tendril yet. He said nothing.

'Right then, guys,' said G. 'Road-trip.'

*

'W-we can't go out th-there!' Nate said.

'Shut up and drink your dew.' G dug deeper.

It was some hours before she had everything arranged to her – if not the pixies' – satisfaction. Nandi's roller-blades were fastened to the bottom of the baby-bath G used for laundry. The bath was filled with a rootball the size of something very big and a mass of greenery whimpered as she wheeled it out to the road. The whingeing grew louder as she heaved it up a ramp and into her Cherokee. The one with the patched radiator-hose.

'So you don't mind going out and leaving a nine-year-old all on her own at night, then, G?'

'Of course I do. But the front porch won't let me down. Nandi will be fine so long as your pixie-dust keeps her asleep.'

'It's as strong as we could make it after all that other stuff you've had us doing.'

And *that* was why Nandi was running towards the jeep calling, 'Gran! Where are you going?'

Nandi was a great help hoisting the baby-bath flower-bed up the fire-escape outside Ellie's office. Midnight stars glittered as Tommo sent a tendril under the window-frame to unhook the catch. They'd already nobbled the box which held the burglar-alarm.

'But Gran!' the girl whispered in a scared little voice. 'This is breaking and entering! I don't want you *and* Mum going to prison.'

'Nothing's broken, lovey, and we're not entering anywhere.'

'But they are.'

Nandi was right but who would believe her? Leaving Nate on watch, Whizz and Prangle followed Tommo into the darkened office.

G would have cuddled her granddaughter except she was balancing several hundredweight of mobile mimulas. 'But the boss's boyfriend isn't in the telephone directory and we've got to —'

'Yeah! Got a trace on him!' Whizz exclaimed.

Two little men skinned back through the window, capering excitedly. Prangle, however, moved awkwardly, his hands behind his back.

G reached over and plucked a leaf out of his grasp.

'Aw, G! It's only a cutting! From that kangaroo-vine on the filing —'

'Put it *back*! We're not stealing *anything*!'

The bath of earth shifted, almost fell. Squashed between it and the wall, Nandi puffed, 'Gran! What's the matter? You nicked that bag of compost you hid behind the shed. They told.'

'But I left the money for it! And it was a garden-centre. I was just a very early customer. Now you guys get that window shut and let's get out of here.'

They bundled back into the Cherokee and drove off, Whizz balancing on the dashboard by the open window. Nandi supported him by his tendril. She kept looking for the sparkling trail of signals but it was too faint for mortal eyes. Round and round they drove, Whizz's nose twitching as he called, 'Left. Now right. Damn! We've passed it.'

So they backed up and parked outside a vast Georgian house with a carriage-drive, a coach-house and a fountain. You could see them through the bars of the gate. A hedge that must have been twelve foot high had holly in it. The garden gang were screened from the house by its spikes.

'OK, Nandi, let's get this grow on the road,' said G.

Nandi grabbed her gran's arm and gasped, 'You can't go in there! It's burglary!'

'Burglary means taking with intent permanently to deprive, dear.' G womanhandled the bath on skates out of the jeep. 'We're getting the money back to its rightful owners. We've hardly got a jemmy and a bag marked *swag*, have we?'

'But look! They've got security cameras! We'll be caught! Oh, Gran, we'll all go to jail!'

'Then you should have stayed in bed. Now shush! Tommo?'

The Tea-leaf fluttered skywards, his tendril straightening behind him in the shadow of the holly. He hovered behind the camera in the hedge and a tiny cloud of dust glittered in the Sunday morning starlight. Then he flew down to settle on one of the wrought-iron gates. Reclining casually in a curlicue, he beckoned mysteriously.

In answer stray tendrils writhed up from the bath, grew in through the keyhole of the lock. The gates clicked and parted.

Girl, granny and tub of growing guys slipped into the grounds. With a *hsshh* of roller-skates on tarmac, the humans tiptoed and followed Whizz's nose. They passed serried ranks of privet with occasional outbreaks of gravel.

Two Rottweilers sprinted out of the shadows, growling. Nandi gasped, retreated trembling into her grandmother's arms. Tommo hid amongst the stalks. It was Prangle who said, 'Here, little kitties!' At a snap of his sparkling fingers, the killer dogs started to gambol after a vagrant leaf.

'He's upstairs in the coach-house,' Whizz said jubilantly as he peered through the crack in the garage doors. 'Whatever you do, don't set off the car alarm.'

'Not yet, anyway,' Tommo said shyly. 'I'm saving that for later. Get us up on that dustbin round the side, will you, G? Whizz, you take five. Me 'n' Prangle will do the rest.'

G, anxiously eyeing her watch, cursed at the sight of J-Day minus one. Nandi was hopping up and down by the time the little men flew back to the dustbin, coiling their tendrils neatly over their arms.

Prangle winked. 'All done, G. Nick'll be caught red-handed just like you planned. Get ready to rock. We're outta here!'

Panting, G and Nandi shoved the tub on wheels. They were just about at the hedge when the car-alarm in the garage started to shrill.

'Right on cue!' Tommo said proudly. Lights sprang out of the darkness. G slammed the gates just as a shout from the coach-house split the night. Footsteps sprinted towards them. Dogs started to bark.

'Ow! Help! Get off, you idiots! I'm not the burglar!' screamed a man's voice. There was a clunk of metal against ribs and one of the Rottweilers yelped.

All aboard,' G said.

'Why aren't we *going?*' Nandi asked in agonies as G floored the accelerator.

A car roared out of the gatehouse, still whooping in unstoppable alarm as the driver gunned it into the road. He seemed to have difficulty steering, probably because of the chain now fastening a briefcase indelibly to his wrist.

G shot the Cherokee cheekily in front of the battered, shrieking Jag. She led a merry chase home through the hot August night, winning by a head.

'Quick! Round the back!' she yelled as the Jag nee-nawed to a stop behind her. Its unsilenceable alarm rang out across the duck-pond. All around the village green, lights were coming on in upstairs windows.

G and Nandi wheeled the tuber-boy tub through the side door, slamming it just in time for the boss's boyfriend to hurtle into the wood.

In nasal distress Nick sputtered, 'Open this bloody door!'

'No tradesmen round the back,' called G. 'If you're an honest man, go round the front.'

They waited in the hall for him. Heard him slam open the front-porch door.

Heard two footsteps and a noise like angry leaves.

Heard him scream and stop in mid-aaargh.

'Gran! Shouldn't we call the police?' asked Nandi tearfully.

G peered out of a window at a bicycle lamp wobbling towards the house. 'I think you'll find we already have. Come on, let's get these guys back in their greenhouse before PC Plod gets here.'

A minute later the constable opened the porch door just as G opened the door from the hall. Caught between them in a writhing mass of rose-thorns stood a dishevelled figure with a brief-case full of lolly chained to his wrist.

'You're Nicked,' mumbled the copper, swallowing the end of the word.

'How do you know?' asked the idiot.

It took a car full of reinforcements to peel the prickly porch-plants off him.

'It's not mine!' he was still protesting as they dragged him off to a Black Maria. 'I don't know how it got there! It's not my money. I mean, it *is*. Oh, knickers!'

The cops didn't take kindly to being called that.

*

It was Sunday noon before Nandi heard her mother's voice downstairs. She recognised the three-tone expostulation Ellie so often used towards G, 'Mu-u-um! I've come straight from the police-station! What have you done?'

In the sunny living-room, G poured her daughter a glass of champagne. 'I preferred the wail of despair, Eleanor. It had a better tune.' G patted Nandi's shoulder, saying, 'You two stay and have a nice chat. I'll be back in two ticks.'

Ellie stopped hugging Nandi long enough to say, 'But why was Nick here with a briefcase full of money chained to his wrist? And what on earth are all those gnomes doing in the washing bath?'

'I told you I'd sort it, didn't I?'

'But what was all that about the front porch?'

G grinned. 'Bad guys have sub-machine guns, sweetie. I have a sub-garden. Now drink your fizz. I've got a date with my compost-heap.'

The Cunning Plan

Sunset painted the tops of the mountains, but on the alpine meadows no goats whatsoever gambolled. Nobody, absolutely nobody, yodelled. Cheerfulness was not allowed.

Crimson light rivered from the sky, seeping like blood into the valley. At the edge of the shadowed village, lights twinkled merrily through diamond-lattice windows. A creaking sign at the front and a stack of empties at the back showed what this place was. As soon as it was full night, dark-cloaked figures began to make their way to the tavern.

Four customers slumocked along close behind. The bright wedge of firelight from the door swallowed them up. Tossing their cloaks over the pegs on the wall, they made their way to their usual table. They sat with an air of cheerful expectancy, watching through the crowd as alleged maidens in black-laced bodices ploughed a path with their ample, up-thrust bosoms.

It was happy hour at the Carpathian Arms.

One such mock-virgin plonked down a tray of tankards for the quartet. Foaming liquid splashed from the steins, staining the table red. Four hands reached eagerly for the scarlet drinks, four sets of pointed eye-teeth plunged into the fluid. Over the rim of their drinks, Sleepless MacBride, Mack the Fang, Long-Tooth McGurkl and Kevin the Killer leered at the wench.

Fräulein Liesl smiled nervously.

Then Sleepless MacBride lifted his face from his tankard to glare around in disgust. Without warning he hurled his glass at the wall. 'Bleedin' Ribena!'

Crash, tinkle, silence. You could have heard a needle drop – except someone would have caught the syringe to suck out the dregs.

But the waitress was indignant. Worse, she owed Sleepless for getting her into trouble. Hadn't he tripped her up the day before when she was carrying a bun full of raw meat, dill pickles and Emmental? She'd fallen on Long-Tooth and the Fang, covering them in goo and soggy lettuce to the detriment of their tempers and her health. And what had he said? 'Big Mack is served with cheese and Gurkl.'

Now everyone was listening, Liesl grinned vindictively. 'Is it my fault you emptied the cat?'

The other three vampyres stared at Sleepless. The rest of the throng came to mill threateningly around him.

'So that was you, was it?' hissed Long-Tooth McGurkl.

A chorus of, 'You selfish bastard!' followed Gurkl's refrain.

Never very tall, Sleepless shrank down even further beneath the weight of the Carpathian's united opprobrium. It if went on for much longer he felt he might disappear altogether. Licking suddenly paler lips, he babbled, 'Er … um … I … er … thought it would give us more rats' blood!'

'Berk! Fang had the last rats weeks ago, didn't you, Fang?'

Next to Sleepless, Mack the Fang leaned forward, shoving his chin out aggressively. He was so muscly he looked like he had whole packs of rodents sliding around under his skin rather than the contents of one scrawny rat in his tum. 'So?' he said. 'I told you it was an accident. I didn't know it was the last one, did I?' His eyes slid pugnaciously round the room. Before they could fall off the table Fang grabbed them and popped them back in.

'Eurgh!' said Liesl. 'I wish you wouldn't do that!'

'Never mind his roving eyes!' Gurkl grated. 'When's this damned boozer goin' to get some more blood?'

Other customers called out, 'Yeah! Can't have a boozer with no blood!' 'Come down here for a quiet pint and you can't even get one!' It was bedlam.

Liesl stammered, 'I ordered a barrel of type O at the dark of the moon but it hasn't come yet. And someone —' she starred at Kevin the Killer ' — drank the last messenger-bat. There isn't even a Tampax to make a cup of tea.'

The crowd, always fickle, was turning uglier. She backed up against the wall, her hands protecting her throat. Not that she could have stopped the baying mob of undead who swarmed towards her.

An unholy thud echoed through the room like a coffin-lid falling into place in a crypt. Again, silence. Except Sleepless stage-whispering to Kevin, 'Now you've done it!' But had he managed to shift the blame?

Toe Knee the barman let the flap drop back onto the counter and stepped through the hatch, the magnet of everyone's gaze. Mack had to peep through his fingers to stop his eyeballs wandering off and getting trampled on.

Shuffle, scrape. Shuffle, scrape. The barman came ponderously forward. Patrons melted out of his path, some of them too nervous to put themselves back together again after he had passed. Beneath his bulk the floorboards creaked. Splinters flew as the claws at the end of his thighs raked the wood. Bears had been known to break their teeth on the monstrous muscles of his arms. He had been known to toss horseshoes with the horse still attached, back in the nights when there had still been living creatures in the valley. He had never been known as patient.

Sleepless' ploy hadn't worked. The blame stayed firmly where it belonged.

'Oi, you!' Toe Knee stabbed a finger at him. 'You're the one that's brought us to this! My poor Tibbles! No wonder she stopped chasing her little tinkly ball. So you —' jerking away from the sickle-nailed digit, Sleepless banged his head on the wall ' — you're going to fix it.'

'But - but I can't bring a dead cat back to life. I couldn't even make it come back to death!'

'Just as well, really,' muttered the Fang, 'or there'd be blood-sucking badgers, killer cattle and deadly ducks on the loose. Some people just have no standards at all.'

But Toe Knee didn't see it that way. The barman's roar

reverberated from the peaks high above. A couple of avalanches crushed passing lycanthropes and clouds of vultures flapped across the star-sprinkled sky. 'Then get fresh blood!' he bellowed. 'Lots of it, you selfish sod! D'you think I don't know what happened to my drayman?'

'Gluh—' said Sleepless. Actually he was fairly sure Toe Knee didn't know what had happened to the drayman. If Toe Knee suspected there was a pile of bones under a certain pine-tree in the woods, Sleepless wouldn't be sitting here now quivering.

'So it's up to YOU,' the mammoth barman gritted, 'to make sure there's plenty of drink. You wouldn't want the Carpathian Arms to go down the tube, would you?'

'Nn-n-n—'

'I'll give you forty-eight hours. After that, you're juice. Got me?'

Sleepless nodded, feeling the eyeballs rattling in his skull. It was long after Toe Knee had gone back to his subterranean lair that they settled into anything resembling a viewing position. But the outlook wasn't good.

'What am I going to do?' he wept, since Ribena was no good at all at stiffening the sinews, let alone summoning up the blood.

Gurkl said mournfully, 'Trouble is, Sleepless, the minute you get out of the valley there's all these gits with garlic earrings and silver bullets and damn' great chunks of sharpened wood just waiting to turn us into a barbie.'

'Besides which,' Kevin added, 'there'd be no point sending you out to bring back supplies. You'd drink the bleedin' lot before it got here.'

'Even if I could cross the ... the stream,' Sleepless said, just to remind them that he couldn't. None of them could. Creatures of the twilight would fall apart if they crossed running water. Hence the shortage, since the stream crossed the only way in or out of the valley.

'See, what we need,' Kevin said, tucking his fetid feet further under his seat and spreading his hands on the table, 'is loads of people coming here.'

Gurkl shook his head pityingly. 'You're not going to get that, though, are you? Stands to reason nobody's going to come here from the outside.' He pushed back his long, lank locks and scratched the great gherkin of his nose. 'People come here—' his voice sank to a menacing whisper '—they don't go back.'

Sleepless grasped at straws. 'Isn't there another film-crew coming soon?'

'Nope.'

'Not even David Attenborough?'

A mass of tongues clicked in disgust.

The quartet sat on in thirsty silence. Mack picked his teeth with a dagger. 'What we need,' he said reflectively, 'is bait.'

'Oh, brilliant!' Kevin sneered. 'Come to the Carpathian Arms and get sucked dry.'

Thud! He looked aghast as the dagger sliced into the wood between his fingers. Mack smiled a smile that turned the Ribena dripping down the walls into crimson glaciers. 'Got a better idea?'

The odour of Kevin's deadly extremities got suddenly stronger. 'No. No no no no no, Mack. Great idea. Fab. Super.'

Mack swung around to squint threateningly at Sleepless. 'You got us into this mess. Don't think I never seen you creeping through the pinewood. I had my eye on you and you never spotted it. Took me days to pick the pine-needles out of it after.'

Sleepless's jaw dropped in astonishment, then firmed in anger. (If asked, it would also thrust forward so the teeth could do a chorus-dance, no reasonable offer refused. Sometimes after parties Sleepless had a heck of a job getting it back again.) He forced his eyeballs to glare balefully at Mack. 'So you're the son of a witch who nicked the barrels from my cellar!'

'I had to. It was coagulating.'

'Clot!' said Gurkl.

'But the question is,' Big Mack said heavily, '*how* are we

going to lure lots of people to the valley?' Mack glowered at the little man. 'It's your fault my glass is empty. So *you* think of a lure.'

Sleepless' nose began to run under pressure. Automatically jamming it back, he sniffed. Spiders swinging in the rafters were sucked into that mighty gale. Sleepless dripped and thought by turns.

They sat and watched him for a while. Then they slumped and watched him for another while.

'How about writing to a university to come and study us?' he asked eventually.

'Pillock! Professors and that, they'd miss their students. Then we'd have the stake and chips brigade on our necks.'

'Well how about tourists?'

They stared at Sleepless, aghast. 'They'd – they'd have to have *running water!*'

'Okay, okay! You don't need to bite my head off.!'

'Oh, bloody hell, we'll just have to think of a load of people that no one would miss.'

'Tele-sales callers,' said Kevin.

'Double-glazing salesmen,' said Mack.

'Politicians,' said Sleepless. Just before they hit him.

But when the candles had guttered low in their sconces and Liesl was pointedly not putting out the cat, Sleepless woke up.

'I've got it!' he yelled. 'Football hooligans!'

Even Gurkl spent a microsecond in reverential awe. 'It's a great, shining, incandescent jewel of an idea, Sleepless. A coruscating nugget encapsulated in crystal clarity. A glorious gobbet of genius. But there's just one fatal flaw.'

Sleepless beamed happily. 'Only one?'

'Well up on your usual score, Sleepless. Football hooligans it is. But *how* are we going to get them here?'

'Coach.'

They hit him again.

Liesl threw a bucket of Ribena over him as he lay on the floor. He propped himself up on one elbow, sputtering, 'No, really, though. Football hooligans travel on coaches 'cause they get chucked off everything else. What we need is a load of fans —'

Kevin stood on Sleepless' head, his hobnails sticking into the little man's tongue. Sleepless tried hard not to breathe as his vast nostrils found themselves under Kevin's fatal feet. Kevin said, 'Which means advertising a stadium they could see we haven't got. And we can't exactly pay Saatchi and Saatchi, can we?'

Mack nodded. 'Specially not within —' he consulted the moondial on his wrist ' — forty-two hours.'

'Well a pub football team then!' mumbled Sleepless, having emptied his mouth by the simple expedient of chewing off Kevin's toes. 'They're always bragging about how their centre forward used to play in the Fifth Division of the Coronation Cup while they pour another pint of that nasty 'orrible beer stuff into their nasty bloated beer guts.'

'Yeah,' muttered Kevin, 'they used to be a contender. Nearly had a trial with Tranmere Rovers' youth team. Long ago, like, when they were footloose.'

'Like you, old son.' Sleepless bit Kevin's toenail. Then slurped on the juicy bone. The way Kevin tasted, he didn't need any parmesan. 'So what we want now is a prize.'

'Like what?'

'Big enough to lure the ageing footie-freaks.'

'Like what?'

'But not so big that real players will want to stick their oar in.'

'Like bloody what?'

Sleepless pulled himself up onto the bench. Wriggled nonchalantly, a self-satisfied smirk scooting across those all-singing, all-dancing mandibles. 'Like a barrel,' he said, 'of beer.'

Mack sent a drowsy eye across to peer at him. 'That,' he said, 'is the best idea yet.'

'But how am I going to get there? I can't cross the stream! I'd disintegrate!'

Mack laid a heavy arm around Sleepless's shoulders. 'Disintegrate, shmisintegrate. I have a Cunning Plan.'

*

Kevin had often played doctors and nurses but he'd never played dentists before. Or, come to think of it, football. However he did a fine line in sharpening up daggers, and at least he had the right tools. So the next night, when they had dragged Sleepless from his hiding-place under a rotting haystack, Kevin waved his long, metal rasp optimistically. "S okay,' he said, 'while McGurk and Mack crow-barred Sleepless's jaws apart and then stopped them scuttling off. 'These particular files have the sharp bits cut in the shape of an X. Makes them extra popular. You know, they're X-rasps.'

'Anyway,' said Mack, 'losing an inch or two off your gnashers is nothing to worry about.'

'Nah,' McGurkl drawled. 'Specially when you're going to lose a foot or two crossing the stream.'

'Mfuh gruh!' expostulated Sleepless in a spray of tooth-shards. But they ignored him anyway.

Soon his prize incisors would never win a show again. 'My victims will have to be catheterised!' he wailed, but McGurkl and Big Mack were already dragging him across the valley and up to where the – the *stream* – ran gurgling in the light of the all but full moon.

'I can't cross that!' he protested, but Long Tooth proudly showed him a length of giant-sized elastic tied between two trees on the river-bank. Sleepless stared, appalled. 'That's not a Cunning Plan!' he said. 'It's a catapult.'

'Pre-zackly.' Kevin helped him ungently into position and tucked a bundle of posters under his belt. 'Correct. So you'll only be above the – running water for about half a second. Stirring deeds are afoot, lad. This is no time to go to pieces.'

As he spoke, Mack nodded, and the combined strength of three large vampyres propelled their small comrade rapidly across the river. He landed in a tangle of his own bodily organs, only some of which were still attached. Replacing his ear with dignity and a blob of Plasticine which Mack thoughtfully fired across after him, Sleepless set off disconsolately with the bundle of posters.

He trudged along the gravel road the Gammer film-crew had made for Christopher Flummer's caravan. The silver star had almost faded from the caravan's door and spiders now inhabited the immobile dressing-room, but at least it had been fun. Except for the guys from Gammer.

Bright under the light of the big, almost spherical moon, the road passed through the only pass out of the valley. Soon Sleepless's feet hurt, and a large blister was developing quite a relationship with his corns. 'Oh, joy,' he muttered, 'pain.'

By the time Sleepless had descended the forty-one hairpin bends it was worryingly close to dawn. Once he'd finally reached the town below, he rushed around pasting his posters on every wall and door in sight. Soon he had only one left: the biggest one, meant for the door of the inn where the prey were bound to see it. But the inn was damned elusive.

Ugly golden light was plastering the fleecy clouds overhead as he raced up and down the crooked streets. Overhanging gables provided some relief, but there was a nasty azure lightening on the horizon. Disgusting birdsong made him want to throw up. Already he could feel the first motes of sunlight ricocheting out of the sky and peppering him with unpleasant sensations, and however hard he looked, there wasn't a convenient cellar or crypt in sight. The nice, helpful darkness had all but disappeared as he skidded around a corner and into the village square.

At last! There was the alehouse, with a red flower painted on the sign. He just had time to slap the sign up below the lettering which read, 'The Pimpernel Bier Keller and Meat Mart'. Then he dived down a manhole cover as the sun peeped nosily into the village.

Gnawing vermin in a sewer wasn't Sleepless's idea of fun but it helped to pass the time of day. Above him in the square, rosy-cheeked peasant women gabbled in the market, kerchiefs wagging as they gossiped. More to the point, rosy-nosed men with beer bellies sat drinking anaemic lager and jabbing their thumbs at the notice:

COME ONE, COME ALL
OVER-FORTIES FOOTBALL MATCH AND BARBECUE
WITH THE MIGHTY CARPATHIAN RANGERS
FREE BARREL OF BEER TO THE WINNERS
CARPATHIAN ARMS, SUNSET TONIGHT
BE THERE OR BE BORING

And by late afternoon there was an air-conditioned Van Hool fifty-two-seater horseless coach parked encouragingly over a certain manhole cover right outside the pub. Someone was cutting out very large letters to stick in the back window. Sleepless could just make out an O, an L, a V, and that was an E, wasn't it? Maybe he should have paid more attention in school but that snaky one, it was definitely an S.

Men were saying, 'I had a trial with Negoi Rangers once,' and, 'See, there was this talent scout from Hategului City but me dad wouldn't let me go,' and thumping each other bluffly on the back in the sunset.

Sleepless wasn't sure the folks at the Carpathian could manage fifty-two plus driver, but he needn't have worried. Twenty of the seats were piled with cans of Pilsner, and half a dozen with onion and black pudding crisps. Only a score or so men shook the coach with their stumbling footsteps as they poured themselves aboard. They were deep in an argument about who'd be the next manager of Focsani Tuesday. They didn't even notice Sleepless creeping into the driver's mate's coffin, the little alcove down by the luggage lockers.

Stopping only twice for pee-breaks, the coach ground its gears noisily up towards the twilit pass. Sleepless heard the visitors singing, 'With a T and an R and an A-N-S,' but he was in no position to care. Faint with malnutrition, he found the swaying of the hairpin bends nauseating. He almost lost the contents of his stomach, and when the coach splashed through the ford he did lose his other ear. In the seconds it took to cross that fiercely running water, his agony made him deaf to what might be happening to the visitors sitting suddenly quiet above.

But it was worth it. It was all worth it when the twenty-seven strangers drew up outside the twinkling windows of the Carpathian Arms. Sleepless slipped out and found himself being hugged gratefully by his mates. With tears in his eyes Long-Tooth said, 'Talk about drinks on the hoof!' Even Mack the Fang whispered, 'Nice one, son,' while pretending to welcome the cocktails.

'There's too many of 'em just to dig straight in,' Toe Knee murmured. 'Better pretend we're going to start the match. Take a few cressets over to my mandrake field, will you? I harrowed it last spring so it should be reasonably level.' Louder he added, 'Have a drink or two on the house, lads. Who's the captain?'

A large, fat, balding man pushed his way forward. 'Pleased to meet you. I'm Hans, that's Nies, and that's Igor, and that's Bumsidasi Junior,' and as introductions do, they went on confusingly for far too long for anyone to find out who anyone else was. But Sleepless hid a mocking smile when he heard the away team's title. Even if they'd brought their own ref they'd had it if they had to make up a phoney name like that.

The challengers were taking it seriously. Some of them had real boots with real studs, and a few of them wore shorts on surprisingly hirsute legs. Once people started taking up their positions there was a fair bit of pushing and jostling. The opposing goalie jabbed an elbow in Big Mack's ribs. 'We're gonna slaughter you, mate,' he bragged.

'Yeah, we're gonna massacre you,' echoed his friend, one of the Hansis.

Now Mack came to look, Hansi was nearly as tall as he was, but he still managed to stare down at the interloper. 'Oh, yeah? You and whose army?' he grated. Sweeping his opponent into a crushing bear-hug, Mack leaned his head in close to the other man's neck, jaws beginning to open.

'Break!' Toe Knee shouted. 'No cheating now, lads. Remember,' he said meaningfully, 'the barbecue's not 'til after.'

Reluctantly Mack stopped, but only because he knew the Carpathianites couldn't take on the team and spectators all in one go. They'd have to wait until the other side were dead drunk and knackered...

Rudolf tossed a coin, Kevin guessed wrong, and the visitors took the downhill goal. Or at least, downwind from Kevin's feet.

The moon wasn't up yet as the players took their positions. Her light was only a dim platinum glimmer on the snow-capped peaks. Still, there were four cressets blazing away to mark the goal-mouths, and the driver helpfully left his coach-lights on to flood the pitch while he snoozed over a crate of beer on the back seat.

Sleepless gave up trying to work out what those letters spelt: WE–O_L or something, and stood sniffing up the odours of fresh grass and living flesh. This was a moment that made him proud to be dead. On the sidelines Liesl was flourishing her dish-mop and yelling, 'Come on you Carps!' While on the other side of the pitch the visitors were chanting, 'You'll never walk alone.'

Then the Big Match started. The hollow crump of boot on bladder rang out as Nies belted the ball off the centre spot. There was a moment of confusion as everyone raced the same way, and Rudolf the Ref blew his whistle at the Carps. 'You lot are going that way!' He pointed sternly at the Carps' goal and the home side drifted sadly away from the men they were marking.

Ten seconds later he blew it again. 'Foul!'

Sleepless had chopped a visitor's shin. A crowd gathered round the man who was writhing dramatically on the turf, a trickle of blood barely oozing out of the graze on his leg. All the same, Sleepless was down on his hands and knees, licking his lips and bringing his head down towards the infinitesimal gore.

Toe Knee, who'd appointed himself team coach, rushed across with a bucket and sponge. He mopped the man's shin and carefully wrang the sponge out into the empty bucket. It was turning into a right needle match.

One of the Hansis threw the ball from the sideline, yelling, 'On the 'ead!' and the ball went flying into the penalty box. Igor belted it into the back of the net with total disregard for the off-side rule.

The Wolves went wild. With their supporters roaring, they ran to hug Igor. And found that the Carps were also swarming around the scorer. Indeed, Long-Tooth was kissing him warmly on the neck.

Rudolf got busy with his whistle. ''Ere! You lot aren't supposed to kiss us lot. Do it again and it'll be the red card, right?'

But the Carpathians couldn't help themselves. The game got bloodier and bloodier. Fouls grew fouler and tempers frayed. Already the Carps were three men down despite the Wolves fielding a grandfather with a pacemaker – their 'secret weapon', Grithi, having mysteriously vanished, presumed drunk. At 17-0 with the Wolves fans chanting, 'We're gonna kick your blasted 'eads in,' even Kevin was getting narked.

'We're gonna make you into mincemeat,' he hissed at the Wolf who'd just chinned him.

'Bugger off, giblet-brains.' The Wolf stamped down with his spikes and Kevin lost a toe he could ill afford. In seconds, fists were flying and the whole thing had turned into a free-for-all with whistle accompaniment.

'Get 'em, lads!' yelled Mack, and the vampyres dropped all pretence of football. The visitors were trounced. Then trussed. Then treated to toothy torment, except for the ones who had to wait their turn. Their bodies shrivelled as bit by bit the blood was drained. Most of it, of course, went straight into the vampyres' stomachs. Sleepless, one eye as ever on the main chance, siphoned off a bit into the football for later.

Now his eye-teeth weren't the right shape any more it would be easier that way. He drank the dregs from the body then stole away with his booty to enjoy it in the privacy of the woods. But he stayed where he could see the field in case there were afters.

Even the driver was not exempt, though he kept pleading that he supported Man U. Lucky for him the pneumatic doors worked quickly. He threw his Van Hool into reverse and scarpered. The coach turned into a little white dot at the crest of the pass then vanished forever down the other side. The hapless visitors were stranded.

Except just then the moon rose over the mountains, fat and white and full.

As one, the surviving opposition howled. Claws burst out from their boots. Shirts ripped apart as hairy chests boiled out of them. Their faces grimaced into lupine masks with dentistry that blinded Sleepless with envy. With several mighty bounds they were free. Sleepless was glad he was under cover in the pinewood.

The Transylvanian Werewolves thought it was all over, but the Carps fought back. Finally the survivors were thrashed to a standstill. In the first grey light of pre-dawn the whole lot of them were panting helplessly, some with their tongues out further than others.

Stalemate.

'We won,' Igor said thickly.

Toe Knee cracked his knuckles. 'Yeah, but you're still stuck in the valley. Without the coach, none of us can get out of here. Didn't you notice the pain when your coach crossed the river?'

The Werewolf captain stood on the penalty spot and shrugged all four of his shoulders hopelessly. He nodded. It hurt. 'What are we going to do? What are we going to eat?'

Slumped on the grass, Mack the Fang groaned and turned towards them. "S all right,' he said. 'No problem. It was all Sleepless's fault so I ... I thought up this Cunning Plan...'

As the moon eavesdropped on his tale, Toe Knee smiled

for the first time since his cat had been nailed up safely behind the bar. Slowly he peered out into the trees, where he could just make out the flash of formerly dancing teeth.

'Sleepless,' he crooned. 'Oh, Sleepless...'

The World of the Silver Writer

Gemma could smell insanity on Arlvad's skin.

*

It was almost the watch of the dead, the time when the night breathes its last and the body is cold. Fatigue gnawed at the willpower keeping her safe and awake, that shrank her in on herself in case she broke through the barrier into Arlvad's world. She was trying to look like she wasn't observing his every twitch. As a silver writer herself, though, half her mind was drawn into the story her chair was broadcasting into the air around her. Light, colour, sound and scent, it was all there, a hologram you could almost feel. She couldn't help but notice where the other silver writer, the one who'd made the story in her chair, had written better scenes than she did, and she winced when he got it wrong. Legs curled under her as if she was on a raft on a cruel and bottomless ocean, Gemma felt/watched/heard the story her chair was telling her even though she only dared have it on half power, and saw —

Arlvad moved.

He slammed his fist on his chair (he'd been watching the 24 hour news). He said loud above the painful kaleidoscope of shattered colour, 'How can they *do* that? How can they put a man down just 'cause she said he'd raped her?'

Gemma tried not answering. Now, though, he wanted an audience for his explosion.

Suddenly he could see her through the metaphorical wall that protected his opinions from reality.

He snapped another capsule, inhaled. Gemma hated the acrid tang of the drug. Higher, straining, his voice forced its way past his fix. 'Oy, you, the tart with the hearing aid. I'm talking to you.'

Gemma tried not to feel her anger or her fear: the bleating of the kid excites the tiger. She tried to find a reply whose contempt wouldn't flay him to violence. An eternal few seconds while she struggled to be super-logical, to explain in calm, simple words —

'The machine found him guilty,' was all she finally managed. And at the same time, not hearing her, Arlvad burst out, 'Bloody typical. What are you, thick or something? Christ, a half-wit could see how unfair it was. But not you. Some geezer's going to be numbed for ten bloody years. She was a prostitute for Christ's sake. What's one more customer?'

Gemma thought, *With a broken bottle? He rammed her with broken glass until her bowel spilt into her womb and he's just one more customer? How can Arlvad even think that? What changed him?*

'Say something, you stupid cow! Christ, you're not on this planet, are you? Living in your own little world. The court's going to freeze that bloke for the next ten years because of some ugly whore. They're going to put him into deep sleep while he loses ten, count them, ten years of his life. A guy got sliced right next to me at the match on Saturday but nobody's going to bust a gut to get the gang who did it. What makes women so special?'

Slow and solid like iced treacle, Gemma's words worked past the guard on her tongue:

'Then they should —'

'The difference is, men don't go blarting, "Help me, help me!"' (Gemma hated Arlvad's stupid high sneer of a pretend woman's voice.) 'But your race think they're God's gift.' *Like women aren't part of homo sapiens?* she didn't say. Triggering another capsule with his thumb, he inhaled. The skin around his nostrils was hardly blue at all. The cobalt vapour lost its colour before it reached inside him but that's where it had left its most ineradicable mark. The indigo dots beneath his nose were almost hidden by his moustache.

He held the drug in his lungs for a moment; Gemma took advantage of the pause to protest, 'Well I think —'

'Don't bloody interrupt!' he yelled. 'I don't give a toss what you think. What do you know about anything anyway? You don't even do a proper job! Just sit in your precious little darkroom all day making up soppy tales. You want to keep your mouth shut 'til you've done seven years in the factory like I have.'

Mistake: she yelled back. Her face twisted with anger (like his), thrust forward (like his). 'I know enough to say violence is wrong whoever the victim is.'

Arlvad threw the table over. Her glass of mulled wine leaped from its heated element to spin scalding through the air. Spears of crimson lanced fire on her thigh. Second mistake: pulling frantically at the blistering fabric of her jeans, she screamed and jumped out of her seat.

Arlvad misread her pain. 'You want violence? I'll show you violence!'

He was between her and the door.

It was only afterwards that Gemma realised: despite all the kicks and blows and strangleholds, the insults designed to annihilate her, he never left a mark where it would show.

*

But in the morning he woke her from her cramped and fitful sleep on the airbed in the lounge – with coffee and a cuddle. He didn't see the wine on the wall or the shattered glass though she'd used all her courage not to clean up his mess. He smiled and didn't know what had happened last night. His touch made her skin crawl.

His gentle hands dropped abandoned to his sides. Eyes bright with unshed tears, he said, 'I wish you wouldn't keep rejecting me,' and left. Huddled on the airbed, she listened to his footsteps, heard the front door slam. His low-slung car roared away, fading off into the distance. Her sobs drew creaks from the airbed. It was the image of the uncomprehending hurt in his face that made her weep.

*

It's from outside that they close the door on the darkroom. When you finally get inside for the only slot you managed to book this side of your deadline, the last slice of light shrinks and is gone. You're in the heart of a black velvet-lined egg. There's nothing but warm, scrubbed air in here. If you lived inside a cavern of jet you couldn't see less. You grope your way along the guide-rope to the console so you can flick the switches. Computer. Driver. The image tank will take a while to warm to that lovely amber readiness. Meantime the clear plastiglass sheet moves up, first one stave … *sky, sea, land, weather*, then the second which is *sun, moon and stars*. It'll be a while yet until *scents* and *movement of hair* appear. Meantime you take the dust-covers off the central keypads: *characters, gestures, face*. The one marked *scenes* has parsed from the history of mankind whether acted or filmed live. Everyone from Conan to Errol Flynn, from Adam and Eve to hedge-fund crooks. All waiting for someone to put them in the image tank and make them live. But the slightest light or noise from outside would kill them quicker than a cobra. That's why even the reception area has only the dim red glow of an old-fashioned photographer's darkroom.

Perfect silence, that's what else you need at a Writers' Guild studio. Do you know what perfect silence is?

It's perfect.

But you panic; you find yourself listening for your heartbeat… Phew! *There* it is! And the silence isn't perfect any more.

Sometimes the black velvet silence is a refuge, but you can't hide for long in silence. Your thoughts go with you: all the emotional encumbrance that's been making you long all week to be here safe in your own darkroom world. *I control the image-tank so nobody can master me.* But you've got to get some potatoes on the way home, and your knee itches, and every worry you've been trying to hide from jumps out right when finally it's your turn and you get in here and you think, *But what's the point?*

Sometimes before you start, when there's nothing, the

dead silence is the black weight of a tomb, a whole necropolis pressing down on you with weights made of missed chances and assorted regrets until they drag you into the grave. And we all go down into the dark alone...

Except...

Except here, impelled by the frightening silence, your thoughts spiral and erupt through your fingers on the keyboard. Silver ink shoots out, radiant marks dance on the staves. Slowly, one phrase at a time, my fingertips gavotte on the keys. My breathing swoops like a barque on the sea, and there, soft and fluid, the figures I've created dance on the stave. I become real with the worlds I make, and someone, somewhere, will see them and connect with the real me.

I – there's no room here for the other Gemma, the one whose body carries the pain I bundle out the door – I love it.

It's laughter distilled in sunlight, joy on the shores of ocean. One of the figures – the hero – switches on music (so I have to go back and put the soundpad in earlier. It's another silver squiggle on the plastiglass).

There's quite a gang of them in the world I've made in my machine. My heroine and her beau, their fun, caring friends – I hope they're having a better time than I am. (I laugh bitterly. Then tears, real, now, drip invisible on my skin. I feel their hot moisture trail down my face. How can you be jealous of a person you've made up? Practice. A wry grin; silent whistling in the dark.

More than that. Loneliness, anger, frustration; all the times you think *I should have* ... but you didn't. But that's the half of my life I try to forget in here. I try to pretend all that's happening to someone else. If it's happening at all. *Arlvad brought me tea this morning. He looked so ... blank, so innocently hurt when I flinched away...* But the scald-marks on my leg are real. *But he loves me! He wouldn't –*)

So, music: I go back and write the song in, glowing symbols on the sound stave, finding snatches of melody in memory, tracing and cueing them via the computer. It finds the sounds in its terabytes of banks. I print them onto the plastiglass, sync the staves and press that magic *Play.* Visual harmony encircles me in the darkroom. And in the image-tank my silver world lives to a cheerful Latin beat. *God! I'm longing for the moment I can fix it on the plastiglass, then watch it through a comfy chair. Or even the one in Reception.*

I play the scene, and replay it, tinkering with it, getting off on it, orchestrating the wind and sky, making the figures dance, eye greeting eye with secret laughter. I write, watch, rewind and delete along all the staves. I do it in a script like balletic notation, and I'm gnawing my knuckle trying to think up just the right words. *Should I make the sky bluer near the horizon? Damn! Why can't I concentrate?* I want my words to hang like stars above the beach in the image tank. I want them to break your heart with your longing for a love like that.

Because words, the gift of conversation pegged on the sharing of a smile, are all that stop us going down into the dark alone.

*

Hell! What time is it? The side-bar of the monitor tells me it's almost half-past seven. *Christ! I've been here all day and only made 37 minutes' screen-time! I've got less than an hour. He'll kill me if I'm late but my backup show's nowhere near ready. If I get the boot for letting the station down we'll never make the rent. We'll be on the street. And it'll be my fault.* A panic-attack drums in my chest. Not now! I've got to...

Alex (that's what I'll call this character. Got to think of the character or I'll never get out of this funk. So, Alex. I've always liked that name. Self-praise is no praise, that's what Mum always said. All the same I had one ecstatic moment of genius when I finally created a sound-shape to tell the computer how to encompass all he is of cheerfulness, of stability and caring). Alex doesn't look anything like Arlvad. I won't let him.

Alex, lean and blond with sunshine weaving rainbows in his hair, stoops to hum a snatch of melody to the soundpad I've just written in. He looks up quizzically to see if his darling has caught his musical reference to their night before. And grins mischievously as he thumbs the remote. Music blossoms in the cove, and she breaks into a smile of delight.

Once Arlvad used to smile at me like that. Not so long ago I heard him laughing on Skype and for a minute I couldn't think who it was in our living room. When did we stop laughing? – When he – my heart beats so painfully my whole ribcage echoes –

Alex. Concentrate on Alex. Checking the image tank, I know that's not quite how he'd move. I press the delete key. It sucks up the silver curves on *gesture* and *face* and there's Alex back the way he was before. Time erased. *If only I could go back!*

So I search visual references until I see the movement-type I want. The computer projects it into the driver for me. When the shape of Alex sums up his exuberance and grace, I tabulate it. There he is, frozen for a second, that movement choreographed on plastiglass, his head flicking up to see her delight, wanting her to share his joy.

Like Arlvad did before there was only him in his world: sun, centre of his team, the staunch hero of his opiate dreams.

We're all centres, I guess, only sometimes it's nice to overlap without hurting. I think of all the people I'm programming this for, all the people who will sit in their chair some night hand in hand or cuddling a cat, and watch the happiness I've made for them. Men too, though Arlvad says I don't like his 'race'. He says all women are men's secret enemies who'll lie and twist and cling. At least I acknowledge we're all the same species. I just wish he did. And if I said that, he'd say it was just me insulting him because, apparently, I'm always putting him down.

Don't have to with Arlvad. He does it for himself. *(When did I get this bitchy? I'm sure I never used to be this way.)*

So, Alex. With the song drifting across the bright beach, everyone's happy. Some of them are dancing again and two lads have a splash fight in the waves. A couple of women unload a barrel of wine from a pickup truck and heft it down the dunes. There's plenty of people to help her so the two lads go on splashing and laughing like kids, and I put in streamers of spray in glittering arcs. Stock characters, more or less. Nice people but rentacrowd. I let the computer handle their bodies. All I put in is their emotions.

But my heroine: what shall I call her? I get the computer to try out several names on Alex's lips. His pleasant tenor voice (so warm!) makes me smile, and I wince. Then he says, 'Astra.' I capture her thrill and mine in swooping shades of silver.

God, I love this world. Thank You for letting me make it.

I rhapsodise about this man, skimming hundreds of scenes from the data bank because I don't want a puppet. I want Alex to be a real person, a man you might meet at a party or on the steps of a bank, so I tame the rhapsody. Still, a man would be glad to have him as a friend (N.B.: go back and write him a best friend), and a woman would be glad to share the warmth of his body.

At their first kiss I can't write any more. It feels like prying. I don't believe what I've written. Their happiness is unimaginable.

Pain. Jealousy. Regret. *Why me?*

I push back from the monitor and stretch my aching neck. My hands are pale in the faint, sunny glow of the image tank. Multiple curves – the kitchen cupboards – gleam half as pale again. The lines come and go with your focus, like charcoal on black. If you blink, you think you've imagined it. Everything's rounded in here, even the edges of the couch in the hollow in the wall. That's so none of us writers hurt ourselves blundering round in the dark. Ergonomics. I cling to the word as I go to the loo, get a glass of Mavrodaphne, eat a Pot Noodle, and all by the eldritch glow of the world I've made. All I've got to hold on to is gossamer words.

And if any light came in, I'd lose them. Any light or sound would turn them into a Jackson Pollock smear on the plastiglass. Until it's finished I can't cover it with fixative so the whole thing would slither down the pan. That's why in

Reception there's a big sign:
DO NOT UNDER ANY CIRCUMSTANCES OPEN THIS DOOR. EMERGENCY PHONE (RED) WILL CONTACT THE WRITER SO THAT HIS/HER WORK MAY BE FIXED BEFORE THE DOOR OPENS.

And Winston's on rota in Reception. He's probably got his feet up on the desk and he's carving a meerschaum pipe. No way would Winston let anyone in here.

I can't put it off any longer. It's 7.20 already! I've been here ten hours and I've only made forty-one minutes' screentime. Even with titles and ad breaks I've got to come up with another nine minutes. Robyn's on tomorrow so it'll be an all-nighter unless I get a move on.

I freeze. When I'm late back, Arlvad is worse than ever, jealous of the time I'm not spending on him. (And what if it's one of the days when he's so kind and loving and I'm not there? Guilt should be outlawed.)

I go back to Alex and Astra, and oh! How their good times hurt me. It's a physical pain, down below the parting of my ribs. My heart starts its flamenco again. I'm afraid alone in the dark. But that side of life belongs to Gemma and I won't mix her up with what I'm doing here. But I'm terrified that her palpitations will turn into a heart-attack and kill me... What if I die alone in the dark between the worlds?

I won't give into it.

Now I have to ramp up the tension and drama. Sympathy for the bad guy that mows down innocent victims? Was it his choice or could he just not help himself? And his girl, she's just swept along by fear because of his cruelty. Will she stab him in the back with a broken bottle? Of course his body has to land at the foot of a whole heap of his victims. Astra and the girl will shake hands. Joke about not being close enough to kiss each other's cheeks just yet. Police. Back to beach party. Happy ending. Even better, small town so the cops come back to join the party when they come off shift. There. Now *that's* a happy ending. Plus I barely killed enough people for the average Saturday night movie. There's a *real* happy ending, especially now I've remembered the minimum body count the contract insists on.

But for me the hokum is a frame for the real picture, which is ordinary people who aren't me having a good time on a beach. Weave the strands of the plot like threads of a tapestry holding the sunny scene together.

(Maybe you have to have the bad times so you can appreciate the good? I mean, we did have plenty of good times before it went wrong… But what of victimology? The fact that some people get mugged again and again because somehow they look like victims? Is that what I'm doing? Somehow making Arlvad take out his anger on me? What have I ever done to deserve this? I must be horrific, evil on a scale like Pol Pot. I loathe myself. But my friends love me. Well they did when Arlvad allowed me to have any. Besides, I used to take a capsule or two back at uni. I just thought he'd grow out of it like everyone else does. Mind, everyone else just gets giggly and falls asleep. With the amounts Arlvad takes you can't tell who he's going to be from one minute to the next. The times I've wanted to hurt myself for being so stupid! How could I have been so thick that I set up home with him? Was he like that all along and I just didn't see it? Was his tenderness simply bait? And how could I have stayed after it got so bad? Because he wasn't always so terrifying. Remember that winter in Devon with him clowning around with cricket-bats strapped to his feet like snowshoes? And our beautiful honeymoon in Crete … Don't I owe him my loyalty? Even if I do manage to get away, how could I live on my own? He'd just come for me anyway. I'd be keeping one eye over my shoulder for the rest of my life. I'm so afraid and I hate myself for being such a wimp. I'm shaking again, and the only way I know I'm alive down here in the darkroom is the way my thorax throbs to my clumsy heart-beat.)

But I've got to push all that outside, let it belong to Gemma. I split myself deliberately. (*Arlvad's mood-swings are fragmenting me.*) There's a deadline. I've got something in reserve – one of those shows you spin out with flashbacks from earlier episodes, but I'm not sure it's good enough to beat the competition, and with ratings coming up … I've got to get this story finished.

So the mobster arrives with his murderous girlfriend. You can't tell they're baddies by looking at them. There are no black hats in real life. Him and his harpy shatter the tranquillity of that party on the beach. Flock of seagulls (have to put some in earlier) take off raucously to show lives being disintegrated. A love-song on the soundpad makes a counterpoint. Guns are waved around, people get hurt. Astra creates a diversion so together she and Arlvad get the baddie.

Arlvad?

Arlvad the addict? The one I've lived with for seven years?

Oh, help me, God. I know it's true. Weeping in the darkroom, I know that almost everything that's good about my hero used to be true about my husband. Still is, some days, even if he is a bit skinny and blue in the face. Friendly, kind, loving, good for a laugh. It's not him, it's the drugs. There's something broken inside that makes him use them to fill the void I longed (long*ed? Past tense?*) to fill. He's too scared to reveal his toxic secret. It's like this great big *thing* puts blinkers on him. He genuinely can't see he's doing anything wrong so he gets frustrated and lashes out at me so he doesn't have to feel his pain. I've begged and cajoled and given him pamphlets but he won't accept help. He says doctors know nothing and there's nothing wrong with him anyway. He holds down a good job, doesn't he? (Not as good as the one he got fired from.) A real job of work, not like my wanking in the darkroom. Everyone outside our front door thinks he's the life and soul. I'm just making a fuss because he acts like a man and I don't like men. He can't be right about that, can he?

*

A long time later, I drink coffee and it's hot and soothing in my swollen throat. The sky in the image tank hurts my sore eyes. I just want to sleep to get away from it all. But I can't. I'm afraid to sleep because I have nightmares where my heart explodes. I never dare go to bed until he's fast asleep. Anyway, Robyn's got dibs on the darkroom from midnight so I'll have to finish this off tonight. There's the seagulls to put in, and a spot of characterisation for the gangster's moll right at the beginning so it makes sense, then the fade-into-the-sunset ending. But I've nearly finished. And it's just as well because – bloody hell! It's nearly half-past ten! Arlvad'll go crazy when I get home.

So, the woman. Show her trying to use her credit card but it's maxed out. And although I start to scroll forward to the end of the story I stop to tinker a bit here, a bit there, and before you know it I've watched the whole thing through, and the scents of the beach-barbecue mix with wine and salt breeze, and in the music-laden dusk (sunset is trite) there are couples breathing soft. I'm on the point of working up a good punch-line for the kicker when I suddenly need to write in some St Elmo's fire on the waves. And what about a trace of pheromones in the closing shot? Every single chair-viewer will feel happy and loved up —

The soundproof door slams open. Yellow light glares in, surrounding Arlvad who looks like a gangling spider hanging in the doorway. He's shouting but I don't hear him. I'm watching the light swamp my delicate silver writing. Sound blurs. Friendship and silver smear dully down the plastiglass. In the image tank my world dies. The characters go nova, then there's only a blood-red pulse fading inside the wrecked machine. Everything I am is dead.

And now the outside world is here in the darkroom. There's an aural assault, Arlvad shrieking. Past him I can see Winston scrabbling across the carpet chasing his phone. His nose is bleeding. I can't handle it. I'm numb.

Arlvad twists his fingers through my hair and I'm not numb any more. Sharp pain tears through my head. It gets worse as I tune into what he's yelling.

'You lying bitch! I thought you were supposed to be home

by nine but I was wrong, wasn't I? I cooked a curry, candles, flowers – but you're just like all your race. Bloody women! Couldn't give a stuff about anybody else. How would *you* like it if *you'd* done ten hours of solid graft and came home to an empty house?'

I wrench away from him, and there's a hank of my hair hanging from his fist. I bark my shins on a storage rack. I just know I'll be black and blue in the morning. They're my bruises, not Gemma's. (Part of me thinks: *ooh, don't forget the accidental injuries you do to yourself – that'll come in handy for a future episode*.) Now Arlvad's here Gemma and I are no longer two separate people. We're coming together.

Safe on the far side of the rack I hiss, 'You know you've not only wrecked the programme I've spent all day on, you've trashed a million pounds' worth of equipment?' I was amazed I managed not to shout.

'I couldn't give a flying fuck. All it is is you playing with yourself anyway. Now shift your arse. I'm taking you home.'

Walking past him, quiescent (a ploy), I kneel by Winston, carefully keeping him between me and the … the bad guy. I use a tissue to wipe blood off Winston's lips and whisper, 'You all right, man?'

'Oh, fine,' says Winston, ever the master of irony. 'How about you?'

Arlvad bustles past, accidentally-on-purpose kicking me. I was expecting it. I raise a grin for Winston and say, 'I'll live.' I dither about, hiding that I'm kicking his phone closer. What if he calls the cops? What the hell would I walk into then?

Arlvad's at the street door, yelling, 'Come on, you stupid tart. You just wait 'til I get you home.' I can see the blue stain on his lip. The drug, bittersweet with just a hint of spice, is already seeping out with his sweat. It smells like madness.

From the relative safety near my friendly bloodstained witness, I look Arlvad straight in the eyes and ask, 'Why don't you get some therapy?'

Arlvad sneers and stalks out to the car but I know he heard. I saw the tight look on his face.

I show my mobile to Winston and say, 'See you soon,' with all the sincerity I can muster. He nods, not quite believing.

Arlvad slams the car door and sits angrily revving the engine. 'I mean it,' I mouth at Winston as I back away. Then, in fearful obedience, I trot across the street. It's a soft May night, and the scent of chestnut candles is in the air. I walk round the front of the car. I know he can't ram me because he's parked in a slot facing the bollards on the curb. Stony-faced, he stares out the windscreen.

I think – and tears stream down my face and I hate myself for crying but I won't be crying soon, I'll be strong one day – I think of my poor broken story.

So he's broken the machine. So he's smashed that silver world. I'll write another. The studio's insured.

Arlvad's not expecting it, and to tell the truth, I'm not sure I am either. To our surprise I've finally found courage.

Instead of getting into the passenger seat, I leave the door open and slip down a side alley. I hear him drive furiously round the other end of it. I'm dizzy with physical fear as I double back and dodge over the side gate of the Writers' Guild. His headlights swoop past just as I jump down onto the wheelie bins. His tyres keep on screeching as he shoots off in the wrong direction.

I phone Winston. We wait in the dark of Reception, Winston and I, until we can't hear the car any more. We lock up and slide over the road to The River Inn. Even though it's after closing time his girlfriend Ceri lets him in. She works behind the bar in her vacations. After Winston cleans himself up in the gents' he asks Ceri how she's getting on at college. She looks over his shoulder and waves at me, then he helps her clean up. I'm too shaky to move right now but I'm getting better. They'll bring out a bottle of bubbly to share in a minute.

I drift out alone on the terrace, shivering as I watch a breeze fragment the ripples on the oily water. The fear – and its destructiveness – leak away. When the breeze has passed, the images on the river come together again, not the same from one moment to the next but always beautiful.

The Seeds of a Pomegranate

I can't stand dogs that don't come in a bun with ketchup. When some enormous hellhound barked outside the station it just about frightened me out of my life.

Heart pounding, I looked wildly round for the monster but it must have been behind a fence. Its throaty roar echoed around the deserted forecourt. I almost ran up the road to the safety of the Himachal Palace. Anyway, I'd been dying for my curry all the way home and they were always so nice on the phone.

Two things happened as I reached for the handle. The door burst open and my phone pinged to announce yet another bloody text.

Mr Chopra barged out, chicken-tikka steam billowing around him. In the shop lights he looked grey. He shouldered past as if he hadn't even noticed me, stopping not three feet away to stare into the darkness.

His haste sent me spinning into the door-jamb. I half-grinned at his wife behind the till, hoping to share a bonding eye-roll of 'Men, huh?'

Nisha Chopra wasn't smiling. She was ducking under the counter. Pale with fear, she ran full-tilt towards the door. Something was terribly wrong. We collided and grabbed one another for balance, both gazing in horror at what was happening outside.

The innocent clouds of spiced steam wrapped around her husband. And froze to hang in the air, shining wreaths of solid fog. The icy mist grew a thousand arms that smothered him from turban to toe. Frost crackled over his eyebrows. Over his skin. He – he *gleamed*. He cartwheeled and crashed to earth like an orchestra of breaking glass. Shards of crimson flesh flew up as though someone had blasted a pomegranate. Icicles of saliva speared his scream to silence.

Nisha lurched towards him. I followed. Glassy splinters melted under our feet. His frosted sheath lost its shimmer though his hands stayed cold and blue. She reached to turn him over.

'Don't!' I yelled, but it was too late. At her touch his jacket crumbled into his half-frozen shoulder. But, horribly, not all of him broke. Rapidly warming to softness in the mild September evening, parts of his face and body remained as they always had, only seamed with canyons of blood where the ice-seeds fell.

Nisha was paralysed by shock but I wrestled her inside. 'Do you know how to stop that – that thing?' I babbled. 'Will the door keep it out?'

The new widow stopped fighting me. 'No idea, Zoe. I don't know what's happening!'

Me neither. We crouched quivering behind the rack of Bombay Mix and peered out through the sudden frost-ferns on the window. Quernmore Road was empty – except for what was left of the cook. He … it … spread on the pavement, blood turning to black shadows that oozed into the cracks. Another text put me off as I shakily thumbed 999, trying to keep my voice out of the bat register to ask for police and an ambulance. How I managed not to request an exorcist I'll never know.

*

While we were crying and clinging to each other, I patted Nisha's back helplessly and wished I'd never come to London. If only I'd never taken the promotion to head office! I could have been home in safe, cosy Rutland where winter didn't come and go in twenty minutes. If only I hadn't needed a bigger salary to pay off debts I'd never incurred. If only I hadn't taken Andy back. If only I hadn't married a lying, chiselling con-artist like him in the first place. But no, here I was on my tod in London with a loan the size of the Matterhorn. It wouldn't have been so bad if there'd been someone I could call for moral support but I'd been in the Smoke for less than a month and didn't know anyone well enough yet. Billy No-Mates, that was me. The sobbing widow in my arms was the only person outside work who called me by my first name and that was just because we'd once been stuck on a broken-down train for three hours.

Shivering on the lino lost in our own thoughts, we nearly had a collective heart-attack when a policeman pounded the door. Constable Ellis, he shouted through the window, though he looked scarcely old enough to shave. He was quite good-looking apart from the sticky-out ears. After a second glance at Mr Chopra's remains he threw up before talking to his radio. He couldn't decide whether to stand guard over the body or arrest us on the spot.

It didn't take long for flocks of coppers to show up. Their suspicions swirled around us. While I wrapped Nisha in shawls and helped her sip sweet tea, they badgered us with questions, tramped all over the house and erected a tent over what was left of 'the deceased', as they called him. They kept leaving the doors open so the balloons saying 7 *Today* bobbled against the walls. Nisha wailed, 'Anjuli's round her friend's at her party. How am I going to tell her her father's been murdered today of all days?'

The police were more interested in why I kept saying the deceased had been frozen since it was mid-September and warm for the time of year?

'But he *was* frozen!' I insisted since Nisha was too upset to talk. So far tea hadn't done much of a job of calming her down. Mind, my feelings were a-bubble like a shaken bottle of pop.

'Hardly!' the woman in the white bunny-suit retorted. 'I mean, it's a good twelve degrees outside. When did you say he died?'

'Look at our CCTV!' Nisha mumbled.

'We did,' said DCI Johnstone, stubbly, over-promoted and disillusioned. 'The cameras froze —'

'Aha!' I cried.

His turn for the eye-rolling. 'I don't mean froze as in freezing, Ms— Ah.' I'd already given him my name. Several times. So I didn't fill in the gap. He went on, 'Froze as in the picture broke up. And, it seems, you were the last person to touch Mr Chopra before he died. What was your story again?'

My phone rang. I ignored it because words like *false imprisonment* and *miscarriage of justice* were polka-ing round my mind. 'Surely he's got frost-bite or something?' I stammered.

The pathologist sighed ostentatiously, raising her brows to show she was humouring me. Guarded by the jug-eared coplet, I followed her outside, flushing under the stares of the assorted ghouls hanging round beyond any crime scene tape: reporters, the crowd off the next train and no doubt the pickpockets and bag-snatchers London Transport advertised.

I was glad to duck under the tent-flap until I saw what it hid up close. When I retched, Ms Pathologist pulled a *tut* face and glanced down at Mr Chopra's bluish fingertips, once casually and one not. Focussed now, she frowned and pinched the skin. 'You're right! The top layer of skin's soft but his flesh is hard as iron. And see here? There's blisters – like he'd been in a deep freeze or something, though he's pretty much ambient temperature now. Inspector, I think those two ought to come down to the station to answer some questions.'

Back inside while Taxi-ears played detectives and the Inspector talked to his radio, Nisha wailed to the WPC, 'We paid a fortune for those cameras! You lot never investigate when they scrawl 'Pakis go home' on our windows so we got the best. Don't they at least have him running out of the shop before…?'

Inspector Johnstone said flatly, 'Let's see your deep freeze.'

Leaning on me as though she'd aged a hundred years, Nisha stumbled down to the prep room behind the commercial kitchen. There stood the freezer, empty and turned off, door sagging on a broken hinge. An Environmental Health label dangled from it. 'See? Three days ago! They said they'd sign it off when it was fixed but we're still waiting for the engineer to come.'

'Aha! So what are you doing feeding the public when you've been shut down?' asked PC Taxi-ears. Whipping out his notebook, he whirled to face the widow.

'We haven't been shut down!' Nisha exclaimed indignantly. 'Nikodem—' she nodded towards the Polish deli next door '—keeps our stuff on ice. The EHO gave Dev a chitty but I don't know where he put it. I wish he...' She broke down again. Obviously the back-patting was no use. I tried holding her hand instead.

DCI Johnstone pursed his lips and glared at the boy in blue. 'Go and fend off the press, Sherlock. Unless you've got a Doctor Watson to do that for you?'

'Yes, sir. No, sir.' Back of his neck as red as radish, PC Ellis practically scampered out of the back room. But he hadn't taken two steps into the shop when we heard him bump into someone. Puzzled, we all looked round but it wasn't yet more police, nor even an intrepid reporter. Instead a short but gloriously handsome man eeled in, keeping one side of his face turned away. Just as I said, bewildered, 'Bosh?' PC Ellis flashed a torch at him. The mystery midget flung up his arms to shield his eyes and squealed, 'Whatever it is, I didn't do it!'

*

After they'd given him a once-over that must have felt like X-rays, they never even asked the pocket Adonis how he'd crossed the police line. Seeming mesmerised, they all watched him answer the inspector's questions. The WPC sort of sighed at each chocolate-brown word. Meantime the young copper's tongue poked out the side of his mouth. He looked up from his scrawly note-taking. 'B-O-S-what, did you say?'

The newcomer rolled his darkly handsome eyes. 'Never mind. It's on my— Don't be a prat! I'm hardly going for a gun. My driving license, see? Boshay Lopez. Usually known as Bosh. Here, give it back! *Thank* you.' With camp irony he rushed to forestall the interrogation. 'Look, I didn't know I was gate-crashing a murder, did I? I just heard Zoe's ring-tone so I knew she was in here and came in for a chat, all right?' This despite the flashing blue lights and the police *do not cross* line. Bosh lowered his voice with theatrical patience. What we could see of his fine features could have been Indian or Mediterranean, but when he moved incautiously we couldn't miss the snazzy black eye he'd been trying to hide. He glared defiance at the cops. 'Yes, I was beaten up this evening and yes, I am thinking of pressing charges. No, it wasn't racially motivated, thank you for asking, and yes, it was domestic and what do I expect with people like me?' Then he hissed, 'Zoe, you stupid mare, why don't you ever answer your bloody phone?'

I waved at the constabulary. 'In case you haven't noticed, Bosh, I've been a bit busy. Goodness knows what you're doing here but you're just the person. Nisha's CCTVs are frozen and unless we get a picture for the, um, time of death – sorry, pet—' I squeezed Nisha's other hand. 'We won't be able to prove we didn't do him in.'

'What, you? Never!' Bosh scoffed.

'But they don't know me and they think I might have. Please. Just do something, will you?'

Bosh scrunched his eyes shut and sniffed while turning his head from side to side. Suddenly he snapped them open again. 'Don't get antsy, Zo, I know you didn't.' He went to jump up from his armchair saying, 'Give us a shufti at the camera then.'

Inspector Johnstone loomed over him. Bosh gave him a falsely charming smile and subsided into the cushions. 'Or don't you want to get the cameras working, officers?'

'He's a techno-wizard,' I said hastily to the boys and girls in blue. 'He can fix anything.'

You'd have thought the droopy DCI would have insisted on somebody from computer forensics but he just shrugged.

'Can't hurt.' I caught myself thinking, 'I'm sure cops didn't use to be like this.' My hand flew up to cover my mouth in horror. Mid-thirties, presentable – but starting to think like a fud. How come Bosh got his own way with the Met like he did at the office? Was it because he was too buff for words? I'd often wondered if he only talked to me because my love-life was as rubbish as his.

Beaming at the inspector, Bosh whipped out a set of tiny screwdrivers. 'Got a ladder, boss?'

*

While I got the family doctor's name off Nisha's mobile, Ms Bunnysuit took the shattered body to the mortuary. Most of the other cops blared off with sirens and lights to enjoy an affray. The doctor chucked me out so I went to see what Bosh was up to. Nobody stopped me. Curiouser and curiouser. I was surprised we weren't in the nick already.

Outside, Ellis held the ladder while Bosh fiddled with the cameras above his head. The mild September night had turned bitterly cold once more so the audience had mostly given up and gone home. It was eerily quiet, and the stars shone brilliantly, promising a frost that hadn't been on the weather reports. Mist haloed the streetlights and I wondered uneasily if it was going to come to life and kill us all, but it just hung about looking romantic and smelling of bonfires.

Now I had time, I checked my phone. Two more voicemails from Andy which I deleted without listening to them. It was the only way I could withstand his emotional assaults. After all he'd done I still loved the bastard - when I didn't hate him. He was probably only playing songs about the chains of love again but I wasn't going to fall for it this time. And six, count them, *six* texts, all from Bosh. He was a good ten years younger than me and while we bantered when he came into work to update the aged IT stuff, we were hardly bosom buddies. He'd plonked himself at my table in Starbucks a couple of times and I'd been glad of the company, but he only had three topics of conversation: his rollercoaster relationship with a loser called Lee, nerdy gizmos and his new puppy. Did I mention I'm scared stiff of dogs? But Bosh was so determined to make me like them that he'd even changed my screensaver to one of his long-tailed pet Alfie. I'd got him back, though. I'd changed the one on his laptop to a kitten in a Barbie-pink tutu. His texts from this afternoon were three more pictures of his dopey dog and then two this evening saying, 'Call me ASAP', 'Lee's chucked me out!' and the one just now. It said, 'Life or death, you dozy mare. Where are you?' Thoughtfully I deleted them as well. Had I got myself a stalker?

'You all right up there?' Ellis called to my creepy follower on the ladder. 'You've been ages.'

'No, constable.' Bosh's hands were visibly shaking. 'All right is about as far from how I'm feeling as you can get. I've just found the love of my life with his hands down someone else's pants and I'm up a ladder getting frostbite because my BFF's a murder suspect.' *'I'm his BFF? When did that happen?'* I wondered, but Bosh blabbered on, 'Come to think of it, constable, after seeing all that blood, I don't suppose you're feeling on top of the world either. Is that puke on your utility belt?'

'I'm all right, sir.'

'Me neither, Constable Ellis. Can I call you by your first name? After all, we're brothers in freaked-outness.'

Could things get weirder? They became Darren and Bosh, with Darren rambling on about how he'd just graduated from Hendon police college and this being his first time on nights. He wouldn't admit it but I could see he was torn between horror and excitement at his first actual murder.

The doctor left, telling me charmlessly that Nisha was sedated and he had no extant next of kin listed so we should stay until she could find someone. It wasn't a question.

Accusingly the WPC told me Inspector Johnstone had gone next door to check the freezer. As time went on she stopped meeting my eye. When her superior eventually came out of the shop next door he was three sheets to the wind and smelling of Polish plum brandy, but much cheerier. Breath puffing white in the chill air, he called upwards.

Bosh answered, 'Yeah, that should about fix it. Let's go in and look at the footage before I freeze my bollocks off.'

We all trailed inside, Ellis making a meal of keeping the non-existent crowds away. The journalists had all gone to the nearest pub for a warm and a whiskey and most other people had realised they'd have to get up for work in the morning so he didn't have much to do.

I ostentatiously put the Closed sign on the door. Nisha, doped to the eyeballs, drifted into the office with us and so did the WPC. With the inspector and Daz Ellis it was crowded.

And Bosh worked his magic. There on the monitor was Mr Chopra, slipping on an old green bottle all covered with frost, somersaulting into the air clutching his heart. The bottle smashed under his fall. That's what caused his terrible cuts. They all remembered the smell of wine. That's why Inspector Johnstone had thought it would be a drunken row. But the two women and the likeable Asian lad had no alcohol on their breath at all. They weren't even on the recording. It was just an accident. Sorry to have troubled you in your hour of grief.

They left, Darren slipping Bosh a wink and promising to call in for a cuppa the next time he was on nights, and Bosh saying, 'Yeah, when I've got somewhere to live.' I locked the door behind Dazzling Darren and followed Bosh and Nisha into the Chopras' living room.

'What on *earth* is going on?' I burst out. 'And what the hell are you doing here in the first place?'

Mouth agape, he fell on the sofa. His sad-puppy eyes welled up. 'What d'you mean, what am I doing here? You don't care at all, do you? My whole entire life's been ruined and you can't even be bothered to answer your phone to see if I was all right. I thought you at least would understand my broken heart but you're too wrapped up in your own self-pity to take a blind bit of notice.'

'Be fair! I had my phone on silent for art class, then I couldn't get a signal on the train, and now—' I waved my hands around '—this.' I turned to Nisha. 'Look, is there someone I can call or do you want us to get out of your hair?'

'Don't leave me alone!' she stammered. 'I called Uncle Saatvik Saatalya but he's in Glasgow and he won't be here 'til morning.' She slapped her face to pull herself together. 'Where are my manners? Your order was ready hours ago, Zoe. You must be starving. And your kind friend.'

I protested but Bosh said something to her in what might have been Hindi. Surprised but pleased, she replied in the same language, then wagged her head and said in English, 'You might as well. Dev's uncle's been trying to shut down the business for ages so he can throw us out. Anyway, it's the last thing Dev cooked. It wouldn't be right to waste it. Stay here.'

Too jangled yet to succumb completely to the sedative, she wafted down to the commercial kitchen. I sat forward, glaring at Bosh. 'So give.'

'I found Lee with his hands down some smarmy beggar's boxers. I went to lamp him one but when they stood up the other guy was about ten feet tall and built like a brick shithouse. He flattened me. And Lee turned round and said, 'You're pathetic, you and your mystic East crap. I can't believe you're still living in the dark ages. Pack a bag and clear out." Bosh gulped back tears and finished Lee's sentence: "Anyway, you had to find out sometime. You can pick the rest of your stuff up in the morning. And don't forget to leave the key."

Bosh's tears were real but he seemed to be kind of enjoying them. Histrionic, I suppose, but I did sympathise. It was only a couple of months ago that I came home to an empty cottage to find Andy had left me a note. And a pile of credit card bills in my name. And a packet of condoms at the bottom of the wardrobe even though I was on the Pill. So I listened to Bosh. And listened. I was just about to brave his wrath and say, 'Yes, sorry, but never mind that. Dev didn't trip over a bottle because there wasn't one for him to trip over. What about freezing fog that goes round strangling people? One of 'em has to be a hallucination. Or maybe Nisha and I have gone cuckoo in the same neck of the woods?'

But I didn't get the chance. Nisha wafted in with great piles of chicken biryani. 'Eat, eat,' she slurred, laying out pickles and poppadoms.

'Won't you need it when your relatives get here?' Bosh asked, magnetised by the smell of food.

'No one will come. We are ... were... I'm not welcome in some parts of the Asian community. I am twice married, too Western, a bad example to dutiful girls. D'you think I'd better call Anjuli?'

I rescued the raita before it slopped on the table. 'Leave it, Nisha. She'll be in bed by now. Tomorrow's soon enough.'

Nisha crumbled a poppadom. 'Soon enough to find out she's lost her father and her home on her birthday. We never told her Dev's uncle wanted to chuck us out. He holds the lease, you see. He's been getting quite pushy about it.'

'Did he send that ice-djinn?' Bosh asked through a forkful of chicken.

'I wouldn't have thought so,' Nisha replied while I sat there like a stuffed trout. 'But his son would sell you the skin off your back.'

'Back up a minute!' I sputtered. 'Djinns?'

The techno-wizard clicked his tongue impatiently. 'Yes, cloth-ears, djinns.'

'What, djinns as in demons?'

'Well what did you think it was? Honestly, Zo, you're the limit sometimes.'

'*I'm* the limit? I'm not the one talking about demons!'

'You saw what happened. OK, you also saw what I made the tape show so the police could wrap it up in a bow and leave us darkies alone but you ought to have more sense. Steam doesn't just turn homicidal on its own, you know.'

'Well why did ... how did you... What's *happening?*'

'Look, I'm a bit of a wizard, and not just with technology. So was my dad, and my mum was a Spanish *bruja* but they've both got ten times the power I have. I can just about push a few pixels around to defend you and your friend here, is what's happening.'

'And enough to shove the police around?' I asked sarcastically.

'Just a neurone or two, as you saw.'

'Ha! If you're a wizard why didn't you sort Lee out with a love potion or something?'

Bosh deflated. 'Faking love takes the point out of it.' He sighed. 'Nisha, sweetheart, you're falling asleep over your dinner. You go on up to bed and we'll take care of everything, OK?'

I caught her just before her face landed in the chutney and helped her up the stairs.

*

I was sure Bosh would have collared the couch while I was in Nisha's bedroom but he wasn't even in the flat. A cold wind was blowing up the stairs. I tiptoed down to check if the ice-fog-freezy-thing was coming for us but as I stepped into the shop I saw it was only Bosh.

Bosh, who I'd only known for a couple of weeks. Bosh, my stalker, who seemed on nodding terms with demons and could make you see things that weren't there. Or that were only I hadn't known about them.

I hid a great big knife behind my back and edged round the counter. 'What d'you mean leaving the door open, you great wazzock?' I cried.

Well, I tried to. I only got as far as 'mean' because then I saw the slavering fiend on the doorstep. Fang-filled jaws agape, its head looked over Bosh's shoulder and its plume of a tail brushed the ceiling. It wasn't a dog. It was a DOG.

With insane courage I grabbed Bosh and leaped backwards, tripping us both over the snack spinner. Packets of Bombay Mix burst across the floor. The monster barked. My heart threatened to explode.

Especially when the dog said, 'Sorry.'

A good job I was sitting on the floor because otherwise I'd have fallen.

Picture a puppy, say the size of a lion crossed with a carthorse, but with enormous paws so you know it's going to be as big as a Number Nine bus when it grows up. With teeth like swords. Give it a long, long tail with little flags of hair tufting up and down it. Fur the colour of a dusty savannah, except for the scales – *scales!* – on its front legs.

In a curry shop in Crouch End.

'Get off me, you daft bat!' Bosh snapped, disentangling himself. 'It's only Alfie.'

Alfie. Who'd looked a lot smaller on my Blackberry. Alphyn, a *genius loci*. I only knew what it was because I'd started watching horror films to make my life seem less bad.

*

Bosh dosed me up with shots of plum brandy and Alfie kindly shrank. 'I didn't know they could do that,' I slurred, but Bosh was too busy foozling with the burglar alarm to answer so it was Alfie who said, 'Sorry to startle you only there's some heavy stuff going down. I kep' telling 'im to introduce us properly. We need you.'

'What as, dinner?'

The Alphyn was now the size of a King Charles spaniel, playing cute games with his tail. 'Nah, you pillock.' He talked like a Cockney geezer. 'You're an empath, ain't you? Which is just what young Bosh is short on. Just what we've been looking for.'

'I'm not anything. Just a project manager with a presentation to do at eleven tomorrow and your freaky pal here hasn't fixed my system yet.'

Alfie snorted.

The burglar alarm gave a tiny electronic sigh and a green light appeared. 'If you've quite finished nattering,' Bosh said, hauling me up, 'we've got work to do. Give me some rage.'

'What?'

He put the brandy glass on the counter and patted my

cheeks between both hands. 'Come on, Zo, get with the program! We've got to lay down some serious protection. They had some pretty serious shields on this place but that ice-demon smashed 'em to bits. We need to get it done before Uncle Pious Neverending shows up. *Cui bono*, I ask you, except dear old nunky who holds the lease? So gimme some rage, dammit! You must have some going spare after what that two-timing toe-rag did to you. '

He tightened his grip. I tried but I couldn't wrench free. It really wound me up. 'Yeah, attagirl! Empath, see? Raw as hell and totally untrained but you can project your feelings when you get mad enough. Think of Andy buying Miss Big-Tits a car on your credit card! 'Specially when he'd forgotten your birthday. That's the ticket, channel it through me. We're making a demon mirror. We want it *outside*, though!' Reluctantly I let him drag me into the pre-dawn street which still had that sticky dark patch on it. Not to mention unseen ice-demons. 'Don't want to spook the customers, do we?' he finished blithely.

But the instant he squeezed my fingers, dark, bitter rage boiled up inside me, far more than I'd ever believed. I felt Bosh's hurt join with it. And something sucked it out through our clasped hands. Syphoned it, spraying frightening quantities of fury right up to the eaves of the three-storey shop and down through the coarse London clay. Alfie weed exactly where it splashed the pavement but Bosh just gave him a thoughtful nod. The *genius loci* was the size of an Alsatian now, but Alsatians didn't usually tell me not to get my knickers in a twist.

When Bosh dropped my hand I felt suddenly lighter, as though something foul had drained away. Grey light was stealing through the trees, and I was cold, so cold I was shuddering. I didn't like any of this. I wanted normal. The streetlights blinked out. 'Just got time to dash home for a shower before we catch the train,' I yawned.

'So you're just going to leave Nisha to face her uncle on her own?' Bosh exclaimed.

'Yes. No.' I glanced at him and groaned. 'We're not going in, are we?'

Bosh gave me a one-armed hug. He smelt only slightly of recycled alcohol. Even as I caught it the smell disappeared. Just like the one last night from that green bottle that hadn't been there. 'Good on you, heartface!' he said. 'And don't despair. You might make your presentation yet, for who is this is driving yon Roller down the highway?'

'Uncle Saatvik Saatalya.'

Bosh grabbed her and hissed, 'Don't say that to his face!' He turned smoothly and greeted the man with a slight bow. 'Chopra-ji, I presume? Terrible thing, terrible thing. And you're standing right where it happened. We haven't even had a chance to clean up the blood.'

The stout Asian man jumped backwards, shiny shoes skidding. Bosh clasped his forearm. For one so short, it was remarkable how strongly he steadied Dev's uncle. Alfie growled so deep it sounded like an earthquake. Mr Chopra recoiled. I didn't blame him.

Where Dev had been mildly plump, his uncle was the shape of a basketball, only taller. His expensive suit struggled to contain him. He was probably in his fifties, white streaks standing out in his curly black beard, and he had all the arrogance of a self-made man. 'Who are you? Where's my nephew's widow? What have you done with her?'

I stepped forward, holding out my hand for him to shake. 'We're friends of the family, sir. We're here to keep Nisha company in her hour of need.'

He dropped his gaze to my outstretched hand and not-quite-sneered. 'Then you're redundant. With me here she doesn't need anyone else meddling in her affairs. Thank you and goodbye.' He barged forward but I held my ground.

'You're standing in the blood again,' Bosh observed, holding Alfie by a collar he hadn't been wearing a moment ago. 'What does that tell us?'

I could have sworn a wraith shaped like Dev swirled up

and pointed at seemingly random spots round the bully. Mr Chopra Senior shivered, leaped aside and scraped his shiny shoes frantically on the pavement. He'd gone a pale, trembly grey.

'Ah, it tells us you're frightened the djinn that killed your nephew might target you next. You are absolved, Chopra-ji. Step inside and allow us to come to your assistance.'

*

There was a lot of chat in their language. I was not only tired, the plum brandy was beginning to give me a headache. I could happily have drifted off to sleep only Alfie (cute version) rested his head on my lap and suddenly I could understand every syllable. We were in Nisha's perfectly normal living room on her perfectly normal three-piece suite talking about feuds and blackmail and djinns. Bosh was some kind of a mage. And I was an empath, whatever that meant. And it was less than four hours 'til my first big presentation at work and I was so going to get fired.

Suddenly Mr Chopra stopped blustering about being the head of the family and sending Nisha back home to save the family's good name. Oddly – well, all of it was odd to me – Bosh had taken my hand and the old gentleman's and all at once the uncle was babbling about his foolish son up to his ears in gambling debts being forced to transport drugs or he'd be murdered. Mr Chopra tried to buy off the blackmailer but it had ended in a stupid shoot-out in Strathclyde. They'd packed the boy off to college in America. It hadn't ended with the blackmailer's death because the clan used his blood to summon a djinn. Words like 'ended' and 'stupid' seemed a large part of Mr Chopra's vocabulary. 'Bemused' was the largest part of mine.

'So I paid a wizard for protection for my family in Glasgow.' The old man was weeping now. 'How was I to know they'd come all the way down to London to target my dead brother's child?'

*

Leaving this mish-mash of terror and weirdness and grief to

do my big presentation come nine o'clock felt all wrong. Still, Alfie stayed to guard Nisha and the tired old man while Bosh carried my laptop onto the train. As if stage-fright and the fear of losing my job weren't enough to set off armies of butterflies in my stomach, the thought of invisible demons had me turning my head like nobody's business all the way down the platform. Once we got on the train at Harringay, though, Bosh said they couldn't get us and I calmed down a nano-degree. He fiddled with my computer until ten seconds before we got off, then led me by the hand towards the office. I could feel all my anxieties draining away, leaving not so much as a chrysalis worming in my tum.

In a daze of unnatural calm, I showed the board what I'd got. Even my boss seemed pleased with it. She smiled, anyway, which was a big step up, and I didn't get the boot. I'd expected Bosh to be hovering outside the door to see how I'd got on but there wasn't a sign of him. Somehow I got through the next couple of hours but there were demons abroad in The Smoke and zig-zags of nervousness started to make me feel like my head was going to explode. I couldn't wait to leave.

I didn't have to. At three o'clock the fire alarms went loco. Malfunction, they said, but they couldn't stop them ringing without turning all the power off so we might as well go home. Why was I not surprised to find Bosh reading a newspaper on the wall outside the building?

'It's all fixed,' he said happily.

'Aren't you even going to ask how I got on?'

'I know how you got on. You're radiating emotions again. Between that and worry about all this magic stuff you're lit up like a firework. Let me fill you in on the plan. You can start by calming little Anjuli. She's cute as a button when she's not crying.'

*

Apart from a strong smell of dog-wee the area round the Himachal Palace was normal in the sunny afternoon. Except, now I came to think of it, for rows upon rows of cars and minibuses lining both sides of the street as far as I could see. Also, I was pleased to note, it was agreeably warm. After the inexplicable frost last night met men may have said more on way but once again they'd got it wrong.

We went in past the sign that said closed due to bereavement. The cosy living-room was crowded, not least because Alfie was big enough for Anjuli to be riding him round the couch. She waved limply at me and snuggled her chin on his furry neck. It didn't seem like she needed me at all. Alfie rolled his gaze ceiling-wards but he seemed happy enough. Lots of brightly-clad Asian women were talking over one another in Glaswegian accents and there were enough samosas to build a life-size model of the Taj Mahal. From inside the rainbow gaggle Nisha gave me a teary smile.

Bosh took me through to a room I'd never seen. Even before I got there a tumult of rage rushed round me in a clash of waves. The place was full of hostile men, some in Western clothes, others in long tunics and baggy pants. Some of them looked like they had daggers under their vests. I wished I were anywhere else. They all stopped yelling to stare at me when I came in. Well, all except a little man as old and craggy as the hills. His thin voice called me and the men stepped aside. Nervously I shuffled towards him.

The moment I looked into his pale blue eyes I had to kneel before him. He didn't demand it. It was just that his aura of serenity spread such power I was overwhelmed. He took my hand and I felt like I was standing in a great golden bell.

As the guru addressed each man, I had to touch their hands to form a living bridge, not for his words that I didn't understand but for the cool rivers of reason that carried them. He had compassion for all of them, for each felt he'd been slighted or wronged. Even those whose relatives would have starved but for their poppy fields learned pity for the ones they'd harmed. Even the sharp-dressed man who owned casinos saw how far he'd drifted from The Path. Even the touchy young hot-heads who competed for the flashest cars with the loudest stereos. Only one man seemed still to have a small dark core of rage.

How strange to touch so many lives. Especially when my own was such a mess.

*

In small bunches most of the men left. They weren't exactly bosom pals but at least they were no longer walled inside private compounds of their fears. Only Mr Chopra and the angry man remained. Several of the women stayed, since Nisha clearly had the guru's blessing. One, a cousin she'd never met, was going to stay and help her expand the Palace. They were chatting like good 'uns about how they'd share the parenting since she was a widow with two small children of her own. Anjuli thought it would be nice to have someone to play with when her par — when her mother was working. She was in bed, cuddled up with her new sisters.

By now it was midnight. When the guru led the rest of us outside, the street was deserted. Strangely, not a light was on in any of the houses nearby, nor any streetlamps either. Orion bestrode the heavens, his great sword at his jewelled belt. And, as warned, Bosh and I had put on warm coats.

Because the little man with the blue eyes stepped into the empty road and gestured. Over Mr Chopra's head appeared – something. A sick, transparent shimmer that made me shiver. It grew and grew, humanoid but not human.

And it was in chains.

It flinched snarling from the old man. All up and down the hills of North London dogs howled in reply, and snow blizzarded around us. Goodness knows what the weathermen would make of this.

At a sign, Bosh led me towards the shifting gleam that was the djinn. I cowered away from it but the old man made little shooing motions that sent me reluctantly closer. 'Not fear, Zoe,' Bosh whispered. 'It feeds on fear. Find out what it wants.'

Tall as the houses, it hung above the rage-filled man and growled at my approach. I was too afraid to touch it. All I wanted was to go home. Back to Rutland, back to peace and quiet and the placid hills and lakes. Back to the life when I thought I'd been loved and wanted and safe. The djinn howled again, rattling its chains.

'It's homesick!' I murmured, and my own longings spiralled sharply up the glimmering links. 'Something's stopping it being where it belongs.'

'You're – you're right,' Bosh whispered, his hand trembling in mine.

And Alfie leaped with a roar like a lion, slashing through the djinn's shackles with one swipe of his claws. 'Well it can bloody well sod off out of my manor,' I heard, and in a wail of swirling snow the djinn rocketed up into the night. The angry man fainted.

I stood staring after it, mouth agape. Somebody shoved something hot into my hand and I nearly died of surprise. It was Nisha, handing me a packet of onion bhajis. The old man had gone and Mr Chopra was scuttling up the road to his car with Mr used-to-be-Angry as fast as they could go.

'So is it all right if I kip on your sofa then, Zo?' Bosh said.

I goggled.

Alfie shrank back to cute fluffy dog and gambolled around us. ''Course it is, mate,' he said. 'She's got pals now. She's right where she belongs. Bags I the outside of the bed.'

'On your bike, Alfie!' I snapped, listening to the silent tinkle of other chains breaking. 'I'll put you a cushion by the radiator but that's your lot. Coming?'

Bride of the Sea

In the art-show brochure on her lap, the copper spires of the crown – her crown – spiked hot and red. Sunset, bursting in through the windows of the plane, all but ignited the photos with their lying captions but they'd still never be as savage as what burned in Sigilind's heart. How dare he? How *dare* Wolfgang, who'd said, 'I love you'?

With her cattle-class seat in the upright position, Sigilind's fingers crunched the pages of treachery while rage roared through her blood. Dutiful daughter, solid old maid, she squeezed it down inside her until it was held in the black bars of her will, a pool of magma just … waiting. There was no room in her for anything else.

Front and rear, plane doors slammed. Her mother clutched Sigilind's arm. 'It's not too late! Let's just get off this contraption.'

Sigi felt her fury assault her throat. 'It's only a plane, Mutti.'

The grip tightened. 'Sigi! My heart! You're killing me!'

'Flight FK703 for Venice is preparing to take off,' a loudspeaker announced.

'I'm not doing anything to you, Mutti! I said you needn't come, remember?'

'Keep your voice down, Sigi! Stop embarrassing me!'

Biting her tongue, Sigi gripped the armrests as the plane rumbled along the tarmac, faster and faster, like the terrible hard pulse between her ribs. Teeth clenched, she could do nothing as the plane left Frankfurt, heading south and west beyond the rosy Alps, down to the sun-blessed lands around the Middle Sea, to the sparkling waters of the Adriatic. To the Most Serene City.

And vengeance.

*

When the plane levelled out, Sigilind dared to open her eyes. She was still alive. As was the shrivelled old witch beside her. Neither of them quite believed it, though they'd known people who'd flown before.

Mutti's face was red, crumpled with the effort to cry noiselessly so none of the people around her would see – except her daughter. Not having a heart-attack, then.

'What is it?' Sigi managed through clenched teeth.

A sob escaped the older woman. 'You – you said you didn't want me to come!'

No, thought Sigi, *I didn't want you to come! I wish you'd stop interfering and just leave me alone!* She swallowed back her guilt and answered gently, 'No, Mutti, that's not what I said! I was just worried it would be too much for you.'

Mutti smiled tremulously, stroking her daughter's wrist with a touch as moist and slimy as a slug. 'All right, dumpling, just so long as you want me, I'll always be here for you.' In an accident that wasn't, the old woman knocked the bright brochure out of Sigi's grasp and slid her boot over it.

As if Sigi could forget her mother's betrayal, or Wolfgang's. Teeth clenched, she bent and ripped the hated thing away from her mother. Sigi shoved the crumpled booklet into her bag.

The film was *Titanic*. Two glasses of wine and Sigi sank drowning in the icy depths like Leonardo di Caprio. The ice felt like fire on her skin. She tried to lift her hands to protect her face but something cruel knocked her backwards. She couldn't fight the knives of fire. Couldn't claw the cellar doors open. The skin on her breast was bubbling blisters. Sparks crackled through her hair, streaking light through the dank basement. In her dream, a mother cackled, 'You were right, Sigilhild! Thorke wants the land, not you. How could anyone love a worthless *thing* like you?'

It's all right, her mind answered. *I'm not Sigishild.* In the dream, the heavy ring on the girl's hand shone silver. Coolness radiated from it. Peace. The knowledge that someone far away longed for her. In the dream the girl, Sigishild or Sigilind, softened. *Hagan loves me. He'll save me.*

Through the trapdoors above, Thorke's words bit like vipers, the Hunnish invader with the bones rattling in the braids of his black hair. 'Do you think Hagan would have left you if he'd cared?' he said, slamming the shutters down with his wolfskin boots. The girl heard the ugly sounds through the crackling of the flames: the door of her tomb closing, the scream and thud as he mother's head tumbled over the cracked cellar doors, trapping her forever.

Then the heat slashed her lungs while her mother's head smiled.

*

When she awoke, sundown was pooling wine-dark shadows across the lagoon where Venice floated ethereal, scarfed in gilded mist below their plane. For a moment Sigi didn't know where she was. Or who. As the plane banked in to land, crimson sunbeams slanted into her eyes. Fear from the nightmare clung about her. On its chain round her neck, the weight of the silver ring her father had bequeathed her seemed first hot, then chill against her skin.

Against the drone of the 747's engines, Mutti's voice brought her fully back to consciousness. 'I've told you, liebchen, that's why I gave Wolfgang your little bits and pieces. You didn't have to drag us away from the farm. He'll come back with your money.'

'That's not what you said before he brought you that gingerbread. You told me he had shifty eyes, remember?'

'How can you say that? He's your one chance at happiness!'

Sigi widened her eyes in disbelief. The grumble of her volcanic ire was drowned by the tyres bouncing on the runway. When the doors opened, even Mutti's protests couldn't disguise the scent of a warm night breeze, full of spice and flowers and aviation fuel. Shoving the art-show literature deeper into her bag, Sigi made her way to the door.

*

Disappointingly, it wasn't a romantic gondola that took them to their hotel in Lido di Jesolo but an old bus that farted its way through the dark. At the front desk they checked in too late for dinner. But a soft, rainbow-lit jukebox was singing by the bar. Through an arch Sigilind could see a barman, black hair and white shirt, polishing glasses. Bottles gleamed all colours and shapes. There were a couple and a young man at the bar, a sprinkling of lobster-skinned tourists at the tables. Laughter shot through cheerful conversations.

Away from the security of home, Mutti was crankier than ever. Sigilind apologised to the clerk with a rueful shrug of her eyebrows, and dragged her upstairs. Only after an argument— 'What will they think of a woman your age drinking alone?' —did Sigilind drift hesitantly back down to the bar.

A woman my age. By the archway she stopped, almost hiding in the leaves of a potted lemon tree, replaying her mother's parting words. *'That dress makes you look like a tart on the Reeperbahn!'* Sigi's hand went to the worn, silvery ring hanging at her neck, the last thing her father had given her before he died. She needed its cool comfort because she'd replied, 'Speaking from experience, Mutti?' She'd pay for that remark in the morning.

Then again, Mutti would make her pay whether she'd said it or not. Trying to pretend she wasn't a tall, self-conscious, muscly woman in her fifth decade, Sigi took a deep breath and strode inside.

It was magical. Fairy lights twinkled all coy in the vine-hung ceiling. Smoke coiled like blue genies on the warm air. As though she were a perfectly ordinary customer the barman watched her sit on the only spare seat, the one beside the blond young man. Twirling his cloth in a glass, the barman said, 'Cosa vuole, signora?'

Sigilind couldn't think. Boring old beer or routine Blue Nun— No, she could have those at home. *How the hell would I know what to ask for down here?* she wondered in panic.

'He's asking you what you want,' said the young man beside her in Italian-accented German.

Frustrated at being considered so stupid, she snapped, 'Ja, klar.' She gulped down the lava and let out a long, hot breath. With an effort, she smiled. She had no idea how pretty she looked when she smiled. It was one of the things Mutti had never told her. 'But I wanted to try something local and I don't know what they drink in Venice.'

The blond youth said something in Italian and the barman filled two highball glasses with ice, sloshed red liquid over it and sprayed in some lemonade.

'Prost,' said the blond man, clinking glasses with her.

Sigi grinned at the adventure of it all. The light shone through her drink like blood, like fire, rags of her nightmare consumed by the atmosphere of Venice. Raising her glass, she said, 'Skol.' She didn't know why. It had been half a thousand years since her people drank from the skulls of their enemies.

'It was your people who helped found Venice,' the blond man said, pantomiming a bow. His name was Mario and he was twenty-two.

Sigi giggled. She liked the way he was flirting with her. Mario was intriguing and said by turns as the awareness of his scars and his loss came and went. Handsome and wheat-haired, not like she thought of Italians, he should have been with his fiancée but after the accident she'd said goodbye. The crown of his head was bald, dimpled, dented, though the rest of his hair was thick enough. More scars marched, parallel pink bands, from his chin to the neck of his tee shirt. He'd long since drunk enough Martini to show her the nest of crimson wounds that hollowed his chest and killed his career as a football star. Now he sold mid-range antiques to tourists and no one knew his name. Sigi was beginning to feel like she'd known him forever. 'My people?' she prompted.

'You said you were from Frankfurt. It was when the

Franks raided in 452 that the citizens of Aquilea fled to the islands in this muddy lagoon.'

Sigi leaned now on the balustrade of the marble terrace, looking out over the regiments of beach-chairs to the silvered sea. If only she could float out along the moonpath, a warrior, Swanhild, trampling the body of the reiver, the sword of justice bloody in one hand and her future glittering in the other...

The movement swung the chain around her neck. Cold as snow, the ancient ring shivered the flesh of her cleavage. Sigi's breath froze in her lungs. For a second terror speared her on an image of her mother locking her in a cellar where flames danced. It wasn't their farm but a log cabin settlement with hides across the windows. But it made no sense. The land Sigi farmed unaided wasn't like that. Besides, surely even *her* mother wouldn't betray her child to keep a plot of farmland?

'What's the matter?' Mario asked her.

She forced a shrug to hide her shiver. 'Nothing. A ghost walked over my grave.'

'You believe in ghosts?'

'Not really.'

'But Venice is full of them! You see them on nights when the moon spins over the waters. You'll think I'm mad but when I was in hospital I'm sure old ghosts echoed through my dreams. They come back to finish the mission of their lives.'

Sigi brushed the ghosts aside. 'Never mind trying to spook me,' she grinned. 'What were you saying about the founding of Venice?'

'When the rest of the barbarians attacked, some of the Franks built homes here too. Who knows? Maybe we're related.'

Lead settled on her heart, squelching the closeness. For the first time since midnight she felt every one of her forty-three years. 'Yeah. I'm your grandmother's great-aunt.'

He raised his eyebrows. 'No. My cousin, maybe.' She

looked sceptical, a woman who inspects armies of wrinkles marching across her mirror. He saw, and laid a hand on the silken hem of her dress. 'I mean it. I don't like young girls. They throw themselves at you but all they see is the parties and the cars. And the paparazzi, of course, let's not forget them. Once that's gone, so are the girls. You're a woman who's … ripe. I'm sure there are dozens of men who are in love with you.'

Sigi closed her eyes so she wouldn't see her rough, farmer's hands. She was ashamed of them, ashamed the burn -scabs from her secret coppercraft made her unfeminine. Now Wolfgang had stolen her creations, the scalds were all that was left to mark her failure. Her face flamed with the belief that her worthlessness was branded on her forehead. As it always did, he mother's voice came out of the dark place just behind her ear. 'I was only trying to help!' And from Sigi's dream came the memory of her self-same hands bloodied with splinters, trying to prise up the door of her cellar prison. Same hands, same black, dank, self-pitying trap that burned around her ears. Who was she fooling? How could she ever have dreamed of freedom from Mutti and the farm? From the open wound that was being herself?

Silence spread sticky as the clay of a grave. Blindly Sigi turned to leave.

From a very long way away Mario's words reached into her. 'Is that the brochure for the exhibition you said you're in? Let's have a look.'

'No!'

She whirled, too late. He'd already lifted the brochure from the top of her bag. Creased and battered, it fell open to the page she didn't want him to see. The page where her name had been erased. Where she had been wiped out.

Copper sculptures, gilded now, each hammered image of warriors and wolves glinting in the lights from the bar. A warhorse trampling a snake beneath its hooves outside a spiring fortress. The serpent's eyes were garnets, the horse's, jet. Brooches and bracelets; chessmen and dwarfs. Thirteen years' work. The spiked crown and the goblet flamed with savage beauty.

'These – these Frankish works are yours?' Mario asked, his words a sigh of wonder.

But the caption read: 'Wolfgang Mannheim, Frankfurt.'

Snatching the brochure, she ran from the terrace.

*

For an hour she stomped up and down the cold, black beach, her nails clawing at the burn-scabs, punishing her hands because they were guilty of giving Mutti and Wolfi a weapon to tear out her heart. The trickling blood tasted of metal and bitter joy. She was alone: a dank sea-fret had driven everyone else to bed. Cloaks of mist kept her company. The sound of the waves came heavy as oars on a farewell tide. According to Mario, from this beach longships had carried her forefathers to their last rest on a drifting bed of fire. Mario – what could he possibly want with a worthless old maid like her? Out to sea flared a yellow light, but it was no warrior's grave, just a fisherman's beacon. And she was another disappointment, Sigi the failure, a disgrace to the warlike ancestors she could see all about her if only the tears weren't in her eyes. Dark pits in their fog-grey skulls stared at her with contempt. She thought of obliterating herself, or blasting her mother and her lying lover with a shotgun.

Only as a salt, pre-dawn wind shredded the sea-fret did Sigi truly feel her Viking forebears had left her. She was alone again. Finally she forced herself back to the hotel. Exhaustion made her feel as ethereal as the ghosts in the mist. Fortunately Mutti was asleep when Sigi crept in.

Guiltily she slipped beneath the covers, needing the reprieve to rebuild her defences, needing the darkness to weep. *How could anyone love a worthless old maid like me?* echoed in the well of her thoughts, but it couldn't stop her perfidious attraction to Mario, nor the habit of yearning for Wolfgang's love. She could still feel the time he had first told her he could sell her work in Venice, hushing her mouth with his fingers when she'd first asked, light as a balloon with excitement, to see the brochure. She'd known there was something wrong even then but she hadn't wanted to see it. Hadn't wanted to think that Wolfi was stealing her name. She'd herded her thoughts away from the dread that Mutti had been right all along and she, Sigi, couldn't still be left, empty and cobwebbed, on the shelf, trapped on a profitless farm. With Mutti. Until one of them died.

In the morning Sigi hid in the shower. The bathroom door wasn't enough to keep her safe. Mutti yelled through, 'Hurry up! I'm hungry. Besides, a woman your age needs something to stop her bones crumbling. I wouldn't want you to be a martyr to osteoporosis like I am. The pain you wouldn't believe!'

She was right: Sigi wouldn't. Her mother needed diseases to keep her interesting, using the constant fear of a heart attack as resin, prisoning her daughter like a fly in amber. Not once in over forty years had Sigi been further than Frankfurt, and rarely as far as that. Mutti's arthritis stopped her milking the cows. Mutti's sciatica wouldn't let her chop wood. That was what Sigi was for. If even a quarter of Mutti's illnesses were real the old harpy would have been dead decades ago.

'After I've come all this way for you, you want to leave me behind?'

Sigi stepped up out of the waterbus, gagging at the smell of the canal. She looked away from the pale, floating guts of a dead rat washing up alongside a chocolate wrapper. The sun was bouncing off peeling stucco, stabbing from the noisome water. But Sigi smiled her thanks at the man who helped her out of the boat.

Behind her, Mutti fluttered like a flypaper in the wind, seeming unable to climb out onto the dock until Sigi stomped back to take her other hand. On the pigeon-spattered flagstones, daughter turned to mother and tried not to spew magma. 'For goodness' sake, Mutti, it's not a rejection of you! I only said I want to … talk to Wolfgang by myself for a few minutes, all right?' Visions of her hands clamped around

Wolfi's throat, an ache in her own as she caught and trapped her scream.

'Ah, young love!' Mutti said archly. It was grotesque. 'Don't worry about me. You go on ahead. I'm sure he just put his name on your little bits so's he could get more money for them. After all, who are you? Don't make a scene now, will you? You don't want to frighten him off. Just let him explain so we can get back to planning your wedding. We'll all be back on the farm in no time, you'll see. I'll catch you up in a minute.'

The old woman pouted for a kiss. Sigi brushed her lips against the moth's-body cheek, not quite repressing a shudder.

In black shade, the gallery shone out like a beacon. Bright, warm lights glinted on the things in the window: Murano glass, crimson and gilt; a little bronze tree with jewelled fruit.

And a dagger, copper hilt in the shape of the world-wolf's head, a crescent of moonstone caught between its fangs. Sigi's fingers clenched, remembering the way her knuckles had cramped as she cut the curve of the gem. Her body filled with feelings from the making: the see-sawing of pride and anxiety, the hope someone would know she existed inside the middle-aged spinster who shovelled cowshit for a living.

Beside the dagger stood a little card: Wolfgang Mannheim, Frankfurt. Not even room for the word *studios.*

Fury escaped its black-barred cage and burned through her skin. The ancient ring tossed on the pulse in her throat. Sigilind swelled.

*

A bell *ting'd* as a gaggle of Americans swarmed into the gallery. Camouflaged inside the flock, Sigi stalked her prey. He was standing pontificating beside a chamfered glass cabinet. From the other side of it she could see three of him. Three mobs of gleaming curls receding from three domed foreheads. Three broken noses above mouthfuls of too-good-to-be-true teeth. Just a sheen of perspiration on those pale slabs of cheeks. But mostly it was the eyes she watched, grey and gleaming like the muddy waters outside. And who knew what further betrayals they were hiding in their silty depths?

Keeping the display case between them, Sigi listened to his patter. The elderly Americans were from Pittsburg and German was their native language.

'Oh yes, these are all my work.' Wolfi stroked his sideburns.

'Every single piece?'

Sigi's hands knotted. So many words were fighting to get over her tongue that they avalanched from her lips as a groan.

'You're very talented,' the fattest American lady said, fluttering her false eyelashes up at him. 'Where do you get your ideas from?'

'Oh, you know,' said Wolfgang modestly. 'It's my heritage. The Franks, the Huns and all that. You should see the pieces in the museum back home. Very inspirational. I'm particularly pleased with the way these little glass and gold flagons came out.'

Chins wobbled as the violet-haired American shook her head. 'No, there's no life to them. No heart, no soul, no … fire. They're pretty enough, but they're not a patch on that wolf's-head dagger, for example. They hardly look like the same craftsman's work.'

A spike of malice prompted Sigi. She stepped forward – Wolfi's mouth slackened – and asked the American, 'What do you think of the goblet in that case?'

'Oh, it's marvellous, isn't it? Simply glorious! Knocks those gaudy flagons into a cocked hat.'

Wolfi's face stretched in speechless shock. Edging angrily towards Sigi, he fumbled for the words to hide her.

Too late.

Sigi stroked the glass of the case. 'I made that.'

Surprised that the words had tumbled audibly from her lips, Sigi looked down, awkward now.

Oblivious to the tension, the blue-rinsed shopaholic said

shrewdly, 'He said it was two thousand dollars. How much did he give you for it?'

Sigi – stopped. *An icy river opened up beneath her. Down into the depths of lightless years the lonely words went sinking: He paid me in lies I thought were love.* All at once she was crying.

And Wolfgang Mannheim smiled. He tried to put his arm round her but she shrugged him off. 'Pay no attention,' he told his audience, 'she does this from time to time. She's well -known to the Frankfurt police.' He made circles of madness by his temple. 'Look.' Unlocking the cabinet, he tenderly lifted out the copper bowl.

'You – you thief!' bellowed Sigi.

The purple princess cowered. The rest of the Americans clustered around her and she glared in shocked fascination at Sigi.

'Don't be alarmed,' Wolfgang told them, pointing at the copper base. 'She can't get away with any of my work here. She's jealous, poor thing – no talent. But don't worry. She knows I'll call the police if she gets up to her old tricks. Now, see here? What's that signature on the bottom say?'

Sigi ran from the shop as the tourists read 'WM'.

*

Sigi whirled through nets of alleys, over bridges, past shops. Art-buffs and critics thronged the galleries, spilling down the steps like pigeons. Clothes bright as butterflies wafted aftershave onto the hot, salty air. Banners proclaimed the Biennale. Everyone was watching her shove past, gossip flaring up behind her. A stitch in her side finally made her stop running. Shame and the blaze of a Mediterranean noon drove her into a church.

In the building's chilly embrace Sigi breathed deeply. Incense and damp plaster poured timeless balm into her lungs. She wandered around, seeing gold flaking off saints' crowns and mould seeping up frescoes of martyrs. It was all so sad. No marriage, no children. No togetherness, no triumphs.

No escape.

'Grüss dich!' said a voice, and she stumbled on the jutting flagstones. Mario stood up in the pews, coming towards her. Sigi wanted to evaporate.

'Do you like Santa Margareta's?' Coming towards her through a patch of jewelled sunlight, he said, 'It's me. Mario. Are you all right?'

Sigi shook her head.

'Come into my shop a minute and I'll get you a drink.'

She took a half-step backwards.

'It's just next door. Look, I'm not trying to hurt you, okay?'

Too wounded to look at him, she followed Mario into the glory-hole next door.

Antiques? It's junk! she thought, watching dust dance like pollen against the gilded carvings. The schnapps was good, though. Warmth and anaesthesia in one. It helped her to explain.

'So it's my fault he got my stuff,' she finished. 'I had to go to the *apotheke* for my mother. I didn't think to lock my workshed. Things I'd been working on for years... He talked her out of the lot. But I trusted him! He said ... he said he loved me.' She tried to blink the shimmering mist from her eyes. 'I shouldn't have left him alone but I was in a panic. Mutti said she wasn't well. She didn't want to be on her own so I just ... left him with her.'

Mario didn't answer. Unconsciously his fingertips were massaging the scars on his throat. Over the dry, fruity perfume of the schnapps she could smell the clean youth of his skin when he took the glass from her. Her mind felt like a desert in a sandstorm. For just an instant the silver ring throbbed, and a picture came to her thoughts: a ghost in the cellar now, Hagan from so far to the south, trying to pull her back from the fire, blood streaming over his blond, cropped head, and an old woman smiling as a foreign sword stabbed him through the heart. Sigi tried to ignore it but the brochure on his desk called her with insistent waves of self-hatred. As the silence went on, mahogany shadows crept across the photos of her work.

'I've got my own grudge against this Wolfgang Mannheim. He's in the moonlit parade tonight,' said Mario, suddenly bending to switch on a computer. 'Do you want to help me get my revenge?'

*

Sigi didn't know how to evade her mother but Mario scarcely looked up from the PC on his desk. 'Simple, *cara*. Just don't go back to the hotel. I spent three years playing for Bayern München – don't you think I was smart enough to hang on to some of the money? Take half a million lire from the safe and buy yourself an evening gown.'

'I couldn't!'

'It's not that much. A small price to pay if it helps me get my revenge. And stop disturbing me. I've only got two hours to nail the *arschloch* down. We art dealers stick together – if only when we're trying to stop someone robbing us blind.'

*

At nine p.m. the marine procession glimmered out of the mist on the waters. The front three boats fairly blazed. Paparazzi shattered the darkness with flashlights from speedboats that set the gondolas rocking. One even paused long enough to yell, 'Hey, Mario! Want to do a 'where are they now' feature?' before security chased the photo-raider off.

'What are we doing here?' hissed Sigi, hunched low and embarrassed in her new gown and scarf, awed by Mario, imposing in his dress suit. An accordion blared in her ear. Wolfgang Mannheim sat in the boat ahead, with, of all people, Sigi's mother clinging to him like a suction cup. Wolfi looked like he was trying to brush her off.

Mario answered from his own perspective. 'That lot up ahead – they're the VIPs. We're only FIP's. Fairly Important People. Last biennale, that's where I was. Probably next year your Mannheim will be on the second boat. Next year,' Mario added bitterly, 'I probably won't be invited at all.'

Sigi was thrown against him as their gondola pitched

through the thickening wreaths of fog. Once out of the watery byway, the high-prowed boat rocked in the current of the Grand Canal. His pain was so obvious that she couldn't reply. 'I still can't understand why you want to help me,' she said instead.

'It's not just you, *cara*. Did you think you were the only one he's cheated? After the accident I used the insurance money to set up the shop. The night before the grand opening I held a private viewing for a few select dealers. I passed out, you know. Two glasses of champagne, no more, and I passed out. Can you believe that? When I woke all the good pieces had gone. And the letters of provenance. And guess where it all turned up?'

Overhead, a news helicopter pinned them in its spotlight. Square and solid, the Doge's Palace reared its myriad arches as they passed the entrance to St Mark's Square. The quayside was lined with foreigners clicking cameras and a loudspeaker said in three languages, 'And so the Moonlight Procession streams out into the lido, where the gondolas will circle the yacht on which the President of the Arts Festival will present the prizes. Not before making an offering to the waves, though. As you know, every year the President of the Republic throws a ring into the lagoon, a symbol of the eternal marriage between Venice the bride and the sea. Some say our moonlit recreation is disrespectful, but it is a homage to Venice's faithful husband who protected her against barbarian raids in ages past. And now the first gondola is docking with the yacht and the president is greeting the Duquessa di Varoli, squired by chart-topping singer Paolorino, a vision in a spangled white suit...'

Surrounded by media and would-be celebs, icon after icon waved and climbed the broad gangplank. Through the fog, Sigi watched with mounting dread. Now their gondola swayed to its mooring. An Olympic skier towed his girl friend up the slope of red carpet to a tumult of cheers. At the top the President of the Festival, a moon-faced man, alternately bowed and was bowed to while the famous queued for their photo-opportunity.

'I can't!' Sigi hissed at Mario. 'If he sees me he'll just tell everyone I'm some crazed faker again! I'll get arrested. Mutti will either drop dead of shock or she'll kill me.'

Mario stood.

Shaking in utter panic, Sigi felt him drag her to her feet.

'Come on! We have to be there when he greets the president!'

Wavelets slapped the hull. The commentator announced, 'Here comes the dark horse tipped for the Small Sculpture Award—'

Mario dragged Sigi onto the red carpet beside her astonished ex-fiancé. Apparently looking down at her notes, the announcer read, 'Signor Wolfgang Mannheim!'

The applause faltered. Sigi's mother went white with shock. In the act of stepping from bulwark to gangplank, Wolfi looked back to see where his acclaim had gone.

And Mario handed the president a sheaf of documents blazoned with the word INTERPOL.

As Wolfgang saw Sigi and his fate, he tottered back, arms windmilling, right to the edge of the gangplank. 'You!' he shouted.

At the same moment the old witch at his side shrilled in outrage, 'Sigilind!' and the moon-faced president ducked Wolfi's flailing fists.

Overbalancing, Wolfgang grabbed for the nearest thing: Sigi's shoulder. She jerked backwards and his grasp ripped the scarf from her neck.

It snagged her chain, broke it. Now there was nothing to keep him on his feet. In slow motion, it seemed, he began to topple. Despairing, Sigi saw her antique ring shining in spotlight and moonlight as, tangled in her scarf, it fluttered and splashed into the misty lagoon.

Still he hadn't finished falling.

And a strand of fog rose, a ghostly hand from the water, cupping her silver ring.

It must have been the flashbulbs that drew a silver sword

of light from that ancient circle of metal. It sliced across Wolfgang's jacket once and then again, too swift to see clearly as pandemonium broke out. He clutched his chest and plunged facedown into the water.

'Sigi' shrieked her mother. 'What are you playing at?' She snatched the Interpol papers out of the president's hand.

Cringing, Sigi heard a voice soft as smoke or fog whisper to the old witch, 'That's twice you've been willing to kill your daughter to get what you want. May your heart be the size of your love for her.'

Sigi's eyes flew open. She glanced wildly around. No one else seemed to have heard the stony words. But her mother gasped raucously, the papers fluttering over the bulwark, and fell back onto the deck of the yacht.

Sigi had seen it all now. What was it this time? Noble pensioner shocked to death by evil offspring? Heartbroken Mutti faints with shame? Anything to get attention. Already people were crawling all over the old bat, and the sheets of paper were drifting on the tide.

More to the point, Wolfgang was lying unmoving, face pillowed on the swell. Sigi saw his hands, pale and nerveless as a jellyfish, washed by the tide. He was drowning! For a moment joy surged wickedly through her but those hands had held hers, had given her a cheap gold ring, and even if it had all been a lie she couldn't let him drown. A photographer's boat almost ran him under its keel, then surged aside at the last moment, swamping the people on the side of the yacht who were fishing for the evidence.

Knowing she'd regret it either way, Sigi dived in. Pewter waves embraced her coldly and she gulped with shock. But four strokes took her to Wolfi, then she dragged him along the side of the wallowing speedboat to the carpeted gangplank.

Blinking in the paparazzi's blitzkrieg, she trod water and shoved the body onto the sodden carpet. He wasn't breathing! Why wasn't anybody helping her?

Then they were. She squinted up through her seaweed

hair and saw the top of Mario's scalp as he squatted, reaching to grab Wolfgang under the armpits and haul him aboard.

Time slowed. Mist silvered Wolfgang's skin. He almost vanished within it. Arched spastically, coughed water. Air whooped into his lungs. His voice, strangled and smoky, shook her as he grabbed her wrist and said, 'They're yours. Your work. Just – tell them you co-own Mannheim Studios. That's why it says WM on your work.'

Mario and the president heard it even if Sigi couldn't take it in.

'But—'

Polished with that lustrous shroud of mist, Wolfgang drew his feet up on the end of the gangplank. There still wasn't room for her to roll aboard. Caught round the buckles of his boots like a hobble was her scarf. Something glinted like platinum within its folds. 'Remember when I gave you this ring?' he said in that borrowed voice.

'It wasn't that one. That was my ancestors'.' Sigi tried to free her hand. People were coming closer now, water-ambulance siren, ghouls and girls who wanted their pictures in the papers.

With a strength that Wolfgang had never shown in the past he held her hand tightly. Muscles rolled in his forearm as he bent to take the silver circlet. 'Oh, but it was. I waited for you but he didn't come.' He fitted the ancient ring to her finger, kissed her hand with a touch like ice and stood abruptly, hauling her out of the water.

But the mist shimmered downwards, pooling off him in a shining coil that sank into the sea. The vaporous, frosted voice whispered, fading, 'I love you, Sigi. I'll protect you 'til the world-wolf eats the sun.'

Was it the spiral of mist or her scarf that belled and drifted slowly under the surface of the lagoon?

Then the world speeded up and spotlights carved open the fog. Police in launches scooped up the evidence and clicked handcuffs on Wolfgang Mannheim.

She glimpsed the president, splashed and dripping, cowled in a grey woollen blanket but smiling at her, then Mario draped one over her shoulders and the president handed over the award.

The announcers got her name wrong, but you can't have everything.

Dragon's Breath

Macao, 1927

Travis had been watching her for three days when she made her move. At first he'd thought she was a boy. That night when she crept out of her hidey-hole back of the bales of copra, the greasy yellow light of Fat Chun's go-down outlined her breasts against her tunic. Besides, her hands and feet were too delicate for a boy, even a half-starved Chinese.

Slim, tanned and hiding his own tensions, the Westerner leaned on the schooner's rail, watching her grope silently between the clutter on the quay. Down there she was safe in the veils of fog. Dragon's Breath, they called it in Macao, that humidity that wreathed from the jungle to ooze between the sampans and the junks. Her destination was the dhow in the next berth. In that place and time where the stink of fish-heads mingled with spices, dyes and all the flotsam of the harbour it had a special reek: the piss and dung of a slaver.

From up by the taff-rail of his trading vessel Captain Travis could see what she could not: the mist clung low over the water. At twenty feet above sea-level, the slaver's deck was clear. And behind the wheelhouse, the watch had tossed the butt of his furtive cigarette overboard. Now he was stalking towards the dockside, ready to look grandly alert the moment the captain came on deck. Which he would to see the cargo loaded. Which would presumably happen any time now. Probably the moment the fireworks started. Travis only hoped she wouldn't upset his carefully-laid plans.

Clearing his throat, Travis went to wave her back. It was a small motion trying not to be noticed by hostile eyes. Apparently she missed it completely. The guard came closer.

Checking the statue cuddled under her tunic and the long knife at her back, Jiao Jianyu crept towards the dhow's gangway. She knew she didn't have long. 'Full tide after the festival,' the gangmaster had said. Any moment the lorry carrying her brother would pull onto the wharf. She had to stow away before the captives were brought aboard. Then the landsmen would be paid off and the skeleton crew would be all alone out there on the China Seas. They'd never expect an attack then. She'd pick them off one by one to be sure though her martial arts teacher had tried her against two and even three of late. The prisoners she freed would help her seize the vessel. They'd all share in the reward. Best of all, Little Brother would be safe. Proud of her plan, sixteen-year-old Jiao set foot on the gangplank.

From the next vessel came a muted cough, the momentary flash of a hand. She froze. That idiot *gwai-lo* seemed to be waving and the guard, however dozy, was bound to see it. In fact she could hear his boots thumping closer. Silently cursing the round-eye, Jiao Jianyu slipped under the handrail, skinning one ankle on the splintery boards. She'd hide by hanging underneath until the guard went on with his desultory rounds.

Except she hadn't realised how weak she was. Jiao couldn't remember when she'd eaten last, but three days' spying from one dawn to the next hadn't been restful enough to stop her feeling every step of the hundred *li* race to save her brother. Only fear and hope were keeping her awake. Yes, she'd waited for the deckhands' noisy game of fantan to end, which it had, remarkably early. Yes, she'd kept out of sight until the players stumbled to their bunks, not as drunk as usual, chased below by the surly mate while the master nibbled honeyed fruit in the go-down. Then she seized her chance.

But she was too innocent to realise the routine would change with the delivery. The usual sozzled guard had been replaced by a battered mercenary with a very large gun, a boss-eyed Lascar who really wanted promotion.

Jiao's hand slipped on slimy weed. She splashed heavily between the dock and the slaver's hull. The guard caught the noise, glad for something to break up the monotony, and clumped rapidly towards the gangplank. He was only a step away when the foul waters closed above Jiao's head.

*

Meantime Ding Xiang couldn't wait to get back to the *Oyster Shell*. If nobody else could, Travis would stop his daughters clucking. They leaned on the oars of the schooner's boat, his Lustrous Jade and Fragrant Lily, sniping at one another like falcons fighting over a kill. Only with bigger muscles. They made Ding Xiang feel so *old*. But once they were back on board the *Shell* they'd be under his command again. Unconsciously he flexed his stringy muscles.

Sadly, the festival was keeping them from the haven of the *Shell*. Red-robed monks and priestesses of A Ma paced along the promenade. The lamps and joss-sticks they carried made a bright cloud over their heads. It was as though their chants and gongs were born in golden mist.

More to the point for two men and two girls stuck in a befogged rowing-boat, fervent believers had hired a three-master to take a statue of A Ma round the harbour to bring luck. A thousand lamp-lit sampans jostled for a blessing from the sea goddess. When they came near enough to the rowboat they shone on the bald head of Ding Xiang's passenger, who clung nervously to the gunwhales. The rickety old gardener had obviously never been on a boat before. The rocking and the strange noises coming out of the fog upset him. Eyes tight shut, both the clear one and the moon-pale cataract, he clicked his Buddha beads. His presence was something else that troubled Ding Xiang. How could such a tottery relic be any help at all? But when the Pirate Queen insists...

The Dragon's Breath thickened, muffling prayers and drunken revelry. More and more often came the clonk of one hull on another. Mostly the response was good-humoured though fights broke out here and there. The whole harbour was a logjam.

Ding Xiang forced his fists to relax. Worrying about his new partner never did him any good but he couldn't help it. He owed Travis so much ... and dickering with the Pirate Queen had been chancy at best. Ding Xiang couldn't think how he'd let Travis talk him into it. Now time was flying away like his luck. The price of the pearls weighed heavy in his sash. He patted it to make sure. Whatever Travis had promised so blithely, only the gods knew whether the Pirate Queen would keep her word – or take revenge. He muttered, 'A Ma, Goddess of Mercy and Lady of the Sea, if you just get us out of this one alive I'll set up the finest statue of you in the wheelhouse. I'll square it with Travis, honest.' As the first rockets carried his prayer over the goddess's throne, he only hoped A Ma would forgive him the times he let expediency trump honour.

*

Jiao Jianyu burst gasping to the surface. She could hear the guard's bootheels ringing on the deck, coming ever closer. The gangway rested a good dozen feet above her, far out of reach. A wave caught the dhow, shoving its curving hull towards the quayside. The stern clashed echoingly against stone. She dashed wet hair out of her eyes and peered through the murk for a way out, but weeds slimed the harbour wall, making it impossible to climb. If she didn't survive neither would Little Brother. Jiao Jianyu didn't want to die. She was too scared to face her ancestors' reproach. Desperately she grabbed a breath and plunged into the silty depths.

Travis saw the dhow begin to swing with the turn of the tide. The hull grated along the dock. He could see her now, tiny against the towering side of the ship. It would crush her – if the guard didn't shoot her first.

With a small pang of regret Travis tossed his half-empty bottle of Tsing Tao over the schooner's bow. Its motion drew the Lascar's eye. Reflexively the man swept up his Sten gun and blasted the beer bottle into oblivion.

Right at that moment the fireworks started. In the cacophony and the jumping flares of colour, the guard grinned sheepishly at Travis, who gave a lopsided shrug and grinned back in an 'anybody can make a mistake' kind of a way before turning into the *Oyster Shell*'s wheelhouse. He flicked the light out and watched from the shadows.

It was less than two minutes before the Lascar got bored and strode to the far end of the dhow's deck to peer at the dockyard gates. Apparently he could make out nothing that demanded his attention. Nonchalantly he ducked behind a stack of life-rafts. A match flared through a strand of fog. Moments later the scent of tobacco drifted across to Travis where he lurked behind the open hatch.

In his soft-soled shoes Travis made no sound. Staying low, he crossed to the *Shell*'s starboard bow where he unrolled a ladder. He heard a faint splash, no more than the sound of a flying-fish speeding into the waves. The ropes creaked as something weighed on them. Travis leaned casually over the rail and grinned.

Hands gripping the rungs, Jiao Jinyu looked up and saw him: a tall Westerner with unnatural blue eyes. For just a moment fear turned her to stone. But surely he wouldn't have distracted the guard if he meant to turn her in? Unless he wanted to claim the reward . But would a *gwai-lo* know about the price on her head? Besides, she could hardly swim through the mass of jostling sampans. In this murk they'd never see her, only feel a bump when they ran her down. Rockets strobed coloured light across his face and she caught his open gaze. Jiao twitched him the briefest of answering smiles, shrugged and climbed the ladder. As she reached the top Travis grabbed her by the waist and deposited her on the *Shell*'s deck. Her muted shrill of outrage died, leaving behind the heat of a blush.

'You're a free woman, princess,' the captain whispered, hand over her mouth. 'You can go or stay for me, only there's a whole bunch of bad men aboard that scow. It's no place for a lady.' He let her go.

Her jaw dropped open, not least at his fluent if flawed Cantonese. She gathered herself enough to exclaim, 'I'm not a lady!' Her voice dropped to gruffness. 'I'm a boy, all right? And … and thank you but I'd have got round the watchman plenty fine if you hadn't woken him up.' She turned away. 'I'll go now.'

'Where to? My guess is the slavers'll be back with their prisoners soon. That's what you've been waiting for, isn't it? They've got someone of yours, haven't they? By the looks of things,' Travis added conversationally, 'you could do with a hot meal. We're not going anywhere 'til the festival dies down and neither are your pals on that tub next door. How about it?'

'You've been watching me!'

'Thought you might be in want, lad.' He watched surprise and then satisfaction flicker over her delicate features. Obviously she thought she'd got away with it. It was no skin off his nose if she wanted to pretend she was a boy. But she said suspiciously, 'How do I know you won't turn me over to them?'

'How do I know you won't stab me with that pig-sticker?' He shrugged. 'Look, I'll go down to the galley and knock up some noodles. If you're here when I come back you can have some, OK?' This time it was he who turned away, a tall round-eye with sun-streaked hair and a smile in his voice. A moment later a towel landed at her feet, followed by a tunic and trousers as patched as the ones she'd stolen to replace her beautiful satin dress. She could hear him whistling as he clanged pans around. As she changed, a delicious odour of chicken-broth floated up from the galley. It made her mouth water.

*

Travis brought two heaped bowls into the wheelhouse. He sat bonelessly on the deck and handed one of them over. His mystery girl glided to a place a discreet distance from his side. She had a feeling he was waiting for something too. His fingers kept straying to the pistol in the small of his back and he never took his eyes off the dock. They ate in the lightning flare of the fireworks. She wondered if she could trust him. After all, *gwai-lo* like him had brought the Opium Wars to China. They were greedy and unaware of how many times they gave offence. And they smelt funny, which was another reason she felt embarrassed to have anything to do with him. If her parents could see her she'd die of shame. Except they were dead. Murdered. But something kept her there, and it wasn't only the food. Perhaps – perhaps he could help. From her seat on the floor she could see guns hooked under the console. He looked as though he could use them, which could be good – or bad.

Gradually the noise of the celebration gave way to the vessel's soft creaks and the everlasting sound of the sea. The silence grew between the Englishman and the delicate Cantonese girl. Travis kept wondering where Ding Xiang and his daughters had got to, and if sending them to dicker with the Pirate Queen was as smart as he'd thought. At least Ding Xiang knew her. She was the one he'd paid protection to – until some of her gang had gotten … ambitious.

Twice Jiao parted her lips to speak and twice filled her mouth to put it off. The second time she choked.

Travis passed her a mug of green tea and patted her back. 'We're leaving on the tide if you want to sail with us,' he said softly. 'So what's your business with the slaver? How many'd want to come with us?'

She put down her bowl. Her dark, almond eyes glared suspiciously from under her brows. Finally she spoke. 'What's your price? And what does it buy for two people?'

'Two, huh?'

Jiao Jianyu clamped her lips then reluctantly nodded.

Travis leaned forward, rainbow sparks dancing across his forehead. 'The price for you is your full story and what you want. What you get depends.'

She planted herself more firmly and settled in to haggling. Normally she enjoyed it, but now… 'First we get silence.'

'Of course. From you too.'

'Swear on your mother's grave.'

Travis grinned. 'My mother's alive and harrying sinners in Eastbourne.'

Jiao's hand shot out to grip his wrist. 'Swear!'

'I give you my word.'

'For how long, barbarian?'

A muscle tautened Travis's cheek. 'Until Hell freezes over or someone lies to me.'

She felt his anger swell that someone should doubt him. It was a good sign. He spat lightly on his hand and reached for hers. Disgusted, she drew back.

'Sorry,' he muttered, using the discarded towel. 'Shoulda known a fine lady such as yourself wouldn't like to share spit with a barbarian.'

Jiao raised her chin. She forgot to deny the 'fine lady'. 'Where I come from they use blood to bind a sacred oath,' she said.

'Hope they don't have malaria,' Travis muttered, and held out his hand. After, when they'd bound the nicks in each other's palms, Jiao Jianyu told her story.

'We live – we used to live – in Zhongshan with my grandparents and parents.' Her face softened as memories enraptured her. Treasured times just last week, a scroll now sealed forever in the past. Gossiping with her friends at their embroidery, she'd sat in the shade of the cherry tree watching Little Brother. The boy shrieked with glee when his arrow hit the target. Mother was taking tea with Father, enjoying the maid's absence to play housewife. Then the grown-ups strolled out to spend time with their offspring.

'Father's an acupuncturist. Grandfather was astrologer to the local nobility. When he and Grandmother became ancestors, though, Uncle Nanzu was jealous that we had more of the family compound.' She swallowed down her guilt. 'It was because of Little Brother and me. Grandfather had said we needed more space because of us children but Father offered Nanzu – a bachelor – another room.

'But it wasn't enough. Nothing was ever enough because Father had always been the favourite. Uncle Nanzu just stroked his moustache and said he wouldn't dream of taking a room needed by the fruit of his brother's loins. He started to go out more, to parties and theatres and viewings of moon -pools, he said. My father wanted to believe he'd given up his obsession and was just spending more time with friends. But it turned out Nanzu's friends were Nationalist lawyers and closet Communists.

'You don't know what it's like in China now.' She looked down to hide her family's shame, then forced herself to meet Travis's level gaze. 'Or maybe you do. Warlords and Chiang Kai Shek and the Reds battling over your homeland, and every spiteful neighbour selling tales about you out of greed for what you own. Don't get me wrong,' she went on earnestly. 'Most people are honourable but so many are afraid. They change with the wind, especially when it carries the sound of cannon to their ears.

'So one night,' Jiao whispered, 'I made a dreadful mistake.'

That memory reeled her straight into the past, hooked on terror as surely as guilt. Now the house with the graceful green roofs was no longer home and safety. Back then, Bohai, their old gardener, had been complaining about his back but wouldn't ask her father for time off in case they fired him. Jiao couldn't convince him they weren't like that so the old man struggled on alone. For him it was a question of not losing face. He liked her. Not so the maid who called herself housekeeper and tormented Jiao where the mistress couldn't see it, but luckily she'd gone to care for a sick relative. Although it wasn't lucky for the relative, of course.

When her homework was too boring, Jiao looked out from her room. She'd see Bohai's bald head bobbing slowly up and down the camellias. And sometimes she'd drop her hated calligraphy and climb out of her window to help him plant the peonies. She'd much rather have been practising martial t'ai chi. But on Sunday she'd been forbidden to see her beloved Ai. It was Bohai's scrawny old shoulder that she cried on.

The next day his tic was worse than ever. That's how she knew his anxiety had grown. Perhaps the sound of mortar shells in the hills had shredded what was left of his nerves or perhaps his rheumatism was playing up. Furtively he showed her the vine that had sprung up behind the bamboo until it topped the compound's wall. He asked her not to tell the master until he'd managed to cut it down.

On the spot she promised to do it for him. 'Only I can't tonight,' Jiao said earnestly. 'I made a mess in calligraphy so Mother's making me do extra practice. But I will, first thing,' she promised. 'Honest.'

But now she knew that vine was there, Jiao could hardly wait for dusk. After yawning elaborately and wishing her parents an early goodnight, she put on her best robe with the blue embroidery and climbed out of her window. She crept behind the bamboos and joyously shinned over the wall. Rolling into a t'ai chi fall, she raced off into the shadows. At last she'd be able to explain to Ai that her parents had made her stand him up but she didn't care what they said. So what if Ai had had a colourful past? He was different now. Only last week after t'ai chi school he'd sworn he loved her. He was so handsome, so charming, that doubts festered. How could he care for someone as ordinary as she? But no. She had to believe their love was eternal. Surely it was a sign that his name was Ai, which meant love? He'd wait for her until her father recognised him as worthy. He would. Really.

Through the wide, dusty streets she ran, sometimes dazzled by torches and lanterns, sometimes in banyan-shrouded dark. She came to the inn on the corner of Ai's street. In her mind she was already climbing the rickety stairs to his attic room, rehearsing her speech as she went. She almost didn't see him.

The breath shrank in Jiao's lungs until they were too tight to draw air in. Despite the lamps glowing on the inn's tables, darkness swirled around her. She grabbed onto a plane tree for support. Because there he was, Ai the handsome, the boy she'd let kiss her cheek. With a girl squealing happily his lap. Ai fondled her cheerfully.

Tears in her eyes, Jiao wheeled and pelted home. She just hoped Mother hadn't come into her bedroom to check up on her. She'd be sent away to school. Or married to a dotard. A rich, ugly one. Jiao wasn't sure which would be worse.

Half-way up the avenue she saw flames leap behind the houses. They were coming from the next street up the hill. The flares of red and orange got brighter as she staggered towards them. They roared from the last building on the upper side.

Her home.

On fire.

Jiao's chest heaved as she told Travis of that run, the one she relived every time she dared close her eyes. At last she'd reached the orchid trees on the corner but the crowd beyond was impenetrable. And unmoving. Nobody organised a bucket chain. Nobody did anything but eye the militia warily. Jiao pushed and shoved and fought her way through. Above the crackle and roar of the blaze even she couldn't hear her own yells.

She was about to barge through the last onlookers when someone grabbed her. Jiao kicked and wriggled but whoever it was just flicked five nerve-points and she dropped like a stone, conscious but unable even to breathe.

A familiar voice hissed in her ear, 'Will you listen, Lady Jiao? There's a bounty on your head. You don't want them to catch you too, do you?'

Even though Bohai released her nerve points Jiao couldn't move. She couldn't think of anything but her family roasted to death. The image was so vivid she could hear their screams. The sound of a truck rattling noisily away made a background. Only slowly did his words penetrate: 'Your parents are ... gone but Little Brother's been taken.'

Slowly she retreated from horror to look at old Bohai. Tears wove clean lines through the soot on his wrinkles. In the dancing shadows cast by the fire's light his cataract stood out pale while his dark eye was invisible. Smoke drifted from his clothes. When he held out a hand to pull her up his spine gave an audible click. He whimpered and folded in two. Jiao put her knee in his back and yanked until he was more or less upright. Now she was the one who had to spirit him into the night. Because once again the political wind had shifted and someone – by which Bohai meant Nanzu – had denounced them to the police.

'But he's got his comeuppance.' Gasping in pain, the old gardener clung more tightly to his mistress as they crept through the night. 'The new mayor was displeased because he'd had his eye on our place. When the Reds said Nanzu could have it the mayor's bully-boys burned it down. Here.' He handed her the family treasure: a hand-sized statue of A Ma in red jade. 'This was all I managed to save.' In the moonlight it gleamed like blood on bone.

A whispered argument at the edge of town decided them where to go: the monastery of Kwan Yin, goddess of mercy, an avatar of A Ma, goddess of the sea. 'And that was where I left him,' she told Travis. 'We heard the truck, you see, the same rattling old truck coughing its way up the hill. I pushed poor old Bohai into the bushes. We were right at the foot of the temple steps when the engine stuttered and died.' Jiao covered her face. 'It was horrible. The sound of children weeping where there should have been the song of crickets. I went and hid under a rhododendron by the road.'

The metal clanked as it cooled. An armed guard strode from the back to see what was up and two men jumped down from the cab. One flinched from the other's slaps as he folded the hood back from the engine. He kept saying it wasn't his fault he couldn't get the parts.

The one with the fly-whisk screamed, 'I don't care! Just fix it or it's goodbye every copper we've laid out. We've got three more collections to make and if we don't get to Macao by Thursday we'll lose our buyer.'

Something crawled onto Jiao's neck. She shuddered. The

man with the rifle came to see what had shaken the bushes. Heart pounding, she inched back into the storm-drain and buried her face in the mud.

'I heard the driver hit something with a hammer, then he climbed in and a guard cranked the starting-handle. The engine just whined and died. I heard the door slam as the mechanic got out again, and the swish of that flywhisk. He yelled, 'That's enough, alright? I'll get us there, don't you worry. The *Desert Rose* can't sail 'til the next day. It's part of the Sheik's plan, remember? Using A Ma's festival to cover the cargo being taken aboard?'

Flywhisk hit him again. Jiao heard flesh give beneath a stinging blow. 'Don't say Sheikh Abdul's name out loud, you idiot!'

'I've just about had enough of you,' grated the mechanic, and the horsehair whisk sailed over Jiao's head to land in the ditch. 'I'm the only man you've got who knows how to drive. Lay a finger on me again and you'll have to hoof it back to your master. Good luck disguising two dozen whining brats on the road.'

'All right, all right! Just get on with it!'

That was the moment when the engine caught. As the truck rattled away Jiao pelted after it.

*

Bohai had known Sister Desire of Infinite Light since before Jiao was born. He had brought the family to this temple one Sunrise Viewing and they'd worshipped here ever since. It suited their own blend of Buddhism and Dao and they were generous with alms.

The nun stepped from the porch where she'd been hiding since she heard the van. One eye out for brigands, she eased herself down the steps and found Bohai in the bushes.

'Where's Lady Jiao?' he croaked.

'She ran after that truck. Did you hear those poor children crying? But she'll never keep up with one of those modern smokepots. She'll be back.'

'You don't know Jiao.' His eyelid twitched like crazy.

For a long time they stood there, the nun in her faded red robes, he in his smoke-blackened rags, but Jiao didn't come back up the hill. Eventually the two creaky old people supported each other to the kitchen, where she dressed Bohai's burns, but she couldn't stop him worrying. Suddenly, as they talked over tea and lychee spirit, he clapped his hand to his head. Even that movement hurt. One moment his left leg felt like it was on fire, the next, snow-chilled.

Bohai swore and apologised. 'I don't think she's coming back. But surely there'd have been some uproar down the valley if they'd caught her? She wouldn't leave me, though, not Jiao. Then I remembered. She heard what I heard. The *Desert Rose* must be the ship they're taking them to, and it's in Macao 'til Friday morning. Sister, I've got to get there before she does something stupid.'

The nun looked at him over the rim of her teacup. 'So you include me in your insane plans? You really think I'm stupid enough to involve myself in a plot where a crippled gardener takes on a gang of slavers to rescue his beloved mistress just so she can die trying to save her arrogant sprig of a brother?'

Bohai shrugged, and winced again. 'Yes. You love Lady Jiao almost as much as I do. And we both dandled Little Brother when he was a baby. He'll grow out of it.'

One either side of the dying embers each fell into their own thoughts.

*

Desire of Infinite Light woke him before cock-crow with a bowl of fish chowder. A night flat on the kitchen floor had gone a long way to straightening his spine. Also she'd put something in the sauce. Bohai so enjoyed the floaty feeling that he didn't argue with her mad scheme.

Not until she actually put him on the train. The frightening, rumbling, racketing train that was headed for Hong Kong. Bohai had never even seen one of the roaring iron monsters before, let alone been dragged in a moving room with smoke belching in through the window.

He was glad to get out before Hong Kong and hire a pony and trap. With a wretched quilt folded beneath him he survived the journey over rutted roads but on the second day when he handed over the letter at a certain temple in Macao, he couldn't straighten from his bow. After reading Infinite Light's message the priestess hid him behind the wall-hanging that backed A Ma's red throne. And there, with drugs and acupuncture and a fierce wrenching that put him straight, Bohai rested until night should come.

*

Bohai wasn't sure he was awake when the young priestess warned him to keep quiet. Pale rainbows hung glowing in the air. Maybe it was the medication or maybe the smoke of the joss-sticks but Bohai thought it was A Ma's aura. The priestess whispered, 'Ssh, Bohai. It's the Pirate Queen. Don't listen.'

So of course he did.

'So, Ding Xiang, after last time your Travis is too cowardly to face me. He knows I don't like owing people favours.' It was a woman's voice, deep and rich. Through a gap in the curtain Bohai watched. The temple doors were locked but the incense braziers and the candles gave enough light to see. The plump woman in the red silk tunic fondled the pommel of her sword.

'He was going to blow up that arms shipment anyway, Your Majesty.' Bohai saw a stringy middle-aged man, Ding Xiang no doubt, kneeling before her, two well-muscled girls at his back. 'The warlord killed his friend. Travis sends his regrets but he had strange things to do for the voices from the air. Little wires, and glass bulbs that glow like demons, and something that clicks louder than crickets before it shouts at you. Otherwise he'd have come himself. He said how much he missed your face alight with laughter and your eyes so full of life. But he sent you this.'

Ding Xiang's daughters pushed forward the small crate they'd carried. 'I saw Travis pack it himself, Your Majesty,' he said. 'He calls it a wireless. He put a paper inside explaining how to make demons carry words from people far away. He says it will help with your … work … against the warlord.'

The Pirate Queen snapped her fingers. One of her henchmen prised off the lid. It was a wireless, all right – in pieces. Valves, wires and strange metal shapes were padded in straw. On top lay a paper – printed in English.

For a moment the Pirate Queen radiated fury. Then she burst into laughter so uproarious it showed her gold teeth. 'So what does your barbarian master want me to do in exchange for this demon box?'

'He merely wants to save you from the traitors who have stolen from you, Your Majesty.'

'And from you pearl-fishers. What is he really after?'

'Do you think he'd tell me?'

From his hiding-place Bohai watched as they haggled. Finally Ding Xiang handed over the pearls Travis had helped them steal back and took a yarrow stick the queen offered. 'This one,' she said, coquetting as though she were twenty years younger, 'is my renewed contract of protection for you and your family. For twenty per cent off the top, I'll make sure my next protectors don't take more than they should. This one –' she produced another twig from her crimson sleeve ' – is my safe conduct back to your vessel. And this one is my demand for Travis to build this demon-box properly.' Mercurial, she scowled. 'Nobody takes over my territory. Tell Travis to meet me ten li south-west of the point at noon tomorrow. Of course if he doesn't...' The gold teeth flashed again. She broke her half of the last yarrow.

Old Bohai had heard enough. He shook off the priestess and stepped through the curtain. At sight of him the Pirate Queen's men drew curved swords. In reply Ding Xiang's daughters whipped metal fans from their sashes. Ropes of tension bound the temple until nothing moved but the leaping shadows.

Then Bohai creaked to his knees at Ding Xiang's side. His

one good eye looked up at her in her red robes while his cataract glowed like the moon. 'Lady of Mercy, you have agreed to cleanse your territory of the thieves who have taken over this man's oyster beds. You and this – this Travis will sail together against them. But there is another threat to the People of the River: a gang of slavers who steal your folk and sell them in a foreign land. They sail in a ship called the *Desert Rose.*'

The Pirate Queen tapped her gold teeth. 'And what has this to do with me?'

Bohai bowed lower. 'My young master is one of their captives.'

She raked him with a glance. 'You are not one of the river folk. I say again, what has this to do with me?'

'Can you be sure these slavers have taken none of your people? Are you not A Ma's general to the people of the river? And though we come from far inland, the river that waters our home is the same mighty Pearl. Will your people trust you if you betray one of their own?' And Bohai prostrated himself, trembling.

For a long moment the queen stared at him, at her followers, at the goddess. Then she cast a glance at her own crimson sleeve. 'My people are those who live on the water. But you are right, old man. These slaver vermin have invaded my territory. Ding Xiang, this man goes with you. He is the last part of my message to Travis.'

*

The truck's tail-lights sent patterns of red light round the bends all the way down to the bottom of the valley. Jiao kept running until it felt like eels gnawed her ribs. The truck dipped across the bridge and its headlights shone cones of light upwards until it vanished beyond the crest of the hill. When she couldn't run any more, she walked. The soles of her silk slippers had long since worn away and her feet were bleeding. At cock-crow she stole a ride in a hay-cart, resting while silently cursing the donkey for a knock-kneed slug. In the first market town she stole tunic and trews from a washing-line, leaving them the tatters of her clothes. The gorgeous embroidered panels had to be worth something. In her peasant disguise she asked around for a lift to Macao but the farmer threw her off fifteen li too soon because she admitted she had no money. She slogged the rest of the way on foot, staggering wearily through the hills of the teeming port until she finally reached the harbour. There, scarcely a stone's throw from the evil ship, she forced herself to stay awake, to spy out the slaver's routine, to come up with a plan. And any time she stopped worrying about Little Brother or crying about her parents, she worried about Bohai.

*

Suddenly Travis cocked his head, and Jiao did likewise. Yes, there came the sound of a motor vehicle chugging uncertainly along the quay. She leaped up, drawing the knife she'd purloined from its scabbard at her nape, but he grabbed her before she got half-way to the door. She ripped herself from Travis's light grasp. He was relieved to see she had the sense to watch from the shadows. He narrowed his gaze at the go-down, eager for the final confrontation with the murderous bastard who owned it.

The truck shuddered to a halt. A slice of light came from the go-down as a tall man in Arab robes strode out, suspicion stark on his features. Travis sneered a grin at sight of his victim: the warlord's spy. By his side trotted a ball of a man in a satin robe who gave a smile blent of terror and fawning. His shrill commands brought the guards down from the truck. They paraded the wretched youngsters for his inspection. The Arab pointed a finger here, pinched a backside there, his face as impassive as if he were buying bread rather than human beings.

Teeth clenched, Travis watched too. He was ready to grab Jiao if he had to, because he had seen how many armed men had stayed aboard the dhow. It was a great brute of a ship and a dozen or more would be needed to crew her. Plus guards.

But if this Arab was working with the foul creature in the go-down, his revenge would be incomplete without the slaver. Trouble was, the Pirate Queen was a chancy ally at best...

*

With all the bustle of locking their captives below deck and raising sail, the thugs on the *Desert Rose* had no attention to spare for the round-eye and his schooner. The man in Arab dress passed a purse to the man from the go-down, then strode aboard. The master of the landsmen loudly demanded his pay, tapping another flywhisk on his leg as he waited. The fat Chinaman wrangled over the price of flesh.

So none of them paid heed to the two burly women who rowed back the schooner's boat. Travis was bemused to see they'd acquired a one-eyed passenger. Jiao stifled a squeal and threw herself into the old gardener's arms. Travis hustled everyone to the galley for explanations. Now he'd seen the whipped children he was more determined than ever. Besides, this was hardly the first time he'd gotten into a scrap. The contents of his locker would attest to that. Fog wasn't the only kind of dragon's breath, after all.

*

It was still dark when the slave-ship manoeuvred out of the harbour amidst a flotilla of merchantmen that had also been penned up by the festival. After a discreet interval Travis nodded to Ding Xiang, whose command sent Fragrant Lily and Lustrous Jade scrambling to raise the schooner's sails. Jiao could hardly contain her excitement at the prospect of freeing her brother.

The *Shell* had hardly got under way when it bumped into a knot of sampans. Insults flew. 'No damage done,' Travis apologised over and over, then disappeared below decks, presumably out of shame. Curses followed them all the way to the harbour mouth. Jiao comforted her poor twitching gardener then went to give the round-eye a piece of her mind.

But he wasn't aboard. Dressed in torn tunic and trews, a

dark wig under a bandanna and a moustache straggling past his stained chin, he had stepped carefully onto a carefully chosen little boat. They ferried him to a wharf and tied up. He knew they'd wait for him. He'd only paid half the cash in advance.

His rope-soled shoes made little sound as he sauntered round the back of the go-down. Now the cargo had gone, Fat Chun wouldn't waste money on guards.

Travis poured his vial of acid around the window-bars. They were metal – but set miserly into wood. Above the sharp burning stink came a waft of opium, the grunts of a fat man in paradise and a whimper.

As soon as Travis eased out the bars the terrified girl spotted him. He laid a finger over his lips. She nodded, and groaned more artistically under the fat bare backside. The earth moved for Chun as Travis punched him to the ground.

The sleazy dealer wasn't out for long, but then, Travis didn't want him to be. He wanted him to appreciate every moment of this payback. With ruthless efficiency Travis gagged the man and tied him dangling from a rafter. The girl giggled and wrote rude slogans on the sagging flesh while the captain searched out every single one of the secret hoards: pearls; strings of cash and bags of gold; exotic perfumes and dark balls of opium. Travis hurled the drugs into the sea – Chun tried to shout his outrage through his gag – and split the rest of the proceeds. The girl sashayed out, her own poor clothes bulging where she'd stuffed her loot.

Then Travis pulled off his bandanna and moustache. Chun's eyes widened in fear.

'Oh, don't mind me,' the Westerner said in his mangled Chinese. 'You may have tortured poor Barney but I'm not like that. I'm just going to rob you.'

Chun sagged with relief.

'But the people you double-crossed have other plans. Goodbye, Chun.'

*

Far out to sea, the dawn came up in veils of scarlet and gold.

There wasn't a sign of Her Majesty's promised fleet but Travis dared wait no longer. The slave junk carried more sail. She'd be hull down in scant hours. Machine guns blazing, he steered the *Oyster Shell* out of the mist.

Scrambling from sleep, the slavers had no idea what hit them. Bullets shattered the wheelhouse. Blood sprayed from the shattered windows as the captain died. Three guards erupted from the fo'cs'l. Fragrant Lily and Lustrous Jade mowed them down without compunction as they headed for the companionway.

Travis tore the yarrow stick from his pocket and hurled it aside with a curse. 'Should've known better than to trust a pirate,' he thought, then drew his pistol and swung to the slaver's deck. Against his express orders Jiao followed Jade and Lily across. Ding Xiang covered them.

From the roof of the slaver's wheelhouse a burst of return fire stitched the deck. Ding Xiang slew the marksman. Now the *Desert Rose*'s deck was clear. Lily zig-zagged forwards and hurled her first missile through the open door. Sounds of choking issued forth. Meantime Travis took cover behind a hatch and risked a peep into the hold.

He saw Jiao sneak into the stinking gloom. A childish treble piped, 'Sister!' and she ran towards the little lad. Jiao bent to cuddle him. From behind the door the Lascar leaped on her. Travis cursed. From this angle he couldn't get a clear shot but to his amazement Jiao ducked, sweeping the Lascar's legs from beneath him with one savage kick. The slaver fell and she snatched his rifle, clouting him with the stock. His head snapped sideways and she filched the keys from his belt.

But Travis had troubles of his own. From nowhere the sheikh leaped out at him, sickle-shaped dagger plunging at his unprotected back. Jade came running towards them as they grappled. Travis twisted, grabbing the knife-hand and bashing it on the hatch but the Arab kneed him in the crotch. Still Jade couldn't risk a shot. As the Englishman gasped, his opponent tossed the blade to his free hand. He grinned nastily and lunged at Travis.

Travis wrenched sideways and the knife left a line of bright fire on his throat before its point spun into the deck. He trapped his assailant's neck between his legs, then kicked, once. Bone snapped and the man lay still. Travis slumped, trying to staunch the blood trickling through his fingers. He managed to lurch upright.

Then Lily tossed her second smoke-bomb. Knock-out gas fumed up through the hatch and all resistance faded.

Ripping the Arab's keffiyeh from his head to bandage his wound, Travis was amazed that the heavy beard came with it. Tossing the wodge of black hair aside, he bound his neck before examining his dead foe.

The black eyebrows had smudged. He rubbed at them. Charcoal! And the walnut dye stopped at the man's hairline. He was a redhead, not an Arab at all!

*

By the time the gas had dispersed, they'd tied up all the miscreants. All the living ones, that is. Travis would have tipped the dead ones over the side for the sharks but Ding Xiang was appalled at such waste. He walked happily among them, adding up the bounty on their heads. Meantime his daughters and Jiao helped the freed youngsters on deck. There were twenty of them, none of them out of their teens.

Travis ordered Ding Xiang and Lustrous Jade to take the slaver's helm while he and Lily crossed back to the *Shell*. The pearl-divers could manage the sale of the junk and the freed slaves could divvy up the bounty. And no Pirate Queen around to demand the lion's share!

Except just as they sailed past the headlands into Ding Xiang's hidden cove, two sizeable ships hove into sight at their backs. They bore the Red Flag of Ching Shih, copied from the greatest woman pirate in history. And Travis's wireless squawked.

He rolled his eyes. 'You missed all the fun, Your Majesty.'

She laughed. 'You are not the only *gwai-lo* who knows

how to make a devil-box, Travis. Of course if it had been working sooner, we'd have got there on time. Still, it looks like you've brought me a fine ship.'

'Now wait a minute!' he protested.

Jiao Jinyu elbowed him aside and pressed the switch that turned off the microphone. 'You're good at fighting,' she whispered in his ear, 'but when it comes to bargaining you need a smart girl like me.'

Travis grinned, not least because she now trusted him enough to give up her pretence. Later, considerably richer, he said nothing when Ding Xiao burned joss before the red jade statue in the wheelhouse. Everyone was happy. Except the captured pirates disappearing into the angry queen's hold. And Bohai, who was sea-sick. But he'd get over it.

Wishbone

The stars fall in their appointed courses, silver scintillation in the flickering sun.

Jenuven ran to catch this one. It knew better: it evaded her gently, settled into its crystal bowl. Like the wind-blown filaments, the stars eddy away from reaching hands. This one was no different.

Halbark played his game: 'No, you can't have it tonight. We'll keep it for tomorrow.' In a vague sort of fashion, he wanted her to want the star now. What else was there to want? Strong man who was the leader; not that the others followed.

Jenuven turned away from him, cartwheeling by way of a change. She knew; he knew; seven people cannot live always together without bits of one becoming bits of the others. They knew whatever he said: tonight the star would shine.

Now Josa and Ranulf came running between the spars, both blindfold. Ranulf's tracker rang musically but intermittently. Ranulf was panting, laughing gamely; fifty-seven was no age to be playing tag, but one had to work hard to find enjoyment. What else was there to do? Josa, forty-something discreet, somersaulted around a spar with indifference; her blindfold would not let harm come to her. Hadn't everything always been safe?

The spars were wide-spaced, flickering aisles between them. Ocular blind-man's buff was too easy. But Ranulf caught her anyway: losing was unthinkable, and together the couple collapsed, giggling and tickling, on the broad, warm steps of the veranda. Their dyed hair didn't show the grey. Now all of them were in or around the House.

'It's here, isn't it?' gasped Josa in her accent of the

moment. She did not bother to take off her blindfold. Semmel didn't stop fretting the strings of his zither; Caspar and Hella kept on arguing in the House.

The star hummed a sweet, insistent note. It told them it was here.

Maybe, wondered Jenuven, *maybe somewhere else another star is shining, on the night side perhaps. You don't know. Random is interest, to keep us alive. You know that because the stars tell you.*

But who made them tell you?

*

Dusk: overhead the storm-clouds of afternoon have parted. The long, wet filaments of the spars have whipped the rain from their brilliant colours and floated their rainbow banners under sunset's flame. Gilt and silver limn the departing thunderheads. The sky is purple and navy, pierced by distant suns.

Jenuven often thought about that, which made the others think she was odd. She might have found it hard to believe those little lights were suns, but it had to be true because the stars had told her. They said other people lived around the suns, that others too lived on their own planet. But apart from Jenuven the others didn't care. Not even Halbark had bothered to go looking. Charitably he put her curiosity down to her youth. Firm, sweet skin; not tall; breasts that were promises of buds. All that, he'd told her, went with still wanting to know. She'd grow up.

But for now she came out with her friends, out of the warm-lit House with its tasty food-smells, their bodies pushing away the mist-wraiths of the evening air. It was at times like these that she felt young and naïve. She wanted to race ahead, see the star shine *now*; she couldn't wait.

But the others could. They didn't jostle or fidget. She was very aware that she wasn't a woman yet, not like Josa and Hella. She hadn't had a baby yet. Soon, though, Semmel would make a baby inside her, and she hadn't needed a star to tell her how it was done. She had seen the others practising often enough, even though they were too old now to have babies at the end of it. Mostly they made funny noises, but they said it was fun and not to worry. So she didn't.

All the same, she still had more fun than they did. There were still some things she hadn't done. But time would change that. Freedom, it seemed, was having everything she had been told she wanted, and nothing more.

In front of the House, they settled down. Between the wide-spaced boles of the spars, the star hovered in its crystal bowl on the tripod, and the tripod stood on the water-repellent carpet. Ranulf and Josa weren't speaking so they sat at opposite sides, pretending not to look at each other. Hella and Caspar had made up passionately before supper. Now they touched each other constantly, knee to knee, and hands caressing neck or cheek. Even apart, they looked as if they belonged together: same blue hair, same blue eyes, young at heart in spite of wrinkles and sagging bodies. Jenuven liked them best of all.

Halbark sat bolt upright, cross-legged, his hair grey with age and eyebrows askew. Against his burly shoulder, Semmel leant his scrawny one.

Semmel watched Jenuven as she dithered about where to sit – who would be offended by the position she chose? – and he patted the ground beside him. For once, though, Jenuven flicked her pale hair at him and the leader, and sat alone. Her eyes were enormous with anticipation; she folded her slender legs and leant on one arm, glad she had put on her best blue tunic with its fringes and silver bells, but she couldn't keep still and the bells chimed softly at each movement. Self-conscious, she wished now she had put on something quieter, and hoped the star would shine soon.

Now everyone was comfortable on the soft, dry carpet. There were no seats, only those built into the House. How could there be with the stones so deep in the soft web of fallen filaments, and the spars of a carbon that shattered but did not break. And of course they don't distribute cutters here, they're dangerous. Scatterguns, yes, you might just possibly need them, but you can't carve anything with a scattergun.

The night settled, fragrant with filaments and scented with fruit, earthy. As yet the star has not started. It knows they're all here, but it's waiting, teasing, pricking some emotion out of the spoilt people, just as it had been programmed to do on some planet far away, where people actually have found tasks to perform. A star once showed them all that.

Expectancy surges in the blood. For sound: a fat raindrop plop, soft breathing and kisses, the breeze flapping the filaments to curtain off the sky. No clawed toes stalking along the broad glades, no wings shivering in the air. No terrifying snap of beaks. All the same, Halbark plays at checking around, but the little eyes in his heavy face see no birds awaiting. Halbark checks the scattergun at his feet. The others watch indifferently. Doesn't Halbark always do that? The stars once said it was a good idea – after all, the birds bore the same maker's mark as the guns and the stars – but nobody else does it. They shrug; it's just Halbark's little game. Makes him feel resourceful.

At last, at last, the star in its crystal cup glows. None of them has seen it start, not even Jenuven, though they all thought they were watching. Its silvery humming twinkled into song.

As far as the seven wanted anything, this was not it. No more warm, soft ease: star-cold radiated, made their homely glade white and bleak. How could white be so many colours at once? A hard cold permeated their bones and the bones of the earth. They shivered, and their sated bodies liked this strange sensation. Over the sudden snowfield the sky was dark, and the tiny distant suns were another white.

Jenuven saw – they all felt and knew and saw – no spars, no filaments. There was no stew-scented House, and the guns threw cutting points. Food did not fall from above – how could it? There were no spars – it ran, and crawled, and tunnelled, or pushed aside the wind-bared earth. You had to fight for it!

Frost crawled up their sudden, shaggy clothes. Jenuven heard around her the voices of a crowd: there must have been as many as twenty or thirty, more than she could count. They were roaring out songs, guffawing, making love by the fires of dung. The illusion – the star-show – was complete. She could even smell the bitter smoke, and wet fur.

Lots – more than two handfuls – of hairy beasts were moaning and stamping beyond the firelight. Picket-ropes tied them head to head. Four in a circle were staggering, intoxicated on yellow lichen.

The shaggy people were stoned on the hairy things' urine. Jenuven, Halbark, all of them, were drunk among the roisterers. They stood and watched a man with a drinking-horn trying to catch some more urine. She howled with laughter when the animal kicked him in the head. Later, out of the star, she would think this was odd, laughing at misfortune. But for now it was a great respite from cold hard work and long hunger.

Beyond the star-thoughts, Jenuven was not aware. But in the morning she would ask the others what they had been in the snowfield.

Only she couldn't.

Physically outside the star-thoughts, the rare birds were coming. The star-makers knew some folk must have a challenge, or die.

The birds paced softly towards the radiant clearing. Their claws bit into the soft mat of filaments as they pushed themselves along. Flightless wings jerked out for balance. Long-fanged jaws wanted sweet, hot flesh.

The stars and the birds were not supposed to coincide, but random is as random does.

Coincidence: flesh scent on warm, damp air.

Plucked from his shaggy bride of the snowfields, Ranulf bled in pain. Another bird snapped Josa's arm off, and Josa didn't understand why the red stump flailed.

Three took Hella and Caspar, fighting over the blue ropes of gut.

Halbark the leader thought something must be wrong. He felt for his unreal scattergun far away at his feet. The snowfield in his eyes was more white than the pearl-damp misted clearing. His first shot took out Semmel's thorax; the larynx screamed as air soughed through it.

Jenuven heard the screams beyond the star-snow-field. One scream was hers. She had no leg any more, but did not know it 'til she tried to run. Jenuven fell, and the pain bit: not a bird, but Halbark's scattergun blazing in the dark. But he knew he was resourceful in his panic-isolated mind. Poor Jenuven! But he had scattered the bird, big and black and ugly. Tomorrow he might enjoy being proud. Now, though, panic was crushing his chest.

Squawking and hideous, the birds tore their meal loudly. They fought and gobbled, and the noise was a desecration of the glade. Jenuven curled up, hands over her ears, but she could still see.

Then Halbark jerked the trigger again, and it rained flesh and gristle, feathers and filaments. Red and black spattered the bodies on the carpet, and the stench made Jenuven heave the home-smelling stew she had eaten in an arc.

The silence shattered her. No-one was left. Halbark's harsh breathing had stopped. He lay under the crystal cup on its tripod, his face grey under the star's light. Jenuven thought suddenly how ridiculous his eyebrows were with his face blenched to match.

Jenuven cried out then, 'I can't find it!' On hands and knee she hauled herself round the carpet, searching. Her spasms of retching had hurt her stomach; shock anaesthetised the leg that didn't know it wasn't there. She was crying, wiping her blurred eyes with muddy fingers, looking for – something. She crawled past Hella's hollow body, felt through the hole in Semmel's chest, but it wasn't there. It wasn't in the pocket of her tunic. It wasn't in the glade at all.

When she realised she didn't know what it was that was

missing, Jenuven laid her tear-stung cheek on the friendly carpet and wept herself into unconsciousness.

*

Pain fished her up to light. Dawn's wind was pink, the filaments gaudy in the loud sunlight. Jenuven was hot and achy, her senses wrongly connected. She saw her stump that Halbark's shot had cauterised, and retched. The pain tasted of metal and bile,. She still saw the stump with her eyes closed. There were no tears in her left to cry.

She lay helpless, alone, feeling very young. She'd never been alone before. Always there'd been someone to comfort her, hug her to their wisdom, and now there wasn't. It was frightening.

Was it one of her friends? Surely they couldn't all be dead together? It wasn't fair when she was alive on her own.

The thing was small and black and fluttery. Jenuven felt too weak to move; she let it flop over her good leg.

The birds! Jenuven sat up dizzily and knocked the thing away with frantic hands. It tumbled, rolled, hopped beyond her thrashing reach.

'They're coming together again!' Her shriek scratched her parched throat. An indrawn breath of wordless horror. Then, 'There's another. And another!'

Black and red, hearts and bones, the birds *were* growing back together, just as the stars had said they could.

Hastily she wriggled to the House, away from the bits of birds that flapped and fluttered together. It would take days, she knew it would, before the birds were whole, scrag-feathered and long-toothed, obscenely hungry for her. But that was a fact she couldn't make herself believe when the dark flesh was writhing all around her.

Her haste, though, was of imagination and will. She fainted again and again, and grew more frantic as she grew weaker. Yards, steps, inches: the sun was vertical above the fanning filaments when she reached the veranda steps. The bits were noticeably bigger now.

Jenuven was so hot when she reached the bright,

welcoming House. Pain and fever throbbed in her head. There was no sweat in her body to cool her.

There was no-one now who could pass the doorspace but her. Still she wished she could block it so the birds wouldn't see her when their eyes grew back in. What she wanted most, though, was to lie in cool, clean snow, suck so much ice she was a part of it, and be with the only other people she knew of on her planet. She was tired of being alone. She wanted it to stop.

The House, obedient to her needs, made a bath for her where she lay. She slaked her thirst with the nutrient bath-water. Its coolness did not cool her fever; she dreamt of the bright, hard snow to the North, but the House would not make snow for her. It had been told there was no comfort in snow.

It did, however, rinse her shattered leg with astringents and antiseptics, and when it thought it should, it turned the bath into a soft, cushiony bed where she threshed and sweated, and it propped her up while it made her want to bind her leg. The floor and walls rippled the dressings box to her but there wasn't much in it. Hella liked – had liked – being ill, and the dressings box wasn't a renewable part of the House. They'd been expecting the stars to drop down a refill sooner or later, but even that hadn't come.

Then she slept again, dreaming of snow that would cool her sweating, and laughter that wasn't just something to do. The House couldn't make her change her dream.

When she woke, she still wasn't really awake; she was sure she wasn't, with this nightmare still oppressing her, but she drank when the House told her to, and sucked the tube of pap that poked through the smothering cushions though she didn't want it. What she wanted was the cold of snow, and the House wouldn't let her have any. She had never *wanted* anything before.

On the third day, a black wing slammed into the door-way. Jenuven screamed herself awake and would not be comforted by anything the House tried. The warm floor rose against her when she tried to scrabble away. The wing knocked and beat wildly but it couldn't get in. Jenuven couldn't get out of the soft pit made by the floor. Horrified, Jenuven watched as a head – a whole head! - sucked out Halbark's dead, resourceful eyes.

She decided then. To get away from the bits of birds, and the House that served but did not wait on her deepest want. To plunge her throbbing not-leg into crystals of ice. To leave the lonely known which held too much absence to bear.

No wheels. No tools – what were they? The House had always done everything— No (her mind would not say it) leg.

The House could not amputate itself to give her a knee, a shin, a foot. It was ill because it could not give the one thing she wanted to the one person left to serve. Its mind retreated deep towards its batteries. The cushions softened away to nothing but floor.

Jenuven crawled out of its doorway, braving the blind-battering wing. The House took into itself the tripod to fill its need which it did not understand. The star crashed to the carpet, and the carpet frayed under its dead. Across Halbark's skeletal toes, two clawed legs hopped to a feathered belly.

Jenuven crept amongst her ruined friends. She could not bear to touch them but the last thing they could give her was cover.

She seized a thigh-bone, stole it from its feathered companion, used it as well to beat off the black things that wanted it back. In her despair she could teach them about want.

Half-birds, wings, gizzards, cawed and flapped but she fought for her prize with the scarlet things and the black. On her insteps were the nervous pricks of fright and her missing knee felt swollen. She crawled away fast – hide and seek for real.

Away North amongst the black-stemmed spars, Jenuven tied on the bird bone, her hands sweaty with fear and pain and fever. She could more or less walk, but the bird's leg was slower regenerating without its companions. Sometimes she remembered to wonder what she would look like when it was grown.

Far in the cooler air of the northern hills, fruit still fell and streams still flowed. Sometimes she thought to feed herself, but she was gaunt and sick. No House looked after her here, and she wasn't very good on her own. Travel and no goal in sight could not give her reassurance; she remembered how they'd laughed, those shaggy men, when one of them got hurt. Her sores from crawling and falling would not heal, and when she tamed her limping steps she felt ugly.

In the last of the forests, the smaller fragments of birds stopped following. Some had got lost, but at night she knew the mouths had gone back to feed on her friends. Death is easier to eat than life. Yet in the lonely dark, each sound still told her something wanted back the leg that was growing into hers. Sleep came very hard.

Jenuven ran and staggered and bled northwards, far from the hot, sticky glade. In the dark hours came eyes of red, and claws; in the day she got no rest. Fear beat exhaustion, but only just, and that with the help of longing. Ice under a wide sky and groups of shaggy friends around many fires – but she didn't know which reality was real. Nor which fear was worse: the trailing almost-bird that wanted back its leg; needing people who die away from you; wanting to belong when she was useless and mutilated. Those men of the snowfields wouldn't need her.

So she came to the lands of snow, where the spars grew short or not at all. Behind her she felt but could not see the one-legged, jumping bird, flapping its wings for balance, stretching its beak for her.

Beyond the spars, into an ice-bound valley, Jenuven found soft mosses to caress her feet. The claws on one of them tore it as she passed. She searched grey, jagged rocks, but no fruit fell at her feet and she carried her ignorant hunger past grains she could have eaten.

In a hollow among the tumbled stones she shivered over a pool of still, cold water. She hesitated her hand, not shattering that limpid reflection of sky and frightened face: the pale mirror showed the face without make-up, hair without dye, eyes empty of laughter. Lines crawled on her forehead and her cheeks were shrunken. She laughed at what Halbark had thought of as want, and trembled in the chilly air because his eyes would never see it.

So many dead! Was anyone alive? Was the star just an entertainment, or was it – please – a lesson?

And how could she go to them – if they did exist – those people who looked after themselves, and fought, and laughed, who would not have been caught?

A failure, a cripple, she struck away the reflection and slaked her thirst again. But the snow-dream was all she had.

On the far side of the hills she jolted down an uneven trail. The sky brought rain and sleep, and at her heels – one brown-skinned, one spurred and scaled – came enough of a bird to kill her.

She slithered at the lip of an abyss. Ice-sharp rocks skittered beneath her odd feet. Twisting desperately over the precipice, she all but wanted to give in, let go, glide out to the crushing peace of death. But her body caught her before she fell, and panted out her fear.

The almost-bird swept down at her, wings outstretched to balance. Its jaws swept snapping past. Its oddness fluttered frantically but Jenuven used its/her claws to kick it over the edge.

It fell end over end into shadow, and she hurled stones down upon its corpse, so that not even its peculiar bones could move again together.

Laughing and weeping, she cried out. Her sense of failure changed to triumph. Lightning flared above her and she echoed back its wildness, running amidst emotions that were fierce and bright.

When she ran, on one foot and one claw, towards the distant light on the snowy plain that was men around a fire at last, she brought pain and humiliation and hungry need. But she brought the laughter and song of recklessness that come when all else is gone.

Fair Phantom, Come I

(From the reminiscences of John H. Watson, M.D.,
late of the Army Medical Department.)

'Bad baronets and fake phantoms? Tchah!'

Holmes's snort of derision was the last straw. He'd already dismissed a lecture on astronomy as irrelevant. I gave up my attempts to bring him out of his dark mood and stormed out to find a cab. If that was his opinion of comic opera he could stay here and stew. Tonight was the final performance of *Ruddigore* and last nights were always a pleasure.

As I stepped down from the hansom, the Crystal Palace dazzled me. Rivers of light spilled from the foyer, promising warmth and gaiety. Glad to get out of the bleak November darkness, I was swept up in a chattering crowd and shown to a box. It all but overhung the stage. It wasn't long before the rollicking tunes banished my vexation. Besides, being so close to the colour and action was rather a thrill. I must confess that when the 'ghosts' stepped from the frames of their portraits I jumped, but only because a thunder-flash exploded at the same time. The acrid smoke of cordite shimmered in the footlights, wreathing around real flesh and blood men. Only Gilbert and Sullivan. Not a Jezail bullet in sight.

The soprano kept giving me strange looks but I could only assume she mistook me for someone else. Right in the middle of the finale she threw something at me. She'd made the movement part of her dance. For a second her eyes burned into mine, then she twirled blithely away. Did I know her? Yes, there was something familiar under the grease-paint, but what? She was obviously certain she knew me. I waited impatiently for the final curtain to fall so I could examine the twist of paper.

The instant the lights went up I smelt as much as saw odd scrawls in grease-paint. There was a kind of mushroom-cap with a long stalk across concentric rings. What could it mean? Only this mysterious woman could tell me. Now where had I seen her before? I shrugged on my coat and rushed to the stage door, smiling to myself. Here was the adventure Holmes had been craving and he didn't know a thing about it! I could just picture his face when I told him. If only I could recall the woman's name! As it was, I waited, racking my brains in vain.

*

It was after midnight when I returned to Baker Street. The performers and stage-hands had long since vanished in the fog and I was chilled to the bone. How I had missed her I didn't know but missed her I had. Still, I thought as I came up the stairs, even if I couldn't place the woman I knew something that Holmes didn't. Time to get my own back.

He sprang up the instant I walked in. 'Was she there?' he cried.

'What? Damn it! Yes, whoever she was. And she —'

'You mean you didn't recognise her?' He clutched at his hair. 'How could you fail to?'

'Who, man?'

'You know, that adventuress we cleared of murder in the Case of the Burmese Ruby.'

'Not Fanny Jensen?' I gasped.

'Yes, yes, get on with it. What did she say?'

I tossed him the scrap of paper. 'I presume it's a message. She flung it in my face during a song, actually.'

But Holmes' gaze was glued to the strange symbols. I might as well have been in the Hebrides for all the notice he took. Crossly I poured myself a whisky. 'And before you ask, Holmes, no, she didn't say a word to me.'

'I know. He told me she wouldn't be able to.'

'*Who* told you?'

'No need to snap, old fellow. Bertie Poole. New client. He burst in, white as a sheet, saying someone was after a valuable scientific artefact. Two someones, actually, a researcher called Barnes and the fascinating young woman to whom Barnes had introduced him. Fanny Jensen, of course, currently the companion of an intimidating Russian who calls himself a count and always has an eye kept on her. He just happens to deal in arms. It seems the lady gives private concerts as well as dabbling in student affairs. Poole knew she had sung the part before so this afternoon he made sure the real soprano and her understudy were taken drunk and got the director to call in Miss Jensen. What colour was her hair this time?'

'Blessed if I know. She wore a wig.'

'Hmm. Anyway, with Miss Jensen and her guards safely at the theatre, Poole dashed back to the laboratory for the cylinder.'

'Look, Holmes, what's all this about?'

'This.' He held up a strange stone, the size and shape of a fine Havana, but glowing with a pearlescent light. 'After he'd refused to let her wheedle it from him he caught her whispering with Barnes. That's why Poole arranged to get her out of the way. At the laboratory he caught Barnes red-handed. They grappled. Poole claims he was winning until three bullet-headed giants barged in. He alleges he escaped by the skin of his teeth and fled here in fear of his life. I don't know what he's holding back but there's something. I suggested he lie low for a couple of days. I believe Miss Jensen's friend the researcher is the nephew of one General Barnes.'

'Not the fellow there's all the talk about in the clubs? Left the Service under a cloud?'

'Exactly. And once Poole knew an arms dealer and a shady general were after his device he was in rather a funk. Oh, by the way, he said not to touch it.'

I noticed Holmes held it gingerly by a handkerchief

wrapped around one end. 'Could that be the cylinder on the note?' I asked him.

'Well spotted.' Placing the object on the mantelpiece, he turned up the gas-jet for more illumination. 'The pestle, as it were. All we need do now is find the mortar.' He held the paper up to the light. 'Can't make head nor tail of these spots and rings.'

'Looks like a map of the solar system, don't you think?' I said, but he ignored me, rushing to his precious books. Once again I was outside his awareness. Piqued, I snatched up the object to examine it myself and it slipped from its wrapping.

A wave of dizziness passed over me. At first I put it down to whisky on an empty stomach and dropped into a chair. The cylinder was as smooth as marble. Something at once warm and cool whispered from it into my fingers. For the second time that evening I was lost to the world.

I seemed to see … *things* … within its radiance. Distant images glimmered, tugging at random emotions. I could not break free.

Was that a battery of cannon? And that, not a bird but something mechanical droning through the sky? It exploded, fragments raining onto a chaos of mud and human remains. A horse bolted, mane aflame. Rage, terror, and infinite loss. Then buildings sprang up, impossibly slender, only to be tumbled by an extraordinary flash of light. Strange creatures roared from stranger seas. Then I was swept along by music that would make angels weep. I lived a thousand lives before I dropped into mine. There was my mother; the gilded elephants at Peshawar; the taste of a mango I'd plucked from a tree. Then the bullet tearing into my flesh…

Next there were stars, only they didn't wheel across the sky in orderly procession. They fell towards me, colours changing from blue to red. Again that sense of longing for … for…

My knee throbbed cruelly. For a moment I saw myself in Harley Street, growing fat off ladies with the vapours. If only I hadn't got shot. Hadn't joined the damned Army in the first place. Hadn't met Holmes with his high-handed arrogance or the cursed artefact to be brought to such a pass…

A storm of outrage blasted through my mind then everything went dark. I was trapped without sight or sound in absolute black.

*

A slap from Holmes jolted me back to consciousness. Something cold soaked into my trousers: the whisky, I realised, because the glass lay shattered on the hearth. Beside it spun the cylinder, unbroken, in the firelight. Holmes scooped it up with my scarf and thrust it in a drawer. 'Watson? Watson! Are you all right, old fellow?'

I stammered something, I know not what. Indeed, the visions had been so intense I hardly knew where I was. I feigned a coughing-fit to mop my eyes. He brought me water then sat opposite, observing me closely as I tried to stop my hands trembling.

'So that's why Poole said not to touch it,' concluded Holmes. 'I wonder what it really is?'

Bertie Poole, it transpired, was a student at the Normal School of Science. 'His moustache is almost bigger than he is,' Holmes interjected sardonically. 'He claimed he made the cylinder last month by sheer accident. He was trying to produce a cheaper form of electric lighting. At first he bragged about it, including to Barnes. Despite Barnes not having a feather to fly with he put on a lavish party at which he introduced him to the delightful Miss Jensen. She tried to wheedle the cylinder from Poole but when he wouldn't let her have it, her watchers began to spy on him and made it clear Poole wasn't to see her again.

'Two days ago his notes disappeared. Suspecting the worst, he hid the cylinder. Then Barnes dropped ominous hints it might be in Poole's best interests to meet his uncle. And that fills in most of the gaps.'

'How the devil did a puny student manage to elude four men?' I expostulated. 'Besides, do you honestly think the kind of chap you describe could have invented such a marvel?'

'Possible, but unlikely. Let's see whether Miss Jensen can shed a little light… Does this paper tell you anything?'

'I'm not in the mood for guessing-games.'

'All right, old fellow,' Holmes patted my shoulder. 'In the morning, then. Oh, and keep your Service revolver handy. We may have visitors.'

*

I could not sleep. I heard him whistle up one of the urchins who called themselves the Baker Street Irregulars and send him off to the telegraph office. Alien sensations plagued me until I sought oblivion in whisky.

A shot brought me awake. I grabbed the pistol under my pillow and leaped to Holmes' rescue, only to be clubbed down from behind.

*

Head pounding, I woke to the jolting of a carriage. For a heart-stopping moment I believed I was blind, then moonlight filtered through coarse weave and I realised a sack was tied over my head. Nor could I speak since a rag had been knotted over my mouth. I recalled the attack. Had they killed Holmes? My pulse thrummed with fear for him and my own fate. I tried my bonds and was kicked for my pains. Two men at least, and I lay on the floor of the carriage between their feet. I smelt furs, and macassar, rank tobacco and sweat. An owl hooted; a fox barked. Not a word did the men utter.

At last we stopped and I was hauled out into the pre-dawn chill. They freed my legs and towed me, still blindfold, over rough country. More than once I tripped on stones or rimy grass until at last I was hurled into a pit. There they left me, hands behind my back, and a distant cock crowed thrice.

Even as their bootsteps faded I struggled sightlessly against the ropes round my arms and legs. Had Holmes bled to death? And Bertie Poole? How had Miss Jensen fared after her daring contact? Was she villain – or victim?

Groping around my dank prison I found rocks, earth and the skeleton of some poor moorland creature. I had begun to despair when a sharp stone grazed my knuckle. With my hands at my back it was awkward to scrape it against the tough hemp. Blood dripped from my wrists long before the strands parted. At last I managed to unfasten the hood, which at least let me see the chamber in which I lay. Soil and blocks of stone made up the walls, roots what passed for a ceiling. Grey light filtered down from far above. With it dripped a sad rain. The faster I tried to carve footholds, the faster the walls turned to mudslides. Then sleet began to ice them over.

I piled rocks into the hardening mud until finally I mounted my slippery steps. I leaped up to grasp a tangle of roots. They held my weight long enough for me to swing to another hold, one closer to the widest beams of light.

Afterwards I always claimed the patter of crumbling earth had covered the sound of his footsteps. He said it was my own feeble cursing. A shadow fell across the opening. His strong arm plunged down and seized me. For a sickening moment my bloody hand slipped in his, then he caught my sleeve and hove me up into the uncanny ruins of some abbey. With those other lives still scrabbling in my mind I half expected to meet the ghost of a monk – or goddess.

'Holmes! You're alive! However did you get here?'

'Never mind that. Let's get you back to the inn. I need you fit for action.' His voice was flat, his cheeks pale. Even by his usual standards his manner was callous.

'Thanks, old fellow. I say, are you all right?'

He shot me a haunted look and strode downhill. Had he, who considered emotion the enemy of reason; he who kept humanity at arm's length – had he too travelled, a phantom in other lives? No. Surely not. He told me not to touch it…

Snatching breakfast before a roaring fire, I listened while Holmes explained.

How he'd lured the intruders by leaving the cylinder in

plain sight then whipped it away from them, intent on trailing them. 'But instead the scoundrels knocked you out. My shot wounded one but I had to follow you.'

'Why those symbols? And how did you decipher them?'

'Obviously Miss Jensen feared they might read our alphabet as well as Cyrillic so she used hieroglyphs. She spelt out devil's stone on Venus with a sketch of a bowl and a gun. When they dragged you out I simply hid under the carriage.

'Quite a convoy we made – they have five prisoners in all, including a general, a researcher and a soprano. Until they knocked her out she shrieked *Fair Phantom Come I* to attract attention. As our carriage was in the rear I hid in the luggage -net. Wherever there was light I studied the note. Also your captors were quite talkative until you woke up.'

His tea-cup clattered and he put it down to disguise his tremors. 'I had a chat with the landlord when I ordered breakfast. According to him this village is rife with tales of druids' treasure and a phantom abbess who sucks out your soul. We must free Poole and the rest for a start. Then we need to find the other half.'

'The other half?'

'Didn't you look at the note? If my theory is right we have no time to lose.'

*

Who but Holmes would have understood the foreigners as he eavesdropped? Who but he would have been in a position to do so? I pondered these questions as he bribed the inn's 'ostlers. Once garbed in their smocks we followed the high street, all but deserted in the dismal weather, and turned into Venus Street.

'Venus!' I exclaimed.

'Assimilated with a Celtic goddess who had a magic bowl – the mortar or mushroom-cap, if you will. Half the treasure-hunters in England have riddled the hill looking for the Venus Bowl. There's a pagan temple underneath the remains of the abbey. Ah, that's what we want.' He nodded at an old-fashioned draper's. The name on the sign was Wells. Bull's eye panes made it hard to see past the frocks in the windows. 'You go in and keep them talking,' he said, and disappeared down a tradesman's driveway.

I patted the pistol he'd given me and plunged inside. No one came in answer to the bell so I called, 'Shop!'

Still the draper didn't come. There was not so much as a 'Back in five minutes' card despite the unlocked door. I felt watched as though ghostly observers inhabited the mannequins. And where was Holmes?

I grew worried. Lifting the flap of the counter, I tiptoed into the rear. Along with dust and dye I detected traces of rank fur and hair-oil. Gun in hand, I pushed open the doors one by one.

The cellar steps were dark. As I struck a match I was shoved down the stairs. Before I could recover my hands were tied behind me. They herded me into a subterranean passage whose odour of damp earth reminded me unpleasantly of graves but they merely forced me up the tunnel. And it was *up*, for twist though it might it always rose towards those haunted ruins. At last we turned into a pool of light and I gasped.

The chamber must have stood since the dawn of history. Stone henges supported a sagging roof and in the centre, what was unmistakably an altar squatted in a circle of candles.

And three men, before whom they hurled me to my knees.

'We await just one more.' It was the fellow in the middle who spoke, a bear of a man with oily hair and a thick Russian accent. A side-buttoned tunic of blue velvet strained to cover his bulk. His moth-eaten cape was flung back to show off a ceremonial sword. To left and right were two trembling youths, hands bound behind their backs.

I glanced behind me. Yes, my two captors were scarred and greasy Cossacks, both towering above me. Muffled voices from an alcove told me other prisoners still lived.

'Yes, we await your friend.' The Russian chuckled, issuing

fumes of ill-digested garlic. 'Each of you shall be the key for another's co-operation.'

He sat on a broken column and took a pull from his hip-flask. 'First, you will help Wells and Barnes move the altar,' he told me. 'Then we shall speak to the general.'

At his nod a scimitar slashed through our ties. 'Proceed. We want everything ready for your famous Mr Holmes.'

At sword-point we began to heave. Soon we were panting but couldn't shift the block. Its bulk was carved with stars like those inside the artefact, and symbols I had last seen in grease-paint. Below were words in Latin but mine was so rusty I could only make out 'she-devil's stone'. Even with one of the Cossacks to help we couldn't budge it. Finally, snapping orders to his remaining guard, the Russian himself joined in.

The altar grated aside, leaving a black hole. Slowly it filled with a pearly gleam. Everyone craned forward to peer at the treasure.

And that was when Holmes clubbed the other guard and stepped over his body, holding the cylinder aloft. It hummed. 'Looking for this, gentlemen?'

For all his bulk the Russian was fast. He leaped at Holmes but Holmes tossed the artefact at him. The Russian caught it bare-handed – and fell to his knees. Face contorted with terror, he was paralysed. I cracked the other Cossack's head on the altar.

'Watson, be a good chap and fish out the Venus Bowl, will you?' asked Holmes, seizing a blade that he didn't quite point at Wells and Barnes. 'Don't touch it, mind!'

'What about the prisoners?'

'In a moment. The vessel, man, the vessel!'

I ripped a piece from a Cossack's tunic and cautiously withdrew the iridescent cup. At Holmes' direction I fitted it over the cylinder in the Russian's deathly grip. I leaped back, feeling almost cheated when nothing happened but a faint brightening of the glow.

'Now, Mr Barnes,' Holmes began, 'shall we talk to your

uncle the General?'

In the candle-light his blade encouraged the trembling Englishmen towards a recess.

'What about the count?' I asked.

'He's safe enough.'

'Are you sure?'

'Quite sure, but tie him up with his sash if it makes you feel better.'

It did, though I was careful not to touch the devil's stones, which cast a ghastly pallor over his features. He flopped like an unstrung puppet while I bound him with his sash.

The General, hands still lashed to a column, was choleric and, once ungagged, vocal in his demands to be released. 'I want my rightful property!' he bellowed.

Holmes turned to the younger Barnes. 'How much do you and your uncle owe?'

It was the last thing the boy had expected. 'What?'

'Look at you. Fine clothes worn to shreds, boots ditto, and you apparently owe Mr Poole, or rather Mr Wells, for attempted theft, not to mention the wrecking of his laboratory. And here's your uncle, left the Service under a cloud – nothing proved, of course, but there's talk in the clubs – without a ha'penny to his name. Luckily for the pair of you, an arms manufacturer from Minsk just happens to be staying nearby.'

'It's got nothing to do with arms dealers!' exclaimed Poole, Wells, or whatever his name was. 'It's a time machine!'

'Don't be an ass!' retorted Barnes. 'It's a sort of phonograph that shows you how to make weapons.'

The general kicked him.

Holmes smiled coldly. 'Which you intended to sell to the Czar, Mr Barnes. Besides stupidity, it seems theft and treason run in your family's veins. You teased the Russian bear and when you couldn't produce the goods, you let him take you prisoner.'

All this while the artefacts grew brighter in the hands of

the inert count. Holmes flicked him the merest glance then searched the shadows for Miss Jensen.

In fact there were two women. One, quite elderly, had gone off in a faint. Wells sprang to her, slapping her face and crying, 'Auntie Vi?' The other was, as suspected, Fanny Jensen. Holmes pulled the muffling folds from her mouth. I noticed he didn't immediately untie her either. In his odd, stilted manner he acknowledged her warning and asked how she had come to be involved.

'My ... employer ... heard rumours of a new weapon and sent me to charm it out of Mr Wells. Not being English myself I had no qualms about his acquiring it on behalf of another power, but—'

'So why did you send me that warning?'

'Warning?' I ejaculated.

'Indeed, Mr Watson.' Sitting knees under her chin against the chilly stone, she smiled up at me. 'The dear count had begun to mistrust me, and with good reason. You see, once I'd inveigled darling Bertie into letting me play with his new toy I knew it was neither a time machine nor the plans for some dread arsenal.'

'What did *you* see in it, then?' Wells snapped.

'A galaxy of knowledge not meant for a world where jumped-up peasants sell arms.'

Suddenly the chamber was lit with a fierce brilliance. The blood in the Russian's hands flared red round the devil's stones. Though his face remained slack his mouth opened. A ghastly vapour issued forth. 'Thank you, Mr Holmes,' it whispered, though I swear the Russian's lips never moved. Nor was there an echo. Indeed, it was as if the artefact spoke in my mind.

Or, rather, painted moving pictures. Its hot, far homeworld, coloured with its tortured longing; the memory of long-ago excitement as it set out upon its quest for knowledge; its crippling fall to chilly, wet England when it flew too far from the radiance of a sun. So cold, so cold it was that it could no longer fly, though it wasn't dead by any means. Lost. Lost and stuck, and used by tiny minds. We watched a British chieftain seize its power to conquer his neighbours. But his tribe could not hold out against the might of Rome so a robed figure – a druid or Venus? – hid both parts separately. And the being was well and truly trapped.

A torrent of emotions swept through us. I was the crone with her joint-ail, terrified lest enemies pervert bowl and cylinder, condemning her tribe to eternal torment. Each piece lay despairing in endless night, growing weaker in their chilly tombs.

The sun! I was the penniless student, hunting treasure to brighten two months' penance behind the counter of his aunt's dreary shop, the one whose fingers scrabbled me from the earth, naked without my shell, the one whose earnest beliefs conjured scenes of a terrible future.

Roses on Mother's table, rajahs in their silks.

I was the Russian, prisoned in terror; I knew the dazzler who was blackmailing Barnes. Most of all I was the being, no longer amputated but whole inside the shell that was its servant and its home. Free!

It stopped, as if to scrutinise us, body and soul. Except for the count, we came slowly back to ourselves.

'The being offers too much knowledge. We cannot let such a plague loose upon mankind,' breathed Miss Jensen into the silence.

'Unfortunately,' replied Holmes, resting the tip of his blade on the spotty nephew's throat, 'I don't think Barnes and his cohorts would agree. Suggestions?'

Miss Jensen shrugged. 'Kill them or let them go. I've already laid on a little reception for them just in case.' She raised her bound wrists and pouted. 'Once Bertie whispered he was hunting for a second piece, this was the only way I could think of to make Grigori bring me.' She was practically hissing now. 'I want both devil's stones buried. Or at the bottom of the sea.' She summoned a smile and went on, 'Personally, I rather favour Nice at this time of year. Grigori has just bought me a villa, though he doesn't know it yet. Do drop in if you're passing.'

Silently Holmes motioned me to cut her bonds.

With a 'Thanks ever so. Ta ta,' she waggled her fingers and glided out.

'Well really!' exclaimed Wells. 'She's a spy! She *kissed* me!' Flustered, he continued, 'And I don't care what she said! I *did* see the future in it.'

'You saw what you believed you would see.' Holmes gazed from Wells to Barnes and his seething uncle. 'I think we'll send our friends here on a little cruise. A certain sea-captain owes me a favour. As for the general, I believe the being has something to add.'

The being in the pearly stones hummed. Oblivious to Well's indignation, the old military man stuck a finger in his ear as though not quite sure he was hearing right. 'Sea-cruise? Just what I said. Thank you, steward. Don't think much of this waiting-room. How soon can we see our berths?'

'Soon, general,' said Holmes.

I jerked my chin at the motionless count, lurid in the crimson light. 'What about – him?'

'He's not going anywhere.'

Holmes was right. Smoke belched from the Russian's mouth, then a tongue of flame. Flesh began to bubble and char. Holmes snatched the artefact from those blackening fingers, Wells hauled up his aunt and we fled, leaving the others to follow if they could.

*

The Cossacks didn't escape the conflagration. Thus it was that some days later we bid farewell to General Barnes and his nephew, who trotted up the gangplank of the SS *Pacific Trader* like a pair of performing dogs. 'Quiet, ain't they?' remarked the scurrilous captain. 'Let's see if they're as tractable climbing the rigging round Cape Horn.' With that he stumped aboard and the ship set sail amid screaming gulls.

That left Holmes, Wells and myself standing awkwardly on the quay. Wells had insisted upon carrying the valise containing the artefact but try as he might, he couldn't get it to communicate with him. Holmes meantime was more otherworldly than ever. Frankly I was worried.

'I take it your aunt has recovered?' I asked, taking the portmanteau.

Reluctantly Wells let it go. 'Doesn't remember a thing. Fancy missing all that! I've a good mind to write it up for the papers!'

The portmanteau hummed unhappily. We all glanced down. Holmes frowned at it and shook his head. 'Not all of it.'

I pled, 'But he's so earnest. It means so much to him.'

A longer tone vibrated. At once Wells looked at us in bafflement. 'Do I know you?'

'You banged your head,' declared Holmes. 'Nothing newsworthy at all. Do you remember your name yet?'

'Poole, is it? No, Bertie Wells.'

'I admire your social conscience, Mr Wells,' Holmes said. 'You kept hold of it though you couldn't recall your name. Three days have passed for us. For you it was but a single step through time. That'll be a story to dine out on.'

We watched him go, slow and thoughtful at first, then he burst into a run. The word 'magazine' was all that drifted back.

'Fancy a trip to Seville, Watson?'

'Not if you're going to spoon with that – that *thing*. Worse than your cocaine.'

'You're right. Seville's far too prone to rain at this time of year. Let's make it Morocco.' He pulled back his cuff. 'Here, this should pay for it.'

I looked at the golden torque on his forearm. It had a nacreous sheen. For a heartbeat I was a phantom watching a bloody-chested Saxon enjoying the spoils of war. Holmes let his sleeve fall and the vision faded.

In my grip the portmanteau was silent now. Holmes knelt to secure it with a strap and padlock, but somehow the thing radiated the joy of coming freedom. 'Some birds —' Holmes flashed an echo of his grin of yore ' —some birds need the sun to fly.'

I couldn't help myself. 'But I thought you'd be dying to know what it's seen. Who it's been.'

His smile went out. He shook his head as he turned and trudged away. Just for a moment I wished I'd never laid eyes on my best friend. I was ashamed to find myself hoping he hadn't felt my life of petty resentments.

That he hadn't heard the cock crow.

Eyes of Day, Eyes of Night

'That way, I said!' The crack of a rifle underlined the harsh command.

In the canoe behind, Verity Fanshaw jerked awake. Stunned, she watched her so-called Red Cross guide send another round past the head paddler's ear. Panicked birds screeched up from the jungle.

For a suspenseful moment the other Burura paddlers stopped work. At once the Amazon's mighty current began to push the boats back downstream.

Cursing, Judson shot the elder in the lead canoe. Before Verity's horrified gaze the innocent man tumbled into the river. The waters seethed and turned red as a thousand piranhas ate him alive. His dying screech drilled through her brain. Hastily the Burura made for the hidden channel.

*

Verity could hardly believe she'd been kidnapped. And not even by head hunters, as her mother had not so laughingly threatened. *'It wasn't meant to be like this!'* she thought. *'It's 1934, for heaven's sake! After all I've been through just to get a medical school to take a 'mere woman'!'* And now she was a 'proper, grown-up doctor' as her father mocked, she thought she deserved a neat, safe adventure. Working for the Red Cross would fit the bill admirably, *and* show her parents the world beyond Rochdale wasn't such a frightening place after all. What she hadn't expected was being stolen away to the back of beyond by a murderer with a loaded gun. Her mother's warnings of white slavery brought shivers down her spine.

Judson yelled, 'Don't worry, *Doctor*. You'll be fine – so long as you keep on my good side.'

The three canoes slipped through tangles of foliage. It was like entering a ghost-train. Jungle blocked off the sky, making it hard to see. Verity tried to shield herself from the creepers dangling in her face. Although the rain had stopped she couldn't avoid the heavy drips from the canopy. Accented by the screams of animals, the hot green gloom whined with insects. Something crawled up her arm. In a panic she brushed the fat bug away. Where was Tarzan when you needed him?

Verity peered into her pocket-mirror, not at all impressed by her green eyes and finely modelled lips. Auburn curls stuck to the perspiration on her lightly freckled cheeks. 'Stop being such a wet nelly!' Verity chided her reflection, reaching for her powder compact. She was sick to death of screen heroines whose only line was, 'Help me! Help me! I'm tied to the railroad track,' but from back here, weaponless, there wasn't a thing she could do. Breathing deeply, she tried to work out what on earth was going on. Why wasn't Judson taking her to the Mission? Not a week before he'd stood on the dock at Manaus, humbly turning his hat in his hands as he said, 'Don't you fret, little lady. I'll take real good care of you. *And* the supplies.'

Huh! Good care indeed. Would she ever see Santa Maria? Surely if Judson could afford three canoes and twelve paddlers, he didn't need to steal medicines? And if that's all he wanted, why hadn't he just tipped her overboard days ago? As though her eyelids were a movie-theatre screen, fates worse than death painted themselves in colours she wished were black and white.

*

It took her far longer than she would have liked to jeer herself out of her funk. She felt pretty much on an even keel again – until the canoe parted a curtain of lianas. Right by her ear a jewel-bright bird struggled in a web until the spider bit it again. Her screech rang through the forest, bringing forth a cacophony of howls. Instantly she clapped her hands over her mouth. From up ahead came Judson's mocking laughter.

Crimson, she clamped her lips and resisted the urge to brush frantically at her blouse. At least she couldn't see the g -g-giant spider any more. How much longer was this going to go on? What did Judson want? And when did it get so … creepy all of a sudden?

Verity felt invisible eyes staring at her. Abruptly she turned her attention to her surroundings. Steam was swirling from the waters, veiling the trees until they were no more than dim shapes. The low sun burnished the river until it looked like cloth of gold. Shadows brown as peat rippled below the overhanging boughs.

Some movement caught her eye and she started. 'River-haze,' she told herself firmly.

But she knew it had moved too swiftly for that. What if it was a jaguar? Or – she gulped – a boa constrictor?

*

Daylight struck her, dazzling off widening ripples. She saw Judson, black against sun-sparked waters, urge the paddlers towards an island. Verity glanced around to see if there were any means of escape.

The armed villain behind her had nodded off, head resting against his rifle. In front of him was the kitchen crate: a cook's knife with a broken tip stuck out of it. Keeping an eye on the American, she lay back, yawning and stretching her arms behind her head. It was uncomfortable but it meant she could palm the blade. When she was sure Judson was looking the other way, she slipped it into her pocket, wincing as she tore through the lining of her jodhpurs to make an impromptu sheath. She looked back and the paddler behind nodded furtive approval. His face was so tattooed it looked like he was wearing a jaguar mask.

She fingered the cheap vegetable knife. What could she do against an armed scoundrel and his gang of desperadoes? Judson sat at the stern of the lead canoe, one of his thugs in each of the others. Every idea that teemed in her brain swooped her from hope to despair as she realised all she could do was wait. She was helpless and she hated it.

All too soon they tied up at a ramshackle landing-stage. Behind it a collection of huts disintegrated along the bank. She'd hoped there'd be a policeman, or at least some benevolent tribal leader who'd rescue her, but at first glance the street was empty.

Unwilling to give in to disappointment, she looked again and saw frightened eyes peeping from doorways. The villagers cringed as a huge white man swaggered past them. Bandoliers crossed over his grubby shirt. He rushed at a youth, making spooky noises, and laughed as the boy fled. As his boot heels rang on the planks, he punched Jud's shoulder too hard to be friendly. His eyes looked like flint. 'Where the hell have you been?'

'Calm down, Walt! The old geezer's still alive, ain't he? I run into a bit of a tight spot but I'm here now. You just wait and see what I got.' Judson shuffled away from the big man to drag her onto the jetty. She tumbled on the planks at his feet, glaring dizzily up at them both. 'See?' Jud said ingratiatingly. 'I lassoed supplies *and* a genuine medical-type doctor.'

Verity struggled upright, sublimely unaware of the smudge on her tip-tilted nose. She faced the man with the bullets strapped across his chest. 'Sir, I am English and my presence has been registered at the British Embassy. This man is a liar and a crook! I can reward you if you take me back to Manaus or on to the mission at Santa Maria.'

'Button it, Your Queenship.' Walt loomed over her. 'We might need your hands but —' he pulled out a machete ' — we don't need your tongue.'

*

They began to haul her towards the biggest hut. She shrugged loose and stalked on, only too aware the white men were laughing behind her back. Whipping round, she shot them a poisonous glare.

It took her a moment to work out what she was seeing.

One of the Westerners – a Cockney, by the sound of it – gestured to the surviving paddlers. If anything he looked rougher than the other two, his massive, scarred face failing to hide the frustration that burned in his eyes. 'Careful with that!' he yelled, jabbing his rifle stock towards a Burura's head.

The paddler threw himself flat. Oddly, he seemed more worried about the kick that followed. He twisted to avoid it and screamed, panic-stricken, when the boot barely grazed his cheek.

The Cockney kicked him in the ribs for good measure and strode away. All up the riverbank tribesfolk darted out of sight as he passed. A small face on his *dustbin* of a head twisted into a sour arrogance. His brutality made her ashamed to be English.

She went back to the fallen Burura, surprised his companions hadn't stopped to pick him up. In fact they stepped aside, not meeting the man's gaze.

Verity knelt to examine him and he cringed. 'Don't be afraid, sir. I'm only trying to help.'

He scrambled to his feet and fled. Judson strode back to tow her onwards.

'Wha— What—?' She couldn't help looking up at him as if for reassurance. 'I'm a doctor, for goodness' sake! They're supposed to come to me, not run away! What's the matter with them?'

He scratched his bristles and forced an unconvincing smile. 'Their shaman cursed us. Now not a one of 'em'll touch us even though Larry wasted 'im. You'd think a guy's juju would run out once he's dead, wouldn't you?' He said loudly, as if to convince himself, 'But I ain't worried.

'Anyways, that ain't why I brung you here. You got a real patient this time, one that's been just a-prayin' for a sawbones.'

*

'In there,' he grunted, and steered Verity into a hut. It was a huge oval, only letting in daylight through the doorway and the smoke-hole in the roof. From the shadows to her left came disjointed cries of fear.

As her eyes adjusted she walked towards the sound. Right against the eaves she came to a low bed, no more than strings across a wooden frame. It had been tipped on its side. Behind it cowered a babbling old man.

'He's off his head again, damn' it,' said Walt, pushing her back with the barrel of his rifle. 'Don't do nothin' foolish, Verity.'

'My friends call me Verity. *You* can call me Doctor Fanshaw.'

Hiding a grin, Judson righted the cot and dropped the oldster on it.

'To examine him I'll need light and clean water. Filtered and boiled.' Verity folded her arms. 'And my bag.'

To her annoyance Walt began to laugh. Judson snapped, 'You wouldn't think it was so damn' funny if you'd had to put up with Her Almightiness for the last ten days. All right, all right, I'll get your damned water.'

'Damned *boiled* water,' she replied, and went spinning as Walt gave her a slap. At least the water was steaming when it came.

*

Judson had a half-naked teenage girl hold the torch. Its circle of light showed a wrinkled man with a greying blond moustache. He too wore little more than a loincloth, though his pale feet showed he usually wore the boots she'd just tripped over in the gloom. There was a massive swelling in his belly. Though she was as gentle as she knew how, he groaned when Verity palpated it. She put a thermometer between his lips and whipped it out immediately because his teeth began to clatter on the fragile glass. But she'd found out all she needed to know: his fever was mounting because his appendix was about to burst.

She swallowed. 'If I don't operate now he'll die. And if I do operate he still might die.'

Walt stared at her granite-faced. 'He dies, missy, and

you'll wish you had.'

The Burura girl closed her eyes when Verity made the first incision and the torch beam wavered. Walt smacked her head. It sent the light dancing across the floor.

'Leave her alone!' Verity snapped. 'She's terrified, poor thing. Don't you want me to see what I'm doing?'

The half-naked girl didn't understand the words but shot Verity a grateful look when Walt backed off. That left her free to carry out her first solo operation. She'd done her best to make the environment as sterile as possible. She'd even thought of rigging up some sort of canopy in case something scuttled out of the thatch overhead, but when she came to think about it, she couldn't hear anything except her patient's tortured breathing. Outside, the silence was so loud it made her ears ring. It was as though nothing lived out there. No foxes, no frogs, not a single bird – though until they came here the jungle had resounded. Now it felt as though the whole world was awaiting a cataclysm. Verity broke out in goosebumps.

Nevertheless her patient's need absorbed her. At last she stitched and dressed the wound. All she could do now was hope the poor old man lasted through the night.

The girl brought her a leaf holding bits of hot meat. Verity worried it down, trying not to wonder what the meat was. Fighting off sleep, she stared at the darkness.

Moonlight danced through the smoke-hole. Judson snored across one doorway; Walt kept guard beside him. Every now and then one of the other men would pass. She recognised the Cockney by the misproportioned head silhouetted against the fire outside. They called the string bean Larry Loco. And all of them were drinking.

She kept vigil, hoping her patient recovered, until, against her will, sleep wrapped her in its welcoming cocoon.

*

Fingers on her face shocked her awake. Verity started; the old man hissed, 'Ssh! They're still asleep.' His accent was upper-crust English, a notch or two more cut-glass than her own. It was all the more startling now she could see his tribal tattoos.

Kneeling beside him in the grey light of false dawn, she was delighted to find his fever had broken. 'How are you doing, sir?'

'Keep your voice down,' he whispered. 'I've got to warn you. They'll make me lead them to the Temple of the Jaguar. If they get their hands on it we're both dead, and half the world with us.'

'Better not let them—'

'They've already killed the Elder Council. Next it'll be the rest of the Burura. They'll save Quenimil and my Iriyani to last. But they don't know what they're getting themselves into.' He coughed, then groaned, grabbing at his stitches.

Verity helped him sip water laced with aspirin and woundwort. He lay back, eased.

'So—' she started.

'No, let me talk while I can. Hector.' His eyes searched her face, looking for comprehension. 'Professor Alfred Hector.'

'I'm sorry, Professor. I don't know the name.'

He sighed. 'Forgive me for my arrogance. I'd rather been hoping for something more on the lines of 'Doctor Livingstone, I presume.' The Royal Society obviously lost interest in me long ago. I'm mad to keep on hoping. I was sure the last lot of specimens I sent would have got through. Arenluka—' she didn't quite catch the name '—took them himself. When I heard you were English I thought he'd brought you back with him.'

Their soft voices had woken the Burura girl. She crept closer. Her hair, cut straight across, shimmered like raven's wings in the nascent dawn. What really surprised Verity, though, were the girl's emerald eyes. She and Professor Hector talked rapidly in Burura.

'My daughter Quenimil.' He squeezed her hand and spoke to her briefly. Slim and bare-breasted, she glided to a bundle hanging from the rafters.

'You see, miss—'

'Verity Fanshaw, MD.'

'Is that right? Well, Doctor Verity Fanshaw, thank you. I didn't think I was going to last the night.'

Quenimil came back with a woven bag. She extracted a glob of smelly paste and reached towards Verity's forehead.

Verity jerked back.

'Let her do it, Doctor Fanshaw,' croaked Hector. 'You're going to need it. It was the last batch poor old Jalkit made before they killed him.'

The paste was greeny-grey and it itched. Every time Verity made the slightest movement Quenilin hissed between her teeth so she swallowed her questions. The sooner this was over, the better. She wondered what Tarzan would do if some stranger wanted to paste tribal marks on him. That talkie she'd seen him in a couple of years ago had made her dream of Johnny Weissmuller. It was the whole tanned chest thing. And the chivalry. And not at all what was happening now.

After endless moments Hector's daughter sat back on her heels. She said something her father translated. 'You bear the mark of the Jaguar Lady. These cads are making me lead them to Her valley. You must respect Her because she will swallow all unbelievers.'

From the doorway came a rude noise.

'*Shh!*' hissed Hector. 'They're waking up. How much time can you give me, Doctor?'

She looked her puzzlement. On the other side of the hut Judson stood, yawning and looking out at the eerily silent jungle.

Hector gripped her hand. 'Do you understand?' he whispered urgently. 'The longer you can keep them from making me lead them to the Eyes, the better our chances. Even forty-eight hours might be enough.'

At Jud's approach Hector collapsed on his rag of a pillow and started breathing noisily through his mouth.

'How soon can we move him?' the gang-leader asked gruffly.

'Move my patient?' Verity leaped to her feet. 'I only operated a few hours ago! It's a miracle he's still alive and you want to move him?'

Jud thrust his face into hers, his morning breath rank. 'He's gonna take us on a little trip, and you're coming too. And if he isn't ready to travel I'm gonna start shooting Burura until he *is* ready.'

'He needs at least a week.'

'We can't afford to wait more 'n another day.'

Verity pinned him with a glare. 'Why not?'

'Because the — Never mind why not. He's guiding us the day after tomorrow or else.'

'Or else what? You can hardly kill him for not doing something that would kill him, not when you need him alive.'

It baffled Jud. He found himself agreeing to three days.

'That's three days of rest, now,' she stipulated, 'or the wound will tear open and your guide will die.'

Swarthy face set in a hate-filled snarl, Jud crowded her. 'You'd better make sure you've stitched him real tight 'cause he's takin' us to the Eyes of Day three days from now or I'll start taking an interest in your welfare. Once we've got our mitts on 'em, he can bleed to death all he likes.' He shuddered. 'This place gives me the creeps.'

*

When he'd left Verity unwound the dressing – and gasped. Under the lint a grey and crimson mess dripped thickly from the wound. 'Whatever did you do that for?' she snapped. 'Do you want to kill him?'

The girl hid her face. Angrily Verity swabbed at the bleeding sore – and discovered that it wasn't blood at all. The skin beneath showed scarcely a pucker and the stitches were ready to come out. She stared in disbelief.

'Gently, doctor,' Hector said. 'Quenimil knows what she's doing. She studied with the shaman.'

Sullenly challenging Verity's gaze, the girl patted the stodge back into place.

Her father continued, 'Just don't let them know I'm doing all right.' He winked and began to moan.

*

'You should be in the moving pictures!' she whispered to Hector as they slipped through the third afternoon. He'd feigned delirium so convincingly they were still in the village by the river.

But with every hour that passed, their captors grew more tense. They snapped at her and Quenimil and cursed Hector and each other. Outside the rain was like a cataract. Larry wanted a drink to calm down.

'You had your share!' snapped Jud. 'Take a nap, why don't you?'

For the next half hour Verity and the Professor hid their smirks as each of the desperadoes pretended to snooze, lifting his head every now and then to see if the others were asleep yet so they could raid the last bottles of bourbon.

'Awright, awright,' Walt snapped in the end. 'If you're that damn' nervy I'll break out the booze. But don't blame me when it's all gone.'

*

'Your turn to stand guard, Cock Sparrow,' ordered Walt.

'No it ain't! I took first watch last night. 'Sides, who's gonna be out on a night like this?'

'Anyone with a boat, numbnuts!' came back Larry.

Jud slapped his thigh and chortled. 'Tain't who's out there that's got him sucking his dummy. It's *what!*'

'You calling me a coward?' the Cockney said in a voice like gravel.

Walt roared, 'Cut it out! That little bit of bother Jud had in Manaus was one of his old pals who figured he was up to somethin'. Jud, bein' the idiot that he is, clobbered him but left him alive. So now Jimmy Half-hand's mob is likely on our tail. You want them getting the Eyes before we do?'

Muttering, the Cockney dashed out into the downpour to stand a lonely guard.

*

Mist began to billow into the hut. Verity cuddled closer to the fire that Quenimil kept effortlessly ablaze. Oddly, the men's fire wouldn't stay alight.

Walt, Jud and Larry ceased their bickering, all three of them crowding round the doorway to scan the night, restlessly seeking the danger they all felt was there. Head down, Jud scuttled to the nearest hut and came back, wringing wet. 'They're gone! Every last one of 'em!'

As though a tap had been turned off the rain stopped. Even the sound of dripping leaves was muffled by the writhing vapours. Verity felt the men's fear creep over her, chilly skeletal fingers that made the fine hairs stand up at her nape. She found herself holding her breath.

Rifles at the hip, the gang kept their anxious watch for what seemed like hours. At last Larry burst out, 'I gotta have a cigarette. This silence is driving me nuts!'

'Whaddya mean, silence?' barked Walt. Ain't that drip-drip-drip enough for you? Drummin' on the roof until it makes a man think there's things out there a-comin' for him that he'd never hear?'

Larry's eyes widened madly. Dropping to the floor, he stuck his head out but the fog was so heavy he could hardly breathe, let alone see. He pulled back inside, hands shaking as he cupped a match. 'Listen, Walt. You hear any of them night critters we usually hear? There ain't no birds, no insects, no nothing.

'Which means there's somethin' out there. Somethin' big enough to scare the whole damn' jungle.'

Jud snorted. 'Ah, did something scare de poor little cry baby?'

Larry pointed past the doorframe. The others hesitated, not sure whether this was some kind of tit-for-tat. 'Come *on!*' he hissed.

They strove to see out without being seen, but the curvature of the doorway made it hard. Walt jerked his head, silently commanding Jud to risk a proper look.

A hideous scream froze them before Jud was two strides

out of the door. A fox ran through the gap, leaving nothing but its stink and a scrap of material that fell at Jud's feet. On it was a painted jaguar with eyes of emerald green.

Jud backpedalled, tripping over. Larry yelled and peppered the jungle with shots. Automatically Walt blasted away, too.

Walt shouted, 'Quit it!' and kicked Larry's gun away.

Larry's fist shot out but Jud stomped a foot on his back. Into the sudden absence of flying lead Walt said urgently, 'Jesus, Larry! Whoever it was, they'll be long gone.'

Jud sniggered. 'Yeah, Larry, what you thinkin'? Save your ammo for –' he made his voice quaver like a kid at Halloween ' – the jaguar.'

Larry crawfished, his sudden movement tossing Jud aside. 'Don't say that!' Larry's eyes flicked to the trees. Glittering with terror, they wheeled insanely to stare at Walt. 'Don't let him say that, boss.'

'Why not?' asked Walt, with a hint of a chuckle.

''Cause whatever's out there, it's treed the whole damn jungle. It's got the Indios more scared than they are of us, and that's sayin' somethin'. So don't you laugh at me, Jud. Don't you laugh!' The two men grappled. Walt, dancing around to try and club Larry, hit Jud by mistake.

'That's me, you idiot!'

Larry leaped back, a feral grimace on his face. 'You're all against me. You ain't gonna let me see one red cent of that treasure, are you? You just needed another sacrifice for the Jaguar's Eyes. The old man told me.'

Jud finally managed to land a blow on the madman's skull. 'Shut up, damn you! Listen!'

Far off, the last echoes of the gunshots rolled against the mountains and died away. Amongst the drips came a Cockney cry: 'You bastards! You've shot me!' Then there was no sound at all.

*

Walt tied up Larry, then stood guard while Jud threw the Cockney's body in the river. When Larry awoke he kept begging, 'Untie me, goddamn it! Whatever I said when I was drunk, I didn't mean it.'

They set off when sunrise was barely a promise. Ghosts of mist played hide and seek through the trees. Verity and Quenimil were forced to carry the litter because every other Burura had gone. Jud didn't trust Larry behind him so he brought up the rear. Walt and a penitent Larry blazed the trail.

At first they had to wade in places but the path soon led them uphill. The long, steep climb had Verity panting despite her years on the lacrosse team at Bart's.

That feeling of being watched persisted. Deepened, even. More than once Larry spun, jerking his weapon to his shoulder as though he'd seen someone. Or something. The graveyard silence had them all jumpy.

At last they arrived at a cavern high on the mountain.

*

After a hasty meal, Walt booted them back on their feet. 'Come on, old man. We haven't got all day.'

'Can't you let him have a rest?' protested Verity.

'He's lyin' down, ain't he? Now shut up. We been here too long already so, no—' he parodied her voice '—we can't let him have a rest. Now shut your yap and get movin'.'

Hefting the pack of medicines, Verity followed the group into the rocky maw. As the darkness grew, so did a stink. It was sharp with ammonia.

Larry lit a lantern, Walt the failing torch. As the lights shone through the stygian cave a rustling and squeaking began. Holding her hat on tightly, Verity ducked as thousands of bats blundered past. She was pleased to see the winged squadrons scratch and claw at the white men, giving Verity, Professor Hector and the Burura girl a wide berth.

Shrieking, Larry hacked off his shirttail and lit it at his lamp. The cotton burst into flames, sending the creatures skittering upwards like burnt paper from a bonfire. With a concerted squealing the bats wheeled out into the daylight.

Her loathing of the gunmen lost its battle with her

Hippocratic Oath. 'Those wounds will be filthy. Let me —'

'Get the hell away from me, you witch!' shrilled Larry. 'I seen the way you made them bats attack us. Get movin', Professor, or we'll cut your daughter's nose off.'

*

Through grottoes that held frozen waterfalls of stalagmites the Professor led them. Higher they walked, ever upwards through tunnels as smooth and round as pipes. Their walls sparkled in the lamplight.

'Emeralds!' yelled Larry, and set to hacking at the rock with his knife.

Hector intoned, 'The jaguar won't let you take her eyes.'

'Ah shut up, you old windbag. Look, Walt! I got an emerald!'

The Professor chuckled. 'Suit yourselves, gentlemen. I look forward to enjoying your regrets.'

*

Ahead Verity glimpsed the first hints of daylight. On the very threshold Larry fell to his knees, dropping the torch. The tinkle of broken glass was the only sound. Everyone dashed to see what had stunned him so.

As she ran, images of Challenger's *Lost World* dazzled Verity's imagination. What she saw when she reached Larry was no movie's mechanical dinosaur. Instead a jaguar a hundred feet tall climbed the opposite peak. Her heart stopped – until she realised the jaguar didn't move.

Larry curled over, keening. Verity knelt beside him. His skin quivered beneath her touch. 'It's all right, Larry. It's only a carving. It's not real.'

Hector chuckled deep in his throat. 'Oh, she is, Larry. The Jaguar Goddess is very, very real. And anyone who seeks to cheat her better watch out. They don't call them the Eyes of Day for nothing.'

The valley lay below them, perfectly round. Wooded peaks sank to grassland ringing a circle of blue lake. At some point an avalanche had torn away the tree-cover opposite. Maybe a happy coincidence had formed the rough outline from thrusting basalt, but someone had carved out a perfect copy of the beast. And painted its claws gold.

And put in two enormous emeralds to form its eyes.

*

The Professor waited until they'd stopped babbling. 'Well, you go-getters – I believe that's the American term – can see exactly where you're headed. Off you go now. Chop chop! You don't need us anymore.'

Verity and Quenimil lifted the litter, ready to leave.

And put it down as Walt aimed his gun at them. 'Ah but we do, Professor. And these fine ladies. Without that shaman, you're our best chance of gettin' in and back. And you don't want to talk to Jimmy Half-hand – so get movin'!'

*

They walked down between lush greenery that could have hidden a thousand jaguars. The only sound was their slithering descent. In the middle of the bowl a ziggurat rose from the lake, strange markings on its sides. Verity squinted but had to wait until they'd gone down another two hundred feet before she could see it clearly.

She stopped, amazed. What she thought were paintings were creepers, grown into pictures that told a story. It was mirrored on the glassy blue waters.

The images were in pairs. Men cut down mountain pines; rain and snow wash the soil away. Heat the air, melt the ice and the world floods. Over and over she saw poisoned earths and all the ways to get there.

But Walt, Larry and Jud walked past without a second glance.

'Please!' Professor Hector sounded desperate. 'We must all pray at the shrine if there's to be any hope of leaving the valley. Truly, we must!'

'If it means that much to you, you can have five minutes – on the shore! Don't want you rowin' off without us, do we?'

*

Verity saw Larry twitch and knew he was becoming increasingly unstable. Either he had no energy or he shouted and cringed. Walt took him for a walk so Jud could have a smoke in peace.

They put Hector's litter by the crystal blue lake, and knelt by him. 'Behold!' he said. 'The Temple of the Jaguar's Home. Let us pray.

'Oh Great Mother of the Earth,' intoned the Professor, his voice swooping like an old-time vicar. 'Oh Lady, fierce as a jaguar, bringer of life and death, let us respect you and the land wherein you dwell. For if we do not, you will punish us. Ice will be our world, or a desert burning under the naked sun.' In a hiss he added, 'Has he gone yet? Right. When I tell you, stand still. No matter what happens, stand still. Don't even yell.'

Jud threw aside his stub. 'What you whisperin' about over there?'

The Professor stood up, shaky but determined. He looked surprisingly chipper and Verity couldn't work out why. Some quality of the light brought out the jaguar tattoos on his tanned blond skin. Now he was recovering, he'd gained weight and rehydrated. As he began to address the thieves he didn't look so old after all. *No older than Father, at any rate. Eurgh! What a thought!*

'That the Earth will punish you for your blasphemy,' he said. 'Those who take the Eyes of Day, beware the Eyes of Night.'

*

They toiled up the slope towards the massive image. It would remain forever branded in Verity's memory: a vast, leaping feline, bounding towards the river cascading almost from the peak. It glittered, dark and uncanny, and the westering sun brought a sinister glint to the jewelled eyes.

The sun was sinking below the mountain-crest behind them now, casting a shadow that slid up the slope faster than the puny humans could climb it. A sudden wind blew chill on Verity's back. She glanced behind and started to scramble faster, irrationally afraid to let the shadow catch her. All around there came a sudden rustling noise, a million tiny clicks all pattering as one. She looked over her shoulder again.

Walt and Larry didn't seem to have noticed anything. 'Leave the litter,' Walt grated, gesturing with his gun. 'The broads can drag you. You ain't gonna bleed to death between now and me holding those gorgeous green babies in my own two hands. But you *will* if you play me any more o' your tricks. Get me them Eyes or your daughter's gonna scream for a long, long time.'

'On your own head be it.' The Professor draped his arms over the girls' shoulders, and they began the arduous climb towards the lowest part of the Jaguar: her great, golden-clawed feet.

Once they began to climb the stone beast's body, the clicking noise came back again. The rock felt strange beneath Verity's fingers: the surface made of millions of shiny bubbles that together made a surface she could clamber up. Tiny sparks shifted before her gaze, glimmering like insect eyes. The cliff grew steeper. She was too frightened to look down. But the pressure of unseen gazes magnified a thousand-fold. She gritted her teeth to begin her ascent of the neck, ignoring a whiff of acid. Above, Larry was racing Walt in a mad scramble to reach the stones.

Then the cold black hem of night swept up over her. Abruptly the darkness raced past, herding the sunlight up the peak.

Walt elbowed Larry out of his way, then kicked him so he went slithering down the rock. Gathering speed the madman latched on to Verity, nearly wrenching her from her hold. As they disentangled themselves, Walt pried free a massive emerald, brandishing it above his head. And as the last rays of sunshine hit the peak, it gave off a flash of green lightning that seared his vision. He spun, trying to hold on, but his clutch failed. He tumbled into the void, crying, 'My eyes! My eyes!'

Larry wasn't as badly burned. But half his face was in cinders, ghastly red pulp seeping from his charred flesh. In shock he missed his footing. It seemed forever until they lost the sound of his body thudding against the rocks. Then dusk covered the bowl and colour left the world. Only the stars that hung so low lit the way.

Verity shook herself and tried to climb up and off the carving but the rock wouldn't stay still. Like grains of wheat pouring down a silo it shifted beneath her hands and feet, threatening to hurl her into the void. Heart pounding, she barely managed to scrabble to hand- and footholds.

From behind, Jud suddenly held a knife to her throat. She'd been too busy to hear him come up. 'Right, Prof,' he barked. 'Tell me how to get the damn' Eyes or the girl gets it.'

'They'll be given to those who deserve,' called up Hector from below. 'Those who don't will be given to the Eyes of Night.'

The knife pricked her deeper and Verity jumped but Jud held her too tightly to escape. She felt a warm trickle over her collar-bone and knew she was bleeding.

'What's it gonna be, Prof?'

'Let her go and I'll tell you. Look up there.' Hector gestured with his chin.

In the last of the twilight a man stood on the crater rim. A man, Verity couldn't help but notice, with a loin cloth and blond hair. And a spear. The Milky Way began to rise behind him. 'Shades of the Odeon!' she whispered.

And the young giant reached out from beside the massive, carven head. Slowly the gem that had fallen on the Jaguar's flank began to rise. Starlight sang in its depths. On a ripple of shiny dark stones the Eye traced its way to its socket and fell in with a bell-like clunk. The light of the Eye dimmed and seemed to go to sleep. There should have been an earthquake but the world held its breath.

Then the demigod pointed at the other Eye and it opened. Verity threw her arm over her face but the Eye was gentle this time as it spoke to its children, its executioners. Verity peeked through her fingers. A faint jade glow washed over the dark, shining body of Mother Jaguar, bringing forth the sparkle of faceted eyes. And the surface began to move.

'Don't be afraid, Miss Fanshaw,' the young giant called down. 'You are of the People of the Jaguar. Just remember what my father said.'

Stand still no matter what happens. Verity strained not to move though she felt Jud's muscles tense to slit her throat. She closed her eyes, then opened them again, determined to show true blue to the end.

And the man in the loincloth made a strange, honeyed sound. Quicker than Jud could move, the surface of the rock swarmed up his body and into his eyes, his mouth, his nose. He shoved her away, clawing at his throat, trying to rid himself of the thousands of ants that were eating away at his insides. His screams choked off. He convulsed and died.

After that she rather thought she fainted.

*

She sat up with a start. 'It's all right, Doctor Fanshaw.' Hector was lying beside the campfire, beaming. In the background, the insects had begun again. After their absence even the mosquitoes sounded like music to her ears. 'Orin and Lucas overtook us in the caves. Orin's gone back down to tell everyone they can stop pretending they can't be seen because Mother Jaguar's saved us all. Not only have we stopped yet more selfish blighters despoiling the valley, Lucas managed to talk to his old Professor at Cambridge. They've recognised the samples and they've asked me to write a paper on indigenous cures! *That* for the Royal Society!'

'Lucas?'

'Sorry, I should have said.' The Professor waved extravagantly. 'My son by my first wife, just come back on a sabbatical to bring me the good news. Doctor Verity Fanshaw, meet Doctor Lucas Hector.'

Verity hid her confusion by checking that the ants had re-formed the living pelt of the Jaguar.

Lucas came across, hiding his grin. His bare chest

displayed a small jaguar tattoo. He squatted at her side like a native and said in perfect English, 'So, Doctor Fanshaw, how does Burura medicine compare with basilicum powder? Good enough to keep you here for a while?'

Verity thought, 'Who needs Hollywood?' and smiled back.

Dragonsbridge

My shoulder's itching unbearably. There, right on the top of the shoulder-blade. I'd give a bloody fortune to be able scratch it. Trouble is, I can't reach it. The only bit I can actually move is my eyes. I look around for something I could use: a bit of bracken, a twig, anything. Every where's so hot, so bright, than I can't make out anything much against the glare.

I can feel the sun beating down, though. My brain feels like it's being fried. Down below, there's the stream, burbling merrily away through ferny dell and mossy bridge, I think sourly. Valley of No Return, for Chrissake. I thought they were joking. You wouldn't think you could get lost in a poxy valley, would you? You just walk downhill 'til you get to where you're going. Or follow the hum of tourist traffic to the castle.

But what happens when you can't walk? When you're stuck at the edge of the bog, can't go forward, can't go back, your head's thumping like a jackhammer's bashing the inside of your skull, and the rocks and trees don't give a damn? That and the endless bloody crickets screeching away. The ancient oaks are alive with squirrels and woodpeckers and all that rustic shit, the leaves are that special green you only get in May when they're opening up, and I'm stuck here with my shoulder on fire.

Yep, there goes the other one. It's worst when the top layer of skin suddenly unglues itself from the flesh, pop! Well how would you like it if someone ripped a layer of your skin off?

I wish I'd listened to Maddy. I know what's going to happen when the sun goes down.

It was seven years ago, in the middle of the building site. He ripped up his returned proposal and scattered it. Then he trampled it underfoot, his toe-tectors slithering in the mud.

'Got a medical appointment, Billy,' he said as he passed the foreman. 'Urgent.'

Billy hid a smile. 'Medical appointment' was code for pissed off and going to the pub. 'Is that right, James Elliott, Dip. Arch.?'

'Stuff the bloody Dip. Arch. Ever since I qualified I've sweated my knackers off drawing brilliant proposals and every sodding time the funding's cut off. If I had that bastard Osborne here I'd teach him to play Ludo with the economy.'

Billy slung an arm round his shoulders and whispered in his soft Irish brogue. 'So you going to quit playin' at bein' a professor and start being a bloody builder? 'Cause you've got it in you, you know. If me 'n' you put our minds together, Jimmy my lad, we can make a bloody mint. I've got this contact up the council…'

Jimmy – formerly James – Swanwick, builder né architect, gratefully let his boss's promise of tax-free wealth hide the size of his debts. Gas and electric. Bastard student loan. Credit card bills…

He thought it all through during his appointment with thirteen medicinal brandies. He'd do it, go in with Billy. Sod the Royal Institute of Bloody Architecture. His wife Maddy wouldn't like it but then again, she didn't have to know.

*

The sun's going down behind the brambles now, thank fuck. It's gilding the trees, bringing out the scent of sap, bringing the end of the relentless sun. For a while it won't be adding to my third-degree burns. But later, when the bats fly through the dusk and the moon rises, what happens will be maybe worse.

Although the waiting's torment enough as it is….

*

He was right, Maddie hadn't liked it when she found out,

not the fear of the taxman nor the endless 'foreigners' he did, the jobs on the sly, but she was just being a snob. Didn't like him working down the sharp end of the building trade. Her and her bloody Bachelor of Fine Arts. What use was that, for fuck's sake? There was sod all she could do about it and anyway, the money came in handy. He liked to get his round in for his gang at the end of the day. A little kindness always helps keep their mouths closed, Billy used to say, and a little threat or two don't go amiss neither. You stick with me, Billy had said. I'll see you right. But for fuck's sake stop going round talking like Little Lord Fauntleroy. Jimmy didn't point out that the boy in the novel had been American. People don't trust poncy gits 'cause they're all on the take. Be Jimmy, my lad, Billy had said, and Jimmy he'd become.

*

It hurts like buggery. Not long to go now. Something's changed about the air, the light. I can't see colours any more, just black and grey and silver. Here in the Valley of No Return, only two or three hundred metres from the Castle of Brocéliande, I shiver. I feel another blister pop, and then the sting as the sweat rolls into it. But I can't move. I'd give anything to be able to move. The stars are bright, owls are making spooky noises in the forest, there's a sniffing noise and the stink of a fox as it trots closer. It sniffs again, pricks its ears to listen, then starts licking my blood. If only I could scream. If only I could scream – but I daren't open my mouth.

*

Maddie lost the baby. It was her own stupid fault, he told her. He'd *said* he was working all the hours God sends so she didn't need to. OK, half the time he was out with his mates, doing a line of coke, going to the casino, there was nothing like it. But she was so stubborn! Paying her stupid bloody student loan instead of getting his accountant to get her out of it. And he'd *needed* that Range Rover, for Chrissake. It'd help him get home earlier, wouldn't it? So why she had to go and act the martyr he didn't know She only had two airy-fairy office jobs and neither of 'em was anything like as demanding as his was. Well, one proper one at the factory and some twilight shift messing about that meant half the time she hadn't cooked his dinner so he'd go up the Dog and Duck. They did a decent steak and chips. He might see Lee and Jason and they could have a game of darts. Leave the old girl to have her cry in peace. She'd be better for it and then they could get back to normal.

*

Now the night wind's rustling these sodding reeds. I never knew the countryside was so bloody noisy! There could be anything out there creeping up on me. After this, rush-hour in London's going to seem really peaceful. That's what I tell myself but fear's bursting through me.

Any minute. Any minute. I can feel it coming. It'll start soft as moth's wings on the raw skin of my burns. The itch'll start to burn like someone's stabbing me with a lighted cigarette. Pain'll sing through me, a vibration of agony so shrill it's above the range of bats. Like last night. And tomorrow night. And all the nights that have ever come.

It's the healing, you see. People say itching's a good sign, don't they? It means things are healing. Bit by bit, day by day, the new skin and tissue grow. A few weeks and Bob's your uncle, good as new.

That's what they say. Or that's what they used to say before I stepped through the Dragonsbridge. It'll take time.

But now it doesn't take time, or not enough. Like fire leaping in darkness the cure goes *Slam!* My heart-rate drops from 126 to 84, just like that. I almost pass out. Healing swarms up the capillaries, stampedes through my muscles. You know when your leg's been asleep and you get killer pins and needles as it wakes up? That's nothing. The edges of my skin crash together like continental plates. It sets up volcanoes of agony.

God, that bitch Maddy! Why'd she have to drag me to fucking France? Leaving me to suffer alone for bloody ever. Just wait 'til I see her.

'Bloody Bella! I never *see* you, Maddy! She's got you like a bitch in heat,' he sneered, sure in his rightness as he faced her over the bills on their Saturday breakfast table. He was *entitled* to a new car, wasn't he? He worked hard enough. He'd earned it! How *dare* she moan?

'Oh, grow up!' Maddie clamped her hands round her mug of tea otherwise she'd have thrown it at him. Only she wouldn't, not really. She always said she wouldn't stoop to his level and start any aggro but she fought back right enough, didn't she? She gazed out at the mothers with their pushchairs going down to the village stores, the families with children taking kites and model aeroplanes to the field at the back of the parish church. She couldn't see the trees at the side. His scarlet and silver Range Rover and now his Porsche got in the way.

She counted to ten, slowly, then said in a voice of saccharine calm, 'Did you expect me to stick around twiddling my thumbs at home when you were five, count them, *five* hours late home? I left you a note where I was, didn't I? Seeing as you'd switched your phone off.'

Oh, she had to get the dig in, didn't she? Bloody dragon. That's what Billy called her. 'How's the old dragon this morning?' he'd ask when Jimmy came to work grumpy.

He tried to say something but she rushed on, 'I didn't *ask* you to wait up. I didn't do anything to deserve this.' Gingerly she felt the swelling that ran half-way up her arm.

'What d'you mean, *this*? It's only a little bruise and you did it to yourself. You're just trying to make me feel guilty, you manipulative cow. All I did was give you a push 'cause you'd gone mental! How was I to know you were going to go and trip into the wardrobe? Got home before you, didn't I? And *you* have the cheek to yell at *me!*'

At least she didn't try to pretend he'd started it. OK, so he'd moaned a bit, but it was her own fault anyway. He got back to the thing that was really narking him. 'You and that bloody Bella. Fat Lesbian whore! I've *told* you.' His blood boiled when he thought of all the times he'd come back late and she wasn't there 'cause she'd gone to bloody Bella's. Jimmy's expression could have stripped paint. 'She's only got to snap her fingers and you go running after her like a baby. Go on, just give her a great big wodge of cash and she'll be your mummy.'

Usually the baby thing shut her up because she felt so guilty about losing the sprog, but not this time. 'It's *work*, Jimmy. It's an investment of *my* time and *my* money. She's a nice woman and she's got a wife anyway. We just work together.'

'That's what you say. You come back sometimes all covered in sweat and I wonder what the two of you have been up to.'

'What we've been up to, Jimmy, is designing a computerised weaving machine. Which means screwing bits of loom together and that's heavy.'

'So long as that's all you're screwing.'

She shot him a glare.

He had to get her off-balance. A guilt-trip would do it. 'On which you spend *our* money.'

'On which I spend *my* money that *I've* earned with my dragon designs in my spare time. And which the Chamber of Commerce in our twin town in Brittany has now started importing so I can pay off our debts. You *know* the money I earn from the factory all goes into our joint account. Which is more than can be said for your bonus. Why you had to squander it on a sports car I can't imagine. You've already got the Range Rover. Don't you *know* our mortgage is three months in arrears? I can't do it all on my own. And your student loan's piling up the interest, and I bet you've got more credit cards than you're letting on. So no, I am *not* running after her. And besides which, I only go over to hers when you're off with your mates.'

He stalked over to the sofa and left it up to her. Put the football on, even. He could see her bottling down her rage. She'd crack soon. She'd come crawling back like she always did. And he'd get something out of it, see if he didn't. Teach her to try and stop him enjoying the Porsche he'd bought with his own money…

She paced up and down the living-room, keeping well clear of the line of sight between him and the telly. He'd taught her well.

At last she sighed, plonked down beside him and slid her arm across his chest. 'Come here, you big silly. It's daft you being jealous. It's you I love, isn't it? It's you I'm married to. Don't be cross. We'll just get through this quicker if we work together, that's all.' She threw her arms round his neck.

So he'd won. Automatically he hugged her to him, glad of the warmth of her body touching his skin. Sometimes he didn't understand why a woman like her loved a bloke like him. But no other bastard was going to have her, especially not some cowing Lizzie. He gave her a long, deep kiss that plunged inside and twisted her mind. Her breathing shifted up a gear with the longing he'd learned to cause her.

'Wish I wasn't going to my darts tournament, gorgeous,' he whispered, and gave her a peck on the cheek. He was half -way out the door when he said, 'Don't wait up.'

*

The moon's sinking now. It's odd when the moon and the sun are in the sky at the same time. At the edge of my vision the fat white disc glows, sheer and pale. On the other side of the valley the blue of dawn flies up like a sodding skylark, heading for the new day's torture. What will They choose for me this time? If only I could have a drink.

The healing's almost finished but my tortured muscles won't stop twitching. Every time I do, the new skin stings as though glaciers are grating over it. I can't even call for help. Surely they've missed me? Surely Maddy'll have le PC Plod combing the woods for me after… Christ! I can't even work out how many days I've been stuck here. Day after day, all the same, except They vary the tortures.

And soon They'll be here. I never know which one it's going to be. They kind of blend into each other. When it's really bad I can't tell them apart, and that scares the pants off me 'cause it makes me scared I'm going doolally. One's a beauty with some kind of pendant glowing on her forehead. The other's a right old bag, her bare arms all stringy and wasted with age.

The beauty's fierce, a proud warrior, wild hair fanning out like a lion's mane, the same colour as Maddy's. The first night I found her irresistible. I was drawn to the passion that flashed out sometimes when we had sex, or when we stayed up all night talking. She seemed, I don't know, all golden and lit up from inside. She made me laugh and taught me glory.

Until that time everything changed. She just couldn't stop rubbing it in when my dreams died but hers didn't. She was so bloody arrogant! Ringing me at work as though I cared a toss that someone wanted to buy her tuppenny-ha'penny doilies. I swear she only wanted to show everyone she was better than me. I *heard* her brother talking about her builder's -bum husband. But he's a posh twat. So what if I like to wear low-riders like Billy and the lads? It's cool isn't it? If she hadn't been such a show-off I'd never have nipped up West with the lads and then I wouldn't have started gambling.

Then she was a fury. Rage sparked from her hair, glittered with the sharpness of her remarks until she seemed armoured in scales. Or she'd cry, a keening that was so bereft, it stabs guilt up right below my ribs.

It might be a relief if it's the old woman who comes. She's got the same delicate architecture to her face though her wrinkles soften the curves. She'll flow towards me through the darkness, lovingly salve my wounds.

Bugger! The pain's so bad I've bitten through my lip and ants are crawling onto my mouth.

Maybe – God! I hate myself! I'm longing to drown in her pity! – maybe she'll brush them away. Set me free. Tell me what's bloody going on!

But as the sun rises up, she hunches beside me, her pity all kept for herself, weeping bitter, bitter tears and wishing she'd never been born.

And I've made her into this pitiful thing.

By the third aeon of torture, I knew They were all one.

*

The sun peeps through the leaves and lances into my new, pink skin. It's like it's writhing over me, crawling over my scraped nerves, stinging like acid.

No! I crane my neck and shudder. There's all these leeches slithering over me, taking a bite. I thought they weren't supposed to hurt? On my arms they are, and on my chest. One's wriggling into my ear. I shake my head – fuck me that hurts! – but I can't get rid of it. The bloody dragons are playing their daylight games.

*

Maddie texted him a month ago to say she'd won them a free holiday, and wasn't it great? She couldn't have made it Agia Napa or Ibiza or somewhere good though, not goody-goody Madeleine. A load of councillors on a minibus to some grotty little town in the arse-end of France? He wouldn't have gone at all except she'd have asked Bella to take his place, the heartless cow.

So here they were, around twenty kilometres west of Rennes. And everywhere they went, they got introduced in mangled English to another load of old fuds or dragged round another bloody chateau. And some old tart would tell them a load of stupid stories about magic and King Arthur and Merlin and that. That first day when they got back to their room and he started taking the piss out of all that New Agey bollocks, she'd practically broken the sound barrier to hiss in his ear, 'Not with the window open! They'll hear.'

'What do I care? It's your bloody jolly, not mine. I'm missing the big match for this so shut the fuck up. Just because they've all been fawning over you and your bloody lizard doilies all day, it doesn't mean I like the sound of your voice as much as you do. They can all go fuck themselves. Where's that bottle of wine?'

*

My skin is like one of those delta maps they got me drawing back in geography, only the rivers are all my blood. It makes me sick just thinking about it. My stomach heaves but there's nothing left in there to come out. The stink of my puke rises up on the hot winds that always blow through this sodding forest but I can't get away from it. All I can do is lie here – hang here? – and bleed.

Maybe she isn't looking for me at all. Maybe she just thinks I'm sulking. Maybe she's had enough, gone swanning on to the standing stones at Karnak with the Chamber of Commerce. I shouldn't have yelled at her last night.

I so, so, so want to call her. Maddie would listen to me. She'd talk me out of these terrible imaginings Or – or if I *am* going mad, she'd take care of me. She always has. I bet she's giving the local rozzers gyp.

But what if that mayor won't let 'em search for me? It was his bloody wife giving me the eye that made me nip down the Valley out of her way. She looked like an elephant wearing face-powder. Mind, if it had been that receptionist in that last hotel I wouldn't have minded getting my end away. Besides, I couldn't stand listening to any more of that bollocks about the gateway to the Otherworld. The tour-guide might have Maddie fooled with all that choosing our fate in the Otherworld shit. I mean, if you crawl under the bridge you face your own dragons or come out into the Summerland. Tir na-bloody-n'Og. Your own choice, the sodding guide had said. I only wanted a quiet fag.

But slugs are swarming up my nose. I'm choking! I can't breathe. I've got to open my mouth.

And a wasp stings my tongue.

*

In the endless noon of the Otherworld, Maddie pleaded through her tears. All around was paradise: friendly beings in lush green meadows, and the sea sparkling under the bluest of skies. And she couldn't touch any of it. She stood in a crystal bubble.

'It's not his fault!' she wept. 'He tried so hard but nobody would give him a chance at a project that might actually get off the ground. And it seems so unfair now Bella and I've got this fabulous new contract thanks to the Chamber of Commerce. Let me go and rescue him, please! I can't leave him there.'

'It's your life,' said the ageless queen in the beautiful gown. 'You're the only one who can decide what path you will take.'

*

'Help me!' I keep trying to croak but the words can't struggle past my agonised tongue. What air I can get whistles round the swelling.

Again that creepy whispering in the grass. I strain to see what's making it. It looks like the earth's walking beneath the grass, and suddenly I realise it's the leeches, red and leaking my blood. All those ones that were piercing my body, she's sent them all away with just a thought. The end of the torture. I'm so grateful to her for just being there. My Madeleine.

She kisses the hollow of my neck. Instantly my breath comes easier. The pain's going, leaving hardly a memory, only snapshots, not the feel of it. Suddenly green leaves shade my skin.

'Are you all right, Jimmy?' I can see the concern in her eyes.

Maddie gestures, and all at once I'm free. I didn't think I'd be able to walk after all this time but I float effortlessly towards her. We hug for the longest time, and nothing hurts at all.

But then I remembered how long she'd left me there, tortured day and night. A wave of anger scalds out from my heart. 'Don't you care about me at all, you daft cow? Fuck knows how long I've been stuck here yelling my head off.' A little dig to make her guilty, not too much, just a cocktail-stickful, but nice and vinegary so she'll know her place. 'Where the hell have you been?'

She backs up, shocked, almost tripping on a tuft of grass.

The sun's behind her now, right in my eyes. 'What's the matter, Jimmy? Have you bumped your head? You've only just stepped under the bridge.'

I give her my best glare. 'Don't you fucking lie to me!'

'You did, Jimmy, no more than a second ago. I was right behind you.'

A ghostly silhouette floats onto her. Into her. It makes her denser, somehow. Gives her – what's the word? – gravitas. The warrior maiden's anger forms a shield. Suddenly my Maddie's more real than I've ever seen her.

Another phantom bursts through her, the old one, kindly arms wrapping her in comfort and protection. She begins very gently to shine.

I'm so stunned I can't move.

'They're not lizard doilies, Jimmy. They're tapestries of dragons and Merlin and the Celtic triple goddess, and they're beautiful. They're made with love and pride, not like you and your corner-cutting crook of a boss with your substandard buildings. Bella's a friend, not someone who uses you like Billy uses you or you used to use me. But no more. Our first order's more than paid our overheads. I know you're in debt so I'll buy the house off your hands.' She twinkles her fingers in mockery, and the light seems to swallow her. The last thing I hear is a derisive, 'Ta-ta.'

*

God knows why they thought they'd bring me a newspaper with *that* in it. For one thing I can't read it 'cause it's in French and for another that's a photo of my wife – my ex-wife – with a giant cheque with lots of noughts on it. It drives me nuts.

All three of them come back to haunt me: the three dragons. Woman the warrior, woman the caregiver, woman the wise. They tried to feed me this bollocks that I'd brought it all on myself.

True, at some time, some age that felt long enough for the whole galaxy to revolve on its axis, Madeleine the mother came to let me go. 'Ta-ta!' Cheeky bloody cow. I swear one of these nights I'm going to go round there and bash her face in just to teach her that if I can't have her, no one else will. I'll read her the riot act right enough.

But not just yet. I'm in some kind of a hospital with some Frog copper standing guard when I have visitors, but Billy says he knows this lawyer.

Buried Flame

Torchlight glinted on … something. Ethan crouched closer, his shoulder scraping the tunnel wall. This abandoned copper mine somewhere in Turkistan had been pretty much his last hope but so far it had been a total bust.

Until he caught sight of that curve of polished stone. Slowly, carefully, he reached for it through a mound of crumbling rock. Dust rose like smoke, making it even harder to see, then a solid shadow blocked the light.

'Get your fat head out of the way, Briggs!' Ethan snarled.

At the same time his minder snapped, 'Crack on with it, boy! Perhaps it won't be a waste of time after all. Maybe your father won't be disappointed again.'

Ethan Quill glanced up with loathing. 'He's not my father! Anyway, maybe it's not for him. Maybe life's not about oil wells or gold mines at all, d'you ever think of that? Maybe it's some fabulous treasure that'll change known history!'

'Idiot.' All the same, Briggs couldn't turn his eyes from the gleaming stone. He squatted at Ethan's back and held his own flashlight closer, muttering, 'Just don't bring the roof down.'

'Number one priority, numbnuts,' Ethan mouthed. Briggs had been bad enough back home in the States. Since Istanbul his bullying had only gotten worse. Taking a deep breath, Ethan went on gently shifting chunks of rock. Once a slither of pebbles made him jerk back. Briggs started and fell over, causing a small avalanche of his own. Ethan watched as the mound in front of him stabilised again. Now even more of the carvings peeked gleaming into view. He gazed breathlessly through the swirls of dust. 'It's writing, Briggs!'

The so-called company advisor tutted and poked him in

the back. 'I *said,* did you hear that noise?'

'What noise?'

'Ssh! I don't know what noise. If I did, d'you think I'd be asking you? Could it be that filthy bastard Akhal looking for shade in here?'

Ethan rolled his eyes. 'I've met his father but I'm not sure about yours. Anyway, didn't you hear him when I suggested that? He's happier frying his brains out there in the desert than come into … drumroll … *the Pits of Shaitan.*'

But even Ethan heard it that time. Voices, plural. So it couldn't be Akhal – unless he'd become a ventriloquist in the last six hours. 'Someone must be forcing him.'

Out of the darkness came a wail of Turkic, a fleshy thud and a curse that whistled through broken teeth. Definitely Akhal, presumably with bandits. Frantically Ethan began to rebury the artefact.

Briggs dragged him backwards. 'What are you *doing,* moron?' he hissed, tussling to snatch the iridescent stone from Ethan. 'Let's grab it and get out of here.'

'If we hide it they won't find it on us, will they? First off we need to rescue Akhal.'

Briggs heaved Ethan backwards and wrenched the thing free. He shoved it into Ethan's hands – a goblet! – and delved the recesses of its former tomb. 'Hide it under your shirt, you fool!' hissed Briggs. 'It must be what they've come for. What else would anybody be doing in the middle of the Karakum?' Digging feverishly, he dragged out a bowl, tossing it carelessly behind him. Ethan just managed to catch it. Briggs resumed his clumsy burrowing. It triggered a minor landslide, making them cough. One of the intruders exclaimed at the sound. The voices hurried closer. Three of them, perhaps four, and the crunch of boot-heels on grit.

Briggs shoved past Ethan, crawling rapidly down the tunnel. He called back over his shoulder, 'Get your skates on, *sir.* You don't want it to go like it did in Armenia.'

'Thanks for the reminder,' Ethan said into the empty passage. He would have left on Briggs' heels except he saw another carven fragment. He clawed it free and stared, perplexed. What the heck was a zig-zag pointy thing for? Or was it the remains of something Briggs had broken? Was there something more back there? Ethan scrunched closer, scrabbling for the camera in his pack. He shielded his eyes from the flash and saw, chiselled into the wall he'd been leaning on, strange hieroglyphics. Quivering with impatience while he reloaded the flash, it seemed hours before he could take a snap of the ancient writing. The footsteps were right around another curve in the maze of tunnels. Then it was time to vamoose.

*

Flashlight hooded, Briggs moved as fast as he could into wider passageways. He didn't need to panic. He didn't. The mine had dozens of mouths and airshafts. He wouldn't be trapped down here forever in the dark. He wouldn't. Anyway, on the way in the brat had marked every turning with a streak of soot. Briggs had scoffed but maybe Ethan wasn't so dumb after all. Now those marks meant escape through the maze of light and shadow and Briggs followed them willy-nilly.

With his barrel chest and short legs Briggs wasn't cut out for running. He was a good decade older than the thirty he claimed. Cigars and port had taken their toll so it wasn't long before Ethan overtook him. At their backs came the pounding footfalls of the intruders, then a new voice shouted from in front. Around a bend a blaze of sunlight sliced through the darkness, scarred with the silhouettes of running men. Before Briggs could blunder into the open Ethan yanked him into a crevice.

Four men sprinted past. The leader and the last one carried fiery brands. Ethan smothered Briggs' flashlight against his chest but he needn't have worried. Dazzled by their own flickering flames, the interlopers pelted off into the shadowy depths of the mine. Just as well. Briggs held his revolver in wavering hands. Ethan pressed down with his thumb to still the hammer. The last thing they needed was a shoot-out with an unknown number of opponents.

As soon as they were out of sight Ethan snatched the pistol from Briggs and whispered, 'Did you see Akhal?'

'Wasn't looking. Didn't want the shine of my eyeballs to give us away.'

'Yeah, your compassion does you credit.'

But as Ethan turned into a vast cavern that sloped uphill, the question became moot. Akhal lay before them, sprawled on the rock, a growing pool of blood drip-dripping from his scalp.

Briggs gasped as Ethan stopped to mop the wound and bind it with his silk scarf. 'We haven't got time for that, boy!'

'You heartless bastard! How about we don't want to leave a trail of blood saying 'We went thisaway'? Take his other arm.'

'He smells like his camels.'

'So do you. Shut up. We're nearly out.'

As they crawled up to the lip of the cavern, the cave-mouths beyond cast ever-increasing fans of light. Dragging Akhal between them, Ethan and his stepfather's spy shuffled noiselessly to the farthest entrance. Here the rock edge was sharp, torn away in some long-ago cataclysm that left a delta of scree spreading down to the desert sands fifty feet below. It was beyond the scree that Akhal had hidden their camp in a narrow wadi. With bandits somewhere below them it seemed a long way off.

They tucked Akhal out of sight and lay flat to peer out. Ahead stretched the endless wastes of the Black Desert. The sheer majesty of it struck Ethan anew and he gazed in awe. A camel brayed somewhere off to the right, dragging his awareness back. Men shouted something he couldn't make out, and a smell of lamb broiling over charcoal made his mouth water. But none of the bandits was looking up here. He edged backwards, Briggs following, and at a safe distance he returned the coward's gun. His own was still on his hip.

Keeping low, Ethan and his so-called assistant hauled the camel driver up the slope above the scree and then on down to the dried river-bed. At every misstep sharp rock ripped their skin, bringing clouds of tiny flies to feast on the cuts. Too tired even to swat the pests away, they paused for a few swallows from their canteens. Around them the wadi lay baked and cracked, waiting for the winter rains. Scattered tamarisks had survived the dry season but they didn't stand a chance against three hungry camels. And there wasn't hide nor hair of the bandits. Much to Briggs' disgust, Ethan gave the groggy Akhal the last of the water while they hastily packed their gear.

'Ride out now?' asked Briggs, snarkily saddling his camel.

'After dark'll give us the best chance.'

'Suit yourself. I'm going while the getting's good.'

'But they can see us, hell! *Track* us by daylight.'

'Haven't seen any of 'em since we legged it. Too busy hunting that treasure inside. Look, shift, will you?' Briggs was pale beneath his tan. 'The longer we stay here the riskier it gets.'

*

Half a day later Ethan wished he'd held out for leaving after nightfall. But Briggs had left at such a pace, not caring where he was leading them except as far away as possible, that they'd ended up in the middle of the open desert. Just as a sandstorm blew up.

He yelled again for his companions but the only answer out of the darkness was the howling wind. The sands of the Black Desert scoured his makeshift tent. Inside, the sheep-fat lamp flared and guttered, leaving swirls of rancid smoke to thicken the air. He dusted the alabaster with his sleeve and held it closer to the meagre gleam. Peer as he might, Ethan couldn't make out the markings on the goblet and bowl. Now pale, now shadowed, the strange alphabet mocked him. It brought back an all-too-familiar memory of his stepfather's disdain.

*

'History is bunk, boy!' Legs wide, stare narrow, Arthur Quantrill stared down at his stepson. Or tried to, because

Ethan had grown over his final semester at boarding school. It had been an April evening in Virginia some ten years ago, with sunlight and birdsong drifting through the windows of Quantrill's study. Ethan knew his mother was listening at the keyhole.

'What's this your principal's written me? You want to waste your time poring over some filthy scraps of parchment? Well? Answer me, boy!'

Ethan could have sworn he heard a gasp from the hall. Nevertheless he swallowed and looked the old man in the eye. 'I met Harvard's Dean of Archaeology when he came to give a lecture. He ... he said I could do well if I applied myself. Sir.'

'I am not paying for you to fritter your time away on dead mummies and potsherds.'

Ethan barely managed to refrain from saying, 'Nobody's going to dig up a live mummy.'

'If,' the old man went on, '*if,* mind you, I decide to let you stay on and try for Harvard, you will study either law or geology so you can work for the family firm. You owe it to your mother.'

'But...'

'But nothing! You know how your mother hates to be disappointed.'

And there was the threat. Ethan knew she had never really recovered from being widowed. From mistress of her own charming Colonial mansion she went to nothing. That's what she'd weep, over and over again: 'Look at me! I'm such a failure. I've come to nothing.' The neighbours called it a breakdown, but only in whispers. Not many of them came round any more when Mrs Quill and her son moved to a dingy apartment in Richmond. Ethan, just barely fourteen, quit school and found a job clerking. Mother got well enough to sew blackwork for funerals into the night, but it still wasn't enough. Ethan gave up his fencing lessons and the shooting club. Bit by bit they sold the silver spoons, the Dresden china, the fine clothes. Well, all except their Sunday best. Mother insisted on keeping up appearances. But her threadbare silks hung off her, so the busybodies said, when she ventured to help at the church fayre. Positively hung off her bony shoulders. Meantime Ethan haunted the history section of the library whenever he could find the time. Then mother's luck turned. Someone introduced her to Quantrill at the Harvest Supper. The old feller wanted a grateful wife. Their courtship was quick, not least because Ethan caught scarlettina and needed a doctor, and Quantrill was prepared to spend money so long as it was in his own interest. They soon married but under his regime Mother never went back to her old sparky self. Instead she drifted round, smothering her fears with chocolate which never quite managed to take the shadow of fear from her vacant blue eyes.

Ethan studied geology at Harvard. Which led him to archaeology. Whenever he could he sneaked into lectures on dinosaurs or Ghengis Khan, Carthage or Constantinople, the Ottoman Empire and Classical Greece, but if his petrogeology grades took the tiniest dip his mother wrote missives whose tinsel of brittle gaiety failed to disguise her anxieties. And now, a year after he'd graduated *summa cum laude*, here was Ethan on his first solo prospecting expedition – with his father's puppet shadowing his every move. Not a hint of an oil-well or a goldfield to prove himself, and he dreaded to add up his expenses.

But with the azure, translucent stone cradled in his fingers Ethan had found something much more to his taste. Sitting on folds of camel-hair cloth to stop the tent flapping way, he tried to decipher the carvings. A particularly savage gust blew the lamp out, spattering him with hot fat. In the stinking, noisy darkness he finally fell asleep.

*

When a gust of wind whisked the shreds of the tent away, morning light scythed into his eyes. Ethan put a hand up against the glare but he was too late. The cloth billowed away to be lost in the thick haze. Beneath his robes, though, the artefacts remained, digging uncomfortably into his ribs.

He stood, rubbing the sand from his eyes, spat the dust from his throat and yelled, 'Akhal? Briggs?' Akhal he cared about. Briggs could go to perdition. Even dear old stepdad couldn't blame him for death by sandstorm so it was with mingled guilt and a sense of freedom that Ethan called into the murk.

Neither of them answered. The whole black desert was swept into fresh ridges, not a footmark remaining. No trace of his camel either, and what little was left in his waterskin made hardly a swallow. He was lost.

The storm had come out of the blue from the west, scattering their mounts. He'd never have imagined he could lose sight of two men on camels within as many minutes. Much as it went against the grain, he knew he'd have little chance of finding them in all the sea of sand. If they had survived, they'd make for water. The camel had bolted with Ethan's maps. The best he could do was head north-east for the Amu Darya. He could hardly miss a river that was over a thousand miles long. There'd be people. Trucks, perhaps, or a caravan. He could pick up supplies in Urgench or some other town along the Silk Road.

If he didn't die of thirst before he got there.

He bundled up the goblet, the bowl and the mysterious wand, slogged up the dune and called out one last time. Veils of drifting sand had him squinting but there was no sign of Akhal or Briggs. He only hoped Briggs hadn't abandoned their injured camel-driver. Ethan turned on the spot. With no sun and no guide, he couldn't even be sure he *was* heading northeast. His compass was cracked and wavering. But to stay was to die. Already the heat was building.

Keeping the wind on his left cheek he trudged on. His thirst grew, consuming hope as surely as its fierce companions, hunger and fatigue, gnawed away his strength, but Ethan wasn't about to lie down and die. Staggering, falling, even crawling when the burning sands had tumbled him downhill, only his indomitable spirit kept him moving until at last he collapsed against a rock and knew no more.

He came to with drops of water on his cracked and crusted lips. An angel in grey knelt over him. As she moved, her robes parted to show a white shift beneath. She tried different tongues until something resembling Farsi made sporadic sense. '…Too much' seemed to warn him against drinking his fill, because she pulled the waterskin away. More worryingly, she said, 'Treasure,' which had him groping for the carved alabaster. And there it was, no longer hidden in his robes but glowing moonstone and pearly on the black sand beside him. She had obviously polished all three pieces.

He gazed in awe at the light shining through translucent stone. The angel had placed the goblet in the wide, shallow bowl. She turned and stirred some cloudy liquid with the wand before floating a needle on a scrap of paper. Round and round it went, drawing his blurry gaze. She asked, 'Do you know what you have?' and pointed to a nick in the rim of the goblet. When the needle finally stilled, she lined the nick up with a groove in the bowl and let the needle settle once more.

'A compass!' he exclaimed, shivering with the fever of sunstroke. Looking around, he noticed the air had cleared. A line of rocks – no, he realised, cairns – threw dark shadows across the burning desert. But the line was irregular and he wasn't sure if he was making a pattern out of nothing.

'Amu Darya,' she said, and 'Urgench' and what sounded like 'buried fire,' but he couldn't pick out anything else from her liquid syllables. She smelt of sandalwood and the desert. A hood covered her dark braids, and her almond eyes were brown. It was her smile that made him think she was an angel, and the wings of her sleeves. Sitting cross-legged beside him, she spread curds on a flatbread. Nothing had ever tasted so good. Nor felt so heavy in his fevered hands.

Afterwards she read the anxiety in his face and bundled the treasures into his robes. Then she half-carried him around the rock. To his surprise a strange, short-legged donkey was dozing in its shade. He argued briefly in gestures but sunstroke took precedence over the manners of a Southern gentleman so he ended up riding while she walked. His thighs ached with the effort of holding his feet above the increasingly rocky ground.

Soon he found himself in a forest of stone spires, and it *was* a forest. Petrified trees cast long black shadows against the setting sun. Some of the shattered stumps looked enormous.

She led him down into a wadi. Its walls rose and rose until the sky was no more than a scarlet gash. As they twisted and turned they sheered through a hundred strata, some sedimentary, some igneous or metamorphic. He longed to explore but she led the ass inexorably downwards until they entered a side-passage. Daylight was suddenly a memory. Feverdreams of succubi dragging mortals to the underworld had him shivering as he clung to the ass. Unnerved, he fumbled at his holster but his revolver was gone. Anyway, it was all he could do to hold on. The hoofbeats echoed for a long time, the sounds coming sometimes from all around and sometimes so close he knew the roof could break his head and he was woozily glad he couldn't sit up. Then, out of the cold darkness, came a gold glow. They turned a corner…

Before them stretched a street. Firelight spilled from windows and doors four or five storeys up on both sides of a canyon. Groups of strollers carried flaming brands to light their way. Women, leaning from their balconies, glanced at Ethan but wouldn't meet his eyes. Conversation stopped. The ass's hoofbeats echoed from the steps of a huge building carved into the rock. Ethan heard chanting, voices low and high, speaking, not singing. The angel joined in, walking backwards to look hopefully up at him but when she saw Ethan was simply bemused her smile faded and she turned away. He felt obscurely that he'd let her down.

Dismounting in a side-cavern, they found themselves mobbed by children. They too were robed in white but chatty as starlings. Shyly touching his sun-streaked hair, they showered Ethan with questions he couldn't understand. The woman – Roshana, he thought – answered, then laughingly warded them off. She left him then, gesturing for him to stay where he was. Ethan wondered if he'd ever understand what was going on.

A vigorous old man thrust his head out of a window in the rock above. 'Hail, stranger!' he called in Homer's Greek. 'Do you understand?'

Ethan grinned with delight and gave the Greek shake of the head that means yes. 'Thank you, sir.'

'Rather thank Ahura Mazda and my daughter!' the old man chuckled, voice fading then coming closer as his sandals slapped down stone stairs. Odd clunks were explained by the silver-headed staff he leaned on. Appearing in the doorway, he beckoned with his whole arm. 'Come in and welcome. Once you've shown me the marvels Roshana describes, we can take our ease. I am Sheda, headman of this village. And you are?'

As he spoke, Sheda helped him up three steps and into a dwelling space of astonishing, if faded, opulence. The old man sat cross-legged and patted a silken cushion on a shelf cut from the living rock. Ethan flopped onto it and stared about him. Embroidered pads that had once been scarlet surrounded a firepit. Tapestries brightened the walls. Magnified by curved mirrors, Aladdin-style lanterns cast cones of light that disappeared into the shadows. The place smelt of rock and incense and food. A giggling girl in headscarf and robe brought them a spicy stew of mutton and cherries. Roshana slipped in, looking flushed, and busied herself serving. Also on the tray was a pitcher of some pale liquid and three cups. Sheda saw Ethan hesitate. 'Have no fear, young man. See.' He filled a bowl and sipped from one side, then passed the bowl across. 'It is camel-milk fermented with our family's secret recipe. Try.'

Ethan brought the bowl close. Its brassy smell was dominated by a more pungent aroma. *Sweet, acid, creamy and*

– he steeled himself and sipped – *yup, a kick like a mule.* Toasting the old man, he raised the drink to his lips again. Then there was a broth of strengthening herbs served over couscous. His head ached ferociously. Besides, he was so tired he could barely talk. More water, and herb-soaked cloths laid on his fiery skin, and Ethan drifted off into dreams. Triumphant, he was lecturing at the Harvard School of Archaeology, gesturing with the zig-zag wand, but it turned into a snake and pursued his mother as she shrieked along the aisle. Professors and students were laughing at him. His stepfather yelled at him to stop being useless while Briggs smirked and stuffed the beautiful bowl down his shirt, running off into tunnels that closed around Ethan, smothering him in tight, cold stone.

*

Daylight and swallows screeling in the canyon woke him. Ethan could barely summon the energy to open his eyes. Coming awake meant facing the burning prickles of heatstroke. Grateful he'd stopped shivering, he lay very, very still and tried to sink back into the void.

Smells tugged against his resistance. Smoke and frankincense. Silver jugs and that fermented camel-juice. And the sounds people made as they sat in the courtyard at the foot of those three steps: a tintinnabulation and the creak of leather chairs that echoed slowly in the chasm.

Nearby, children chanted something over and over, perhaps to learn it since a deeper voice corrected them. Hoofbeats and the trundling of wheels echoed from stone walls. Lying perfectly still – moving hurt too much – Ethan took stock. He'd stopped shivering, which was a plus, but his head didn't so much ache as feel like his brain was going to drill its way out through his skull. And in the courtyard just three steps below a quiet argument erupted into a noisy one.

Suddenly he remembered the treasures and groped beside him. They were gone – and so was Roshana.

He peered into the shadowed yard. Sheda used his staff to

haul himself to his feet so he could shout back at the younger man facing him, although *young* was a relative term. The newcomer was a little past his prime, the fading embers of a bruiser, it seemed, with a shaven head but features very like Sheda's, only sunk in rolls of fat. Face distorted in rage, the stranger bellowed, 'Angra Mainyu!' and brandished the goblet right under Sheda's nose. A shaft of sunlight cast harsh shadows, intensifying the cruel possessiveness in the man's face.

Sheda snatched the thing back so fast the other was taken unaware. Or, judging from the look of surprise, in sheer disbelief that anyone could challenge him. Silk embroideries and flame-shapes of beaten silver made him resplendent in his rage. By contrast Sheda's linen with its subtle patterns of interlocking squares looked plain. The two men yelled at each other. Ethan heard 'Mazda' and 'Asha,' and 'Angra Mainyu' again. Before further hostilities broke out, a shaven-headed youth rushed in, aligning himself against Sheda, but Roshana arrived breathlessly, followed by a burly teenager streaked with rock-dust. They flanked Ethan's host. In that unknown tongue the hawk-faced stranger barked something that could only be, 'You haven't heard the last of this!' and stomped out, his acolyte on his heels. The others began an animated discussion.

Then Roshana glimpsed the strain on Ethan's face. Gesturing to him, she gathered the artefacts and brought them inside, pausing only to say over her shoulder, 'See you later, Gailor.' So that was the beefy lad's name. She settled on a cushion at Ethan's bedside and soon Sheda joined them.

'Well, young man, you have set us a puzzle.' Ethan struggled with the strangely-accented Greek. 'My brother the high priest insists you are a thief and a heretic, sent by Angra Mainyu to destroy us by leading us down the path of the father of lies. I believe you are a gift of Ahura Mazda on a holy mission to return us to the heart of truth – despite the fact that you do not know the rites of Zoroaster. What do you believe?'

Ethan shrugged and wished he hadn't. 'I dunno about this Angry Mania feller but I have heard of Ahura Mazda. Wasn't he the forerunner of Mithros?'

Sheda shook his head, leaning heavily on his staff to sink to the padded stool beside Ethan. A graunch of arthritic bones accompanied the gesture. For a moment the old man's face twisted with agony but he smiled so quickly Ethan wondered if he'd been mistaken. 'No,' the old man said, 'Mithros was an invention of the Romans, an anaemic avatar they drowned in a sea of sacrificial blood. I've always believed he was Angra Mainyu, the demon of lies. We worship the Spirit of Wisdom, the Essence of Being, he who is Light itself. And you bring us these holy relics because Asha – the truth, the right way – has heard my pleas for my people and brought you to us.'

Ethan never even wondered why the headman needed divine aid. 'What, me, a god's champion?' he scoffed. 'No no no no. It was just luck. My companions and I found this stuff abandoned in the Pits of Shaitan while we were prospecting for minerals. We had no idea what it was, just that it shouldn't be left for the bandits who attacked us. We were going to take it to a museum. Have you seen two men, an American and a tribesman? We got separated in that storm and I'm worried. Akhal was wounded and I have no idea if those bandits captured them.'

'Then we shall send out scouts. Your compassion does you credit. And what do you believe of truth?'

Ethan blinked. 'Not sure what you mean.'

'Is it stone or air? Slavery or freedom?'

'Uh, freedom, I guess.' Ethan thought of Step-pa Quantrill crushing others to his whim. 'Yeah, freedom.'

Sheda beamed. 'Well said. And tradition?'

Ethan put his head to one side and thought. 'Show respect but don't let it force you into someone else's cage.'

Sheda kissed the head of his staff and waved it happily. 'Good, good. And what of women? Surely a fine young man such as yourself has many children.'

'Not me. Only just striking out on my own. Sure, one day I want a wife and kids, but not until … until I find a woman who isn't a doormat or a shrew.'

The oldster looked from Ethan to the silver head of his staff. It was worn, the remnants of fine carving visible only as darker threads, but recognisably the horned head of a bull. 'You see? Asha,' he said to it, then grinned at Ethan. 'Take the medicine my granddaughter's prepared and you shall see us find the true way.'

And I'm guessing that's not Mr High Priest's way, the adventurer thought to himself.

To his astonishment, half an hour later he felt almost human. It was miraculous. The cream Roshana had slathered on his burns took the sting out and the potion, washed down by more of that fermented milk, had him feeling strong enough to walk out into the noon light.

Passing along the street that was the canyon's floor, they came to a place where it opened up into a pocket valley. Asses turned water-wheels to irrigate the fields that rose in terraces to the towering scarps above. Young crops greened the earth and orchards blossomed alongside palms. Rich, moist soil perfumed the air, and cheerful groups plied hoes, waving and greeting Sheda. It was a paradise hidden in the desert.

Sheda led him to a cave hollowed out of the rock. Its cool depths smelt of musk and something sharp. As his eyes adjusted Ethan saw they were in a mews. Sheda unhooded one of the hawks and set it on a leather brace on his arm. Stroking the soft feathers of its breast, he crooned to the bird. Man and beast gazed into one another's eyes in wordless communication of love and need. The tawny creature blinked and took off, circling the valley once then climbing rapidly into the heat-whitened sky. With a shrill cry it shrank to a dot and disappeared.

'We will know by tonight. I have this much authority at least. Now rest in the shade. Roshana will bring you food.' The old man strode back into the canyon. Ethan, lying on a pile of rugs, wondered whether this was courtesy. Or whether he was being kept in a cosy jail. That high priest fellow hadn't liked being thwarted. And where were Akhal and Briggs?

*

The dust-storm swirled round Briggs. Within moments it was darker than the inside of a cow. What with the wind battering his ears he had no idea where Ethan was, or that damned tribesman. Briggs' camel bolted, almost throwing him. Tossed around by the awkward gait, he barely managed to cling on between the humps.

And the stupid beast took him straight back to that blasted mine into the arms of the bandits. They looked a murderous crew with their scars and bandoliers. Or, he thought as they offered him mint tea and some weird kind of stew, perhaps they weren't bandits after all. Perhaps everyone carried guns around here. Maybe Akhal had just tripped and bashed his head. Wherever the fool had got to. And that dratted boy. The old man would cut off his expenses if he didn't bring the brat back in one piece.

Now, surrounded by what looked like Ali Baba and his Forty Thieves, Briggs nodded his thanks to the one-eyed man who brought the bowl. In surprisingly good English, the bearded man with the green eyepatch went on, 'So you will reward us if we find your son?'

'That arrogant pipsqueak? He's not my son! But yes, we can pay. Get us to Urgench and we'll give you more money than you've ever seen.'

Squatting beside him, One-Eye toyed with a curved dagger and said, 'Does your word hold weight?'

'That it does! Just what are you implying?'

'That I was a translator at Gallipoli. You Crusaders aren't known for honour.'

'I'm an officer and a gentleman.'

Now One-Eye spun the dagger glittering in the firelight. 'So were they. Now, just what did you steal from the Pits of Shaitan?'

'It wasn't stealing! It was archaeology.'

Suddenly the point of the dagger was an inch from Briggs' eye. He jerked back, stew spilling down his front in a scalding wave.

'And just what were these pieces of archaeology from my land and not from yours?'

Briggs could hardly speak fast enough. 'Gotta be worth a fortune!'

As soon as he described the zig-zag wand, One-Eye smiled with satisfaction. 'Then if your master lives, we will know where to find him.'

*

Over supper Sheda and Roshana questioned Ethan, and vice versa. He was getting better at their odd style of Greek.

'The angel-girl said, 'Uncle Ardrax – you know, the priest, wants nothing to change. He says we are safe here, away from the pollution of the world outside.'

'Yes, daughter, but what is safety? Every year we dwindle, prisoned by his fear of discovery. And every year his power grows.'

'Why's that?' interrupted Ethan.

'Zoroaster lived long, long before your Christ. He preached compassion and respect for all life. Parts of Judaism and even Islam carry some of his messages. Yet the Romans, the Seljuks and Mamluks, the Crusaders – men of every faith and none – have persecuted us ever since he preached the holy word. Conversions at swordpoint or rape and starvation and murder. I cannot swiftly reckon the year by your calendar but about seven hundred years ago the Mongol Genghis Khan outdid them all. He diverted the river to flood Konye-Urgench. Its inhabitants either drowned or fled, but not many escaped the archers. They say now there is a new Urgench, and they use the old city's ruins as a graveyard. But we who left have never gone back to see.'

A chill wind seemed to whisper through the cavern, dousing the lamps. Ethan shivered. 'Your ancestors? Surely you mean your *ancestors* left?'

Sheda looked bewildered then laughed uproariously.' You think I am seven hundred years old? With *my* arthritis?'

As Ethan flushed and stammered, 'Uh, nossir, of course not,' Roshana rekindled the lanterns. Then Ardrax came in, all smiles, bringing dates. Except the smiles grew into a rictus of hate when the priest darted a look at Ethan. Making nice to a bigot didn't appeal so Ethan left them to it and went to explore the firelit town.

*

At first light Roshana woke him. 'Make haste to pack the treasures! We leave at dawn. My father has insisted some of the community go with the priests, because it's the citizens' job to protect the sacred ones. Uncle Ardrax doesn't like it. Nor that father says you are to come with us to find the treasure we have sought for a thousand years. He says you are the bearer of the keys to truth, but uncle says you'll have us mixing with all kinds of heretical scum. Fortunately, Uncle Ardrax cannot *force* the elders to vote with him. Keep out of his way, if you can.'

*

When they assembled at the far end of the valley, each group, the priestly and the town militia, had plenty of support. Half a dozen townsfolk, men and women, carried bows or spears while six acolytes with halberds flanked the high priest. The holy ones sneered at the female warriors. Ardrax glared at Roshana but she strode beside her father, one hand on her recurved bow, determination and excitement marking her exquisite features.

Ethan was puzzled as the party tramped towards the closed end of the valley, and more puzzled still when they didn't come back from the camel pasture but mounted up and rode towards the seemingly impenetrable wall of rock. At a gesture from Sheda, repeated a moment later by Ardrax, burly men pushed aside a slab of rock, revealing a tunnel. At the further end men closed off the passage with a pivoting door of stone.

Ethan found himself jogging along on an ancient camel,

Roshana on one side of him and Sheda on the other. Acolytes flanked them, great halberds at the ready, trying to shoulder the civic force out of the way. Behind them, though, came the townsfolk who made very sure the headman stayed in front. It seemed to be a clash of ideologies, and Ethan was the one sparking the ready-laid tinder.

The old man winked at him. Ethan winked back, feeling a little better. With her father to translate, Roshana quietly plied Ethan with questions about the world beyond. Everything seemed strange to her: automobiles and aeroplanes, wireless and the existence of the New World. She drank in his words, eyes shining, and Sheda looked on with a smile of satisfaction, which turned sombre as he viewed his brother's hostile glare. The hawk perched on Sheda's saddle was hooded and quiescent, while overhead, Ardrax's own hawk circled, emitting shrill whistles from time to time as the travellers descended the foothills to the sea of black sand. Off in the distance Ethan saw those strange cairns half-buried in the desert, and wondered what they were.

When a new range of hills broke the horizon Ardrax rode back, demanding the zig-zag wand. Sheda told Ethan, 'Go with him. Be sure you don't let it out of your sight.'

Puzzled anew, Ethan moved up to the front of the caravan. Ardrax held out his hand imperiously. Ethan handed over the slim alabaster shape, intrigued despite his qualms. The high priest, earrings ajingle in the hot wind, held the rod horizontally and turned, scanning the skyline. He flung out an arm and the caravan moved in that direction. Several times he stopped and repeated the performance. At last he cried, 'There!'

It was obvious now. The curves of the wand matched the distant hillcrests. Whatever they were looking for, this was the first step on the map. Joyous, the whole party dismounted, clustering round as Sheda urged Ethan to place the bowl and the goblet on a damask rug. What Ethan had taken to be chips out of the rim turned out to be shallow copies of the skyline. Ardrax threw himself to his knees, filling the goblet with muddy liquid and floating a needle as Roshana had done. Only this time it showed exactly where they were going. Checking the compass in his pocket, Ethan saw the needle didn't swing north but off towards the east. He couldn't help wondering if the photos he'd taken of the writing in the cavern would have helped but there was no way of developing them out here. He had to hope the mad compass wasn't leading them to die out in the desert. But the high priest seemed to believe he knew where he was going.

Apparently he did. With a whoop Ardrax mounted his camel which set off at an ungainly run. Hastily Ethan tipped out the liquid, snatched up the goblet and bowl and pelted in his wake. The others followed, while overhead two hawks now circled the sky.

Twice more Ardrax dismounted to consult the wand and its alabaster companions. Finally he halted the caravan at the foot of a black escarpment. This time he paced out a spot, consulted the writing around the rim of the bowl, moved left then right until he found what he was looking for: a symbol incised into the rock. Worn dim by the winds of the desert, it wasn't easy to make out. Squinting, Ethan saw it was a bull's head above a fiery heart. Ardrax pressed it. Pressed harder, swore, then hit it with the heel of his dagger. Stone splinters flew; the onlookers hissed in horror but a door cracked open. Blind to Sheda's sending his falcon into the skies, the priest ordered his acolytes to push the slab wide, not easy with the heaping sand, but at last their struggles were rewarded: the door shifted just wide enough for them to push their way inside.

Snarling, Ardrax yanked his followers back and plunged into the tunnel at their head. He didn't get far. The inside was black as a crow at midnight, the floor uneven. Strange currents of air warned of side passages. Ardrax stumbled, skinning his knees . Sheda smothered a grin, lifted the skull of the silver bull at the top of his staff and dropped some tinder into the hollow. He blew gently and flames flickered up. He and Ardrax tussled briefly for the lamp, then rushed on together.

The acolytes tried to shove ahead but Ethan skipped forward, dragging Roshana to the front. 'Ladies first,' he said, with his courtly Southern bow, and grinned as he tucked her hand in the crook of his arm. That sturdy young guy shot Ethan a look and grabbed her other hand. Roshana smothered a grin of her own.

Although the entrance was stygian, like the Pits of Shaitan, once past a certain point this underground place had odd shafts of light streaming down from above. Unlike the Pits of Shaitan, the light grew broader as the rock above them split. It funnelled the sun's heat down around them. Inch by inch the sun climbed towards noon; inch by inch the glare crept down the wall so that Ethan felt he was broiling At last the trench snaked underground. Winds whistled softly from places they couldn't see. A few more bends and it was dark. The high priest edged closer to Sheda's staff-lamp. Around them the walls hollowed, strata pitching and falling in all shades from black to red to … gold?

But it wasn't gold. It was veins of ammolite. Ethan gasped. Now thick as an eyebrow, now thinner than a hair, the crystalline mineral refracted every colour of the rainbow. Great ink-dark columns bulged from the walls, studded with fossilised mother-of-pearl where the ammolite poked through. It winked like amber or amethyst, or garnet shading to emerald. But Sheda and Ardrax sped on regardless.

The tunnel ended in a vast, echoing cavern. From its centre a single narrow shaft of sunlight faded outwards, failing to touch the walls. Amidst the darkness that one ray was focussed on a gleaming outcrop of stone.

Everyone jostled to get a look at it. Shadows sunk into the hollows only drew attention to the glittering bas-relief. Surely it must have been carved by the hand of man? But there were no chisel-marks on what looked like a bull's head and torso wreathed in fire. The horns curved upwards, seemingly made of flame. Great golden eyes glowed either side of the muzzle. In the beast's chest blazed a scarlet heart that was crowned with gilded fire.

Ethan knuckled his eyes in disbelief, and edged forward to get a better look. Half-buried in the crumbling rock, he saw a great shining ammonite, a spiral shell wider than he could reach. Here and there broken edges revealed the membranes inside the petrified shell. Not a miracle, a coincidence of fossils.

Ardrax threw up his arms up with a great shout of wonder. Sheda knelt humbly, staring at the symbol of all he held dear. The murmurs faded to the silence of awe, and the winds hushed a ghostly harmony. Sheda shouted, 'Thank you, Asha, for your gift from outside!'

Then wings whirred, startling everyone. Sheda threw up his arm and his hawk swept in to perch there, shrilling a warning. He climbed awkwardly to his feet, the bird's wings fanning.

'No! Defiler!' yelled Ardrax, whirling to point accusingly at Ethan, then at Sheda. 'Puppet of lies and darkness! Ahura Mazda has revealed his truth to me. I reclaim this holy place in the name of Asha.' He jerked his chin at Ethan and sputtered, 'Your unworthy gaze ... your outsiders' greed... Ahura Mazda has sent this creature of daylight to stop you defiling this holy place. Had you planned to steal our treasure like a thief in the night? Bring heathens to profane ... even *this?*' He shook his fist at his brother. 'And *you're* his accomplice! Kill them!'

He swung his halberd towards Ethan, who jumped back, his hand going fruitlessly to his empty holster.

But Sheda raised his staff in a half-circle. Maybe it dislodged dust-motes hanging in the shaft of light, but it seemed to draw a golden wall in the air. The acolytes recoiled. Ardrax himself had no such fears. He was too sure he was right. He threw himself forward. His weapon gonged and recoiled, sending out shimmering ripples as he fell back.

Sheda yelled, 'We've been followed! Unite!'

The acolytes might be confused but not so the militia. Roshana nocked an arrow to her bow, swivelling to see where to aim. Somewhere out in the dark rang battle-cries: a confusion of echoes. Ethan heard the scuff of feet, the rasp of swords being drawn, but from where he could not tell.

A shadow shifted through the outer darkness. Roshana shot hastily but her arrow clattered to the ground. More silhouettes out there played hide and seek, then several arrows whizzed out of the night.

Suddenly Sheda's hawk had tripled in size. It screamed and took flight, the abrupt thrust of its powerful legs shoving the old man towards a deeper patch of shadow. Itself lost in the gloom, the bird screeched a war-cry of its own. Unseen, a raider shrieked with pain.

Meantime Sheda part-closed his beacon. 'This way!' he hissed.

'No!' bellowed Ardrax. 'We have to defend the Heart of Flame!' One of his followers wavered, but the rest ducked and scuttled off behind those pelting in Sheda's wake.

Without his gun there was nothing Ethan could do but watch impotently as the mass of thieves hacked the high priest into shreds. Wait a moment! That was Briggs, fighting as desperately as any of them – against Ardrax's henchman! Ethan had suspected Briggs was many things but this treachery was a shock.

A hand shot out of the gloom. 'Keep up!' whispered Roshana 'Father's found the old cistern.'

'Cistern?'

'It leads to the aqueduct. We can get round behind them!' She dragged him into a side passage, and the darkness and disturbance of the main cavern faded behind them. The wind wuthered along the tunnel at them, surprisingly chill and damp.

Before long Ethan heard water dripping. The sound grew louder as they drew closer to the rest of the group. Bobbing heads and weapons stood out against Sheda's light. It seemed brighter now, blue-white flames pouring up between the silver bull's horns.

In front of Ethan, Roshana came so abruptly to a halt that

Ethan bumped into her. He put an arm around her waist to steady her, only to draw quickly back when he felt a hairy, muscly arm holding her from the other side.

She cleared her throat. 'Mind you don't trip into the cistern. It goes down hundreds of feet but the water wouldn't reach above your ankles.'

Sheda rapped the butt of his staff for attention. 'Keep to this wall here. The first six of you, town or temple, you're with me. At the first passage, the rest of you go with Gailor and Ethan. You lot, make as much noise as you can. We'll come at them from two sides, so wait 'til you hear my signal.'

Ethan couldn't help wondering why he got to be one of the mission's leaders. After all, he was a heathen defiler. But maybe his reactions earlier had given the old man the impression he could take care of himself.

Gailor, Roshana, Ethan, two acolytes and a blacksmith waited breathlessly where the tunnel debouched into the main cavern. Tension mounted until Ethan found himself grinding his teeth, but still they had to wait out of sight. Where were the other group? Where was Sheda's signal?

The hawk's scream rang out above the echoes of the hostiles' shouts. Ethan yelled, 'Come on!' and led the charge. They dashed straight to the knot of men crowding around the heart of fire. Roshana couldn't shoot for fear of striking a friend but she had a short sword. Ethan held a dagger as they raced bellowing towards the intruders.

At the racket the bandits spun. They had no compunction about shooting, but they were in the light while Ethan's group were shadows among shadows. An arrow tore through Ethan's sleeve. The fletching whipped his shoulder but the point missed entirely. Then he was in the thick of the fray.

Ethan thrust, then ducked a scimitar driving straight for his throat. He came up inside the other man's reach and planted a left on his chin. The bandit's head snapped back. He collided with another brigand, the two of them crunching back into the bull's head. It seemed as though the horns took on an extra curve, plunging into their chests. Lightning flared along the twin horns. The thieves turned into pillars of fire, their shrieks terrifying. They died and fell, blackened husks, and the bull's head glowed serenely.

The battle had lasted an instant and forever. Sheda's hawk was everywhere, great wings cutting a swathe through the enemy. It seemed to Ethan that the bandits were limned by the great Mithraic light while he and his companions stayed in twilight. Panting, Ethan looked around but there was no one left to slay.

Sheda walked to his brother's corpse. 'But, Ardrax, we have to survive to protect it. The Heart of Truth has decided who is evil and who is fit to live. May the Light wash all stain from your soul.'

Ethan didn't observe this private moment. Captured torch in hand, he was going from body to body, searching for Briggs. He found him, just beyond the eldritch glow, crawling away as fast as he could with one leg cut off at the knee. Briggs heard him and cringed. 'They made me! I swear, Ethan, I only pretended I wanted a share in the spoils so they wouldn't kill me.'

But that wasn't what he babbled as Roshana bandaged his stump by the flaming heart of truth. And despite her efforts, Briggs didn't make it through the night. Oddly enough, all the wounded on Sheda's side did. Roshana wept in Gailor's arms.

Ethan turned away. He wandered over to study the icon that had caused so much death. Drawn by the ruby gleams, he hunkered down to examine the heart in the bull's chest. Quiescent now, and shining brighter despite the cracks where the brigands had tried to prize it free, it radiated both peace and watchfulness.

'We are not ready to face it, are we? We the human race?' Sheda spoke at his shoulder, startling him. At his words the spectral chorus of winds began an aetherial song. The hawk gave a muted cry.

Ethan straightened slowly. 'So, what? You're going to kill me so I can't tell anyone?'

The old man chuckled. 'You won't tell anyone. You'll keep our secret for the good of Roshana and my people.'

Pulling a face, Ethan nodded. 'Guess I'll have to go home and 'fess up to my mother's husband that I haven't made our fortune. Bet he and mother will tie me to a desk from now on.'

Sheda laid a hand on Ethan's shoulder. 'You already know you cannot take our treasures to found your career in ancient studies. But fear not. I think a scroll I made for the archive will give you much useful information about the wonders of Old Urgench. Especially since you'll know exactly where to dig.'

Roman Games

Rome station seemed to rattle as the train began its farewells. A hand, freeze-frame black-and-white, banged silently on the outside of the Pullman's double glazing that slid away. Inside, a boy with his leg in plaster babbled in anguished Italian. In her corner, Sister Thomas read a detective book so that – for once – she could pierce the secrets of men's souls. It was typical, so it was, that she almost missed the Drama of the Ticket as she hid in her book from her failure in Rome. And when she got back to Ireland – ?

'My ticket!' The boy pulled at her skirt. 'I no have the my ticket!'

Sister Tom looked: saw the boy with his crutches, whose ticket was outside the window. The poor bobbing uncle, distraught, tied to the train's motion by the ticket he could not pass in to the nephew, trotting along the platform walloping the panes. A frenzy of silent shouting like a fish outside its bowl.

Sister Thomas ran to the door, hurled its back in its track; the corridor; the carriage door; slammed down the window and snatched the ticket.

'*Grazie! Mille grazi –* '

The platform fell away to gravel: goodbye uncle Outside the station it was dark. Sister Thomas pushed the window up, no longer leaning on the sign that said 'It is dangerous to lean out of the window.' Where her head might have been, a telegraph pole whizzed past. A miracle that passed her by.

Nephew, his leg horizontal in graffiti and gypsum, was very thankful in his heathen tongue. A pity our somewhat good sister didn't understand one word of the canticle. But she smiled.

The train headed north as Sister Tom tried to remember what faith was like. It was impossible. So she tried to sleep instead.

Stops and stations, then a long blank journey towards dawn. The boy and the graffiti on his leg were gone. The Rome-Ostend express was a world of light and life travelling through the outer darkness of Italy.

*

What of Thomasina's opponent? She's hungry, that's what. Dawn is brilliant up in the mountains, and on this particular dawn she blunders over the valleys, hunting. Her scales, like her teeth, need cleaning. As her wings crank her stiffly over the rosy Alps, she thinks of fresh marrow and picking her fangs afterwards with a nice, juicy rib.

The trouble is, people don't believe in her any more. There isn't room in this bright winter's sky for her and jumbo jets: their slip-streams dull her scales and bring on her bronchitis. Draco Vulgaris is mucky with other people's neglect.

She turns her head, trying to spot a victim. Hope – and memories – of feasts always make her nostalgic. Those Romans were nice and crunchy with brass and spiky iron. There's been a virgin or two – knight-bait, they were, a morning's sport *molto bene*, very good. Thieves and murderers, fat millers with lungs *en croute*.

Draco spotted the train as a stream of colours, hugging the snowy side of the pass. She spiralled in lower. Sulphurated saliva dripped from her jaws. Her last meal was partisans with gunpowder sauce. Dinner was forty years ago and she was ready for breakfast.

*

Round One

In her compartment, only Sister Tom was awake. It was incredibly hot, redolent of garlic and bodily effluents The double-glazing, of course, maintained its efficient seal. Five-feet-eight-inches of Irish nun did not fit the seat; her short-cropped head was jammed at an uncomfortable angle, so that every time her unwilling eyes jolted open she could see the frightening mountains. Little faith and less hair did a poor job of cushioning her. Her curls had stopped growing by themselves thirty years ago. She sometimes thought her hair was more religious than she was.

'Is this a dragon I see before me?'

Sister Tom rapidly checked her watch, set to this foreign time. Not yet six o'clock. Besides, when the frost-jewelled cliff shot by – Holy Mary! – the abyss held no dragons.

Back in her village in the Mountains of Mourne – proper mountains they were, nice and soft and gentle – it would be just past three o'clock, the witching hour. Many's the night Sister Tom had sat up with the dead in a candle-lit room. *She* knew that midnight was nothing. But three o'clock in the morning, when death squeezes the souls out of bodies, that was when horrors enter the mind of a nun. For doesn't a nun see only the underside of men, now? At three o'clock by God's time in would slide a banshee, maybe, in the soft mist around the corner of vision. Or a large, creaky dragon over the sudden, jagged Alps.

It was nothing, now. Just a bad dream. And it was gone.

Draco dimmed a little more, wounded by disbelief.

Dragon 0 – Sister Thomas 1

*

Round Two

Draco singed a pine tree out of pique. Disbelief always put her in a flaming temper. No doubt she had once been a pure, innocent hatchling, but she'd soon grown out of a diet of sheep and chamois. We are what we eat, and she had eaten liars, cheats, cowards and killers, man-unkind with all his little failings. In short, she had eaten people.

After the nightmare, Sister Tom needed air. Yawning and stretching, she staggered along the corridor as the train swayed round the cornice. At the carriage door, she lit a filthy, cheap, foreign cigarette, all the better to savour the cold air. She rested her forearms on the window, trying not to see the river right down in the black depths of a gorge. Sure the Alps were pretty now, but better with a picture-frame safe around them.

More importantly, could a nun who apparently believed in dragons not have a little more faith in God?

There it was again! Dull bronze, dull green, dull soot – Mother of God, it was there before her eyes! All it needed to be believable was a tongue of —

Flame ripped out at the smart carriages crafted by robots in Milan. The blue paint blistered, that was all.

No is like the old days, thought Draco nostalgically, going through her gizzard to find another belch. *Then I really make them blaze!*

Pride was just one of the sins she had consumed.

'Oh God, I wish I wasn't an atheist,' a humorist once said in danger. Sister Tom prayed, for real this time, as if it might do her some good. Too long had prayer been a comfy, cosy thing, like her night-time Guinness or warm slippers.

Hands together, eyes closed – but with one eye cheating, because the dragon was closer than God – Sister Thomas *prayed*. Harder still, when the dragon's talons raked along the roof, and in fear Sister Tom closed her other eye.

Draco back-winged, puzzled, and hauled herself higher in retreat. Why hadn't her claws ripped through the metal? The pink sun shone in her eyes and she shook her head in annoyance. She must be getting old.

Arrowing her tail, she dived like a cormorant, trying, trying, trying again. A downdraught from the snowfields gave her a helpful shove.

It *was* dangerous to lean out, and the good sister didn't need the notice to tell her. Head and shoulders crammed through the window, Sister Tom howled her prayers upwards, eye to eye with the dragon, only partly so she wouldn't see the chasm below.

English, Latin, Gaelic – Sister Tom tried everything. *What did the dragon speak? What would work?*

Draco was an omnivore. That is, she'd eaten men of all tongues, and so she spoke the lot. And she knew the power of prayer, whether the deity was called Mithras or God.

Nonchalantly she wheeled away over an arête.

'Saints be praised!' cried Sister Tom, falling to her knees in the corridor the minute the beast was gone. The sky was as blue as Mary's robe, the mountains white and majestic. Pale sunlight gilded all, even the battered old face with its thorny crown of Irish hair, even the bulbous nose her mother had passed on from the tinker who'd made her laugh – until she'd conceived Sister Tom. She'd not laughed then till the dates worked out, and it might have been her husband after all.

Sister Tom shook her head. What a terrible confession to hear from her own darlin' mother on her deathbed. Had that started her doubts?

What if it had? She'd done a Saint Patrick! Smiling, full of faith, she resolved to give up the weed for good and put the money in the poorbox. This would be her last cigarette.

Faith! She could do it now.

Dragon 1 – Sister Thomas 2

*

Round Three

Draco was in a bad way. *Quindi* – she'd pretended she'd just changed her mind, but the prayers had made her sick *de vero*. Perched on a black rock in the corrie, her tail draggled on the snow and her head drooping, she gave way to the pains that griped in her stomachs. She almost overbalanced when she put a claw down her throat, but the indigestible prayer gave her hell. It wouldn't come out but it wouldn't stay down.

Sister Tom walked back along the bouncing corridor, bouncing herself with joy. The spring-door fought back when she slid it open, but what did it matter today?

The boy with the broken leg had got out at Turin; now two tubby men slept in his seat. One was a salesman, one an accountant: besuited but naive in sleep, their scepticism dormant in their pockets with their spectacles. It was too early yet for businessmen.

What time was it? Sister Tom's watch on its old leather

strap still said before six: she could tell by its single pointer.

'Must get a big hand,' said Sister Tom to herself, and opened her one bottle of Lambrusco. 'Never too early for a heroine to drink,' and she thanked God for screw-caps. She was in that rare, generous mood that ascribes to the Creator all the good things He – or She? – had dreamt up. Sister Tom would have thanked God for the Velcro on her veil if she'd thought of it.

Imagine her surprise, then, as she swigged surreptitiously from her bottle – silently, out of consideration for her sleeping partners, watching the cars on the autostrada – and Draco appeared!

For Draco had eaten atheists, and their proteins swallowed prayers in the stomach of unbelief. It just took time.

Sister Tom gulped wine from the bottle. The beast was still there, though, hovering behind a big motorway sign, lurking until the sparse, early cars thinned out.

The cheek of it! Thought Sister Tom, pushing the damned door sideways. Pound, pound went her boots along the corridor, and her heart did the same. Back to the carriage door, where a dog-end lay before the open window.

What weapon could she use this time? If it was sweat, she'd have won hands down. Sister Tom lit a cigarette with shaking matches.

Sure the beast was so vain, wasn't she creaking over the train now? Making sure Sister Tom had seen her. And on the stilted autostrada, no cars but one for miles. A mother – black hair, blue coat – was peering in its bonnet that was open to curses, if not to coercion. For the thing wouldn't start.

Lazily cocking her tail as a snook at the nun, Draco strolled across the sky. What could the nun do, but nothing and rage?

On its corniche, the train had stopped for no reason, as trains do. On the flyover with delusions of grandeur, the woman was slamming shut the boot, putting up a *pushchair*, wheeling her *baby* to the emergency phone! Mother of God, the dragon was going to —

'You're no dragon at all! Just an overgrown lizard, so y'are!'

Draco balked in surprise, and had to flap twice to stay up.

'Dragons are noble, glittering beasts,' yelled the woman who'd kissed the Blarney Stone. 'Hordes of treasure they've got, and never eat less than a virgin princess. You don't want her – she'd not make a mouthful for ye.'

And she prayed again in desperation for a natural catastrophe, just a little one. Dragon-size, for preference.

Vanity, vanity, all is vanity. Our present imperfect Draco had eaten plenty of it. She leered at her puny foe – grubby grey serge and skin, waving a fist through the window of the train – and Draco showed off her vanity.

And for all Sister Tom's prayer, there wasn't a cloud in the sky, not a ghost of an avalanche.

Flaming, terrible, Draco dive-bombed the mother.

Madonna of the motorway! Yes, she ran – but she snatched her baby and fled – towards the phonebox.

Draco's breath hurled the pushchair *through* the parapet. Sister Tom watched the pushchair's parachute progression. Held on its web of metal, it tumbled into the gorge, a gorgeous red flare of fire on its charred black frame.

Sister Tom almost collapsed – vertigo was catching.

Two all.

*

Round Four

Then Draco, seeing no other cars about, nor anyone else astir on the sleepy train, craftily burnt up the phone Vain, yes, about her ability to destroy, to scare, to terrify. But smart enough to know that armies in the nineties have tracker-planes and bombs. And all for the price of a phone-call.

She settled, wings spanning the concrete carriageway, teasing tufts of fire towards the mother. The woman stopped. Stood still, while a wind from nowhere picked up her skirts. The baby wailed – wouldn't you? But the woman didn't. Pale face, pale legs – only the blue of her clothes was colour against the white of the concrete and the black of the cliffs. Mouth slack, she didn't scream. She could see the monster's eyes.

With an insolent wink at the nun, on the train on the hillside helpless across the yards and yards of air, Draco advanced. A step at a time.

'My prayers are useless!' Thomasina – she'd be Sister Tom no longer! – slammed her forehead on the window.

Prayer was no good. The trip to Rome had done no good. A lifetime's savings gone to *prove* faith had no virtue. The Vatican was just a museum. All those monuments of marble and gold, canvas and flesh, to glorify God. And what had God got to show for it? People.

And Thomasina had heard enough confessions to know what people were.

Draco strutted another step. Her wings rattled in a sudden gale while she concentrated on grandstanding to the arena. Even her cockscomb crest was playing to the crowd.

Even the mother's tear-ducts were frozen with fear.

Like a gladiator, Draco minced forward. Step by step. Closed in for the kill. Belched like hell.

Will the Madonna die? Will her infant?

Thomasina couldn't watch faith's final death.

Out sprang the fire –

Two things happened. All over Europe on the farmers' news, weathermen moved symbols to show wind over the Alps. A small, natural catastrophe, just dragon-sized: the mini-hurricane blew the dragon's flames in again. In short, Draco backfired.

And while Draco skittered in surprise and the child cried and the woman's shaky legs tottered her away as far as the parapet, and while the weathermen pushed stick-on isobars around their maps, and the full-cheeked wind roared off down the valley, carooming off the train – while all that was going on, our doubting-again Thomasina from the back of Ballymartin groaned a prayer for the effectiveness of prayer. Despairing, self-loathing, eyes shut, she missed the lot.

Around another cigarette she wailed, 'Oh Lord, help Thou mine unbelief!'

Slowly, slowly, slowly, lace appeared on Draco's skin. The woman saw the cliffs through Draco's wings. She saw the veins, the viscera, the ichor.

Draco glanced wildly at herself, the inner dragon. *Ecco qua!* She hadn't known her guts were *that* colour.

And Sister Tom opened one eye just a crack, peeking to see where the thunderbolt had got to. She couldn't believe her eye.

The train started up again with a jolt. Away on the autostrada hung a surprised outline of a dragon, made entirely of soot. The tail end of the wind pulled it along to play. Like a newspaper kite, it fell to bits.

As the train rounded a bend, all Sister Tom could see was the woman in blue with a baby, the Madonna of the Flaming Phone-Booth. Sister Tom hoped her car would start.

Dragon 3 – Sister Thomas 4.

*

Oh – and Sister Tom took out a cigarette to savour with her heroism's wine. And sent the rest of the packet spinning into the abyss.

Story Origins

"By Right of the Stars" first appeared on the Alchemy Press website. I loved the idea of stars having different meanings, and that writing is its own form of magic. This was the first piece of fiction that appeared under the name of Anne Nicholls though my agony aunt work and self-help books already used my new name.

"Howie Dreams" was originally published in 1989 under the name of Anne Gay. It appeared in *Arrows of Eros*, edited by Alex Stewart, published by New English Library. Back in the eighties when I wrote this there was a compulsory topic in A Level and even post-grad language syllabi. This was called "The Battle of the Sexes". In one interview for a teaching job I was asked not only if I was using contraception but what form it took. (I nearly told them I safety-pinned my vest to my knickers but I needed the salary.) Men, of course, weren't asked things like that because they didn't get inconveniently pregnant. I was even told to my face that women shouldn't work because it forces men into unemployment. Things are better, but pay is still unequal; glass ceilings still abound. In some societies women are still stoned if they show their faces in public, and female genital mutilation is practised, fortunately illegally, even in Britain. I'd still like to make a Dream machine, though, to improve confidence and communication.

"Pixellated" began with the thought of the capabilities of people who are overlooked: old hippies gardening in purple kaftans, working mothers, children and other little beings. Although it was first written in the '90s, I decided not to update it because I thought it had a certain period charm. Besides, I couldn't have a gnome twizzling on a memo-stick.

This is its first outing in print.

"The Cunning Plan" was written for *The Mammoth Book of Comic Fantasy*, edited by Mike Ashley. Carroll & Graf of New York published it in 1998. At the time everyone would have known that Blackadder's Baldrick was the one who came up with Cunning Plans. They never worked. I just transferred that to pub football contenders I used to know.

"The World of the Silver Writer" was originally published under the name of Anne Gay in *Digital Dreams*, edited by David V. Barrett for New English Library in 1989. As a trainee psychotherapist I heard so many stories of how survivors of abuse found themselves fragmented that I had to explore this concept.

I wrote "The Seeds of a Pomegranate" for *Urban Mythic*, a collection edited by Jan Edwards and Jenny Barber for The Alchemy Press in 2013. I just love the phrase *as many as the seeds in a pomegranate*. And the idea of three friends (and an Alphyn) rescuing each other seemed as cosy as all those lamp-lit houses in Crouch End in autumn. It's another Anne Nicholls story.

"Bride of the Sea" was written for *Phantoms of Venice*, an anthology edited by David Sutton, in 2001. Lire had yet to give way to euros though the new notes were being printed, and mothers were as they always have been: some good, some bad. Much like footballers and antique dealers. And forgive me for taking some liberties with how the Italians celebrate the biennale. Every year there is a bride of the sea though.

I was thrilled to be invited to contribute to Mike Chinn's *Pulp Heroes #2*. "Dragon's Breath" was published by The Alchemy Press in 2013. I adore pulp fiction with all its adventures and I'm fascinated by China. *Wo xing* Nicholls Anne, as they'd say in Beijing.

"Wishbone" was the first SF story I ever had published. Not, however, the first one I'd ever written. I shoved it in the drawer with the rest of them, not brave enough to send it off. Then I heard Paul Simon's inspiring song *If you want to write a song about the moon, Just do it! Write a song about the moon.* So I screwed up my courage and sent it off to the Gollancz/ Sunday Times competition, and was thrilled to bits when it was published as a runner-up in their anthology *SF Competition Stories* in 1987. Paul Simon, you changed my life. Thank you!

"Fair Phantom, Come I" was written under the name of Anne Nicholls for an anthology that never happened. There are more things in Heaven and Earth ... but Sherlock Holmes dismissed the Solar System as irrelevant. Yet his creator, Sir Arthur Conan Doyle, became fascinated by the idea of the Otherworld, the world of the spirits, that was so prevalent at the end of the 19th century. What would happen if these two belief systems coincided? If Sherlock, who abhorred the way emotion clouds logic, had to experience other people's feelings?

"Eyes of Day, Eyes of Night" appeared under the name of Anne Nicholls in Mike Chinn's first *Pulp Heroes* anthology for The Alchemy Press. Jungles! What a rush! Ancient mysteries and hidden civilisations where the boundaries of *real* aren't quite where we know them.

"Dragonsbridge" appeared in 2012 in *Ancient Wonders,* an anthology for The Alchemy Press edited by Jan Edwards and Jenny Barber. By now I was getting used to my stories coming out in the name of Anne Nicholls. Here we have the bridge but what of the dragon? Who is it? Or he? Or she? I wrote this after Stan and I got back from *Les Féeries du Bocage,* a great little fantasy festival in Voulx, south of Paris. The Forest of Brocéliande was brought vividly to life for us by Pierre Dubois, artist, author, TV presenter.

"Buried Flame" was written especially for this collection published by the good people at The Alchemy Press. My first researches into Zoroastrianism led me to think it was a religion of pure goodness – until I got to the bit where the ones in California forbid intermarriage with folk of different faiths. It's never the religion that's the problem, though. It's the fanatics corrupted by absolutism. John Brunner used to stamp his envelopes, *Where books are burned, in the end people will be too.*

"Roman Games" was first published in *Other Edens*, edited by dear old Rob Holdstock and Chris Evans, for Unwin, UK, 1988. Since I wrote it not long after my divorce it was still under the name of Anne Gay. It was reprinted in *The Year's Best Fantasy*, edited by Ellen Datlow & Terry Windling, for St Martin's Press, USA (two editions). It's urban fantasy, Jim, but not as we know it.

— Anne Nicholls, 2015